May Day
A Sam Cable Mystery
Scott Bell

May Day
Red Adept Publishing, LLC
104 Bugenfield Court
Garner, NC 27529
http://RedAdeptPublishing.com/

For Alvie Bell, who taught me how to rebuild a carburetor, shoot a gun, and play poker. All the mistakes I've made are my fault, not his.

Chapter 1

"But wildlife experts say a black panther in east Texas is near-impossible." — report from *KLTV News* regarding black panther sighting in Upshur County, Texas

Sam

Tree limbs scraped the paint of my Ford Expedition as I navigated a backwoods trail in the dark. The SUV pancaked into an axle-deep rut then bunny-hopped out; all four wheels churned sand. The seat belt saved me from a concussion by cutting me in half. *Hashtag, grateful for small mercies.*

"Oof," Reyes grunted from the passenger seat. "Are we there yet?"

"Do you see the fossilized remains of an Airstream trailer sunk up to its windows in weeds?"

Ferdinand Reyes, a detective from the Gregg County Sheriff's Department, peered through the windshield and shrugged. "I saw the Boggy Creek monster a ways back. He was seven feet tall. Taller than you, even."

"Really? They made a movie about the Boggy Creek monster. Not a good one."

"This one was better looking than you too."

"Now I know you're lying."

Reyes tapped out a Marlboro Red and rolled down the window. Muggy night air huffed into the cab. Engine noise and dust came with it, followed by the smell of pine trees and weeds.

My nose twitched, anticipating a sneeze. High beams whitewashed the narrow tunnel of vegetation lining the track. Grasshoppers flickered through the light, buzzing away or ticking against the grill.

Other night bugs kamikazed into the windshield. I smeared their greenish remains with the wipers every once in a while.

I caught a whiff of acrid back draft when Reyes lit his cigarette off a disposable lighter and blew smoke toward the open window.

"At least tell me you know where you're going, Ranger Cable."

We rocked and swayed through another series of dips before I answered, "Mostly." It was my turn to shrug. "Beaver said the Thigpen brothers have taken up an old trailer on Ten Mile Creek. The only abandoned trailer I know of is back down here somewhere. I saw it about two years ago, pokin' around."

Reyes's cigarette flared, and he nodded.

"Unless he meant the Ten Mile Creek in Rusk County, in which case, that's a whole different trailer, and we're way 'n hell gone the wrong direction."

Smoke snorted from Reyes's nose. "Middle of the night, I should be in bed with my wife."

"And ruin her sex life?"

"You know what today is?"

"Laundry day?"

"Friday the thirteenth, man."

I grunted a laugh. "You're not superstitious, are you?"

"No, not me." Reyes shook his head. "Besides, I got on my lucky socks."

A low-hanging limb slapped the windshield and squealed across the roof. Beyond it, the headlights picked out a jumble of rotted barb-wire fence posts—part of a gate built before man discovered fire. Arcs of rusted wire twisted around the gap in the trail, just begging to give someone a bad case of tetanus.

"This is as far as we go by car. Any farther, they'll hear us for sure, or see the headlights." I shut off the motor and killed the lights.

"Holy shit," Reyes said, "it got *dark* out here."

"Did you bring your blankie?"

Reyes's teeth gleamed, and the metallic sound of a slide action clattered in the dark. "Yes, I did. Mr. Glock is all the blankie I need."

"You say that now." I stepped out of the SUV and settled my Stetson. "Junior and Ray Thigpen are poison mean and lower than armadillo shit. They belong to the infamous club of crazy-ass gun nuts. You may want something heavier than a puny nine-mil if things go to hell."

Reyes joined me at the tailgate. He was built on an R2-D2 frame, so his flattop haircut came to my shoulder.

"Take this." I handed him a Rock River Arms LAR-8. "Three-oh-eight caliber, two-stage trigger, twenty-round mag, and a red dot sight."

"Holy mackerel," Reyes whispered, taking the weight of the rifle.

"Safety is on the left. Bolt is *here*. The mag is full, chamber empty."

"I'm feeling warmer already." Reyes used the same voice he would for a full Hail Mary. "What's that?"

I held up the weapon I'd removed from my gun locker. "My new toy: an HK G36C. Seven pounds of space-age fire stick."

"What was that about gun nuts?"

"Hey!" I fitted one of the HK's translucent magazines in place and seated it with a slap. "I'm not a gun nut. I'm an *enthusiast*. C'mon, Rambo, let's go find some Thigpens."

I flashed my Maglite to negotiate the gutted remains of the gate then switched it off.

Two days ago, Ray and Junior Thigpen had held up a convenience store bait shop near Cherokee Lake, on the border of Gregg County, Texas. They'd shot and killed the owner, a Pakistani immigrant named Tarik Bhatti, for reasons unknown. The silent security video footage showed a lot of shouting and gesturing by Bhatti and the Thigpen brothers. Then they crashed their way out—two bowling balls in a china factory—with seventy-eight dollars and a case of Michelob Ultra. A snitch—Mason "Beaver" Cleaver—had given up a potential nesting ground: a rusty trailer on a mosquito-ridden bank of God's sewer line, a trickle of snake-infested muddy water known as Ten Mile Creek.

Guided more by feel than sight, I led the way down the pitch-black tunnel of pine trees, squelching through the occasional mud puddle and stumbling into wheel ruts. Behind me, Reyes slapped at vampire mosquitoes and griped under his breath.

Thirty sweaty minutes later, a patch of lesser gloom ahead indicated a change in the trail. I slowed from a stumble to a creep then hissed at Reyes to stop.

"What is it?" he whispered. He sounded a little hoarse and out of breath.

I snuck back to where he was, nearly bumping into the deputy before I saw him. I put my head down next to his and murmured, "I think we're close. Looks like a clearing up ahead. Fan out to my right and watch where you put your feet."

"Booby traps?"

"Snakes."

"*Tu madre*," he breathed.

We split up, and I crept forward, rolling my steps from heel to toe, feeling for twigs with the sole of my boot. I wasn't Deerslayer, but I could move a *little* more quietly than a gravel truck when I wanted. Reyes, not so much, though.

The end of the rutted track cut through a ring of high brush and weeds that tapered off to shorter grass covering an area the size of a high school stadium. On the far side, the weak light from a cloud-covered moon revealed the muted gleam of a silver Airstream trailer plonked down under a copse of trees. A nearly new Silverado pickup sat in front of it. The same type of vehicle used in the robbery.

I went to one knee, trying to see, hear, or smell any sign that Ray or Junior had sensed our catlike approach. To my right, Reyes found the edge of the field by stumbling into the high grass. He kept his voice down, but by the faint sounds of his cursing, I would've said Ferdinand wasn't an experienced night stalker. He thrashed and muttered more Spanish curses.

Thwok!

"*Mierda!*" Reyes snapped. His voice wasn't low anymore. More like extra volume with a side of hysteria. "Goddamn motherfucker!"

"Shh!" I stage whispered. "What happened?"

Reyes wasn't having any part of *shh*.

"I've been bit! Goddamn snake. He bit *me*!"

"No way," I hissed. "Are you jacking around with me right now?"

"Jack this, motherfucker! Fucking snake bit me!"

I could barely make out Reyes hopping around in the dark, right up until he tripped and fell on the road somewhere near the edge of the clearing. The clatter of metal made my skin shrink.

"Did you drop my rifle?" I kept my voice pitched low. If we were lucky, the Thigpens were heavy sleepers.

"I'm bit!"

"Calm down and stay put. I'm coming to you."

Reyes grunted, and I could hear the rustle of clothing followed by a bright splash of light flaring by his huddled body. He twisted to see the outside of his right calf.

I duck-walked over and put a hand on his shoulder. "Let me see."

"You gonna have to suck out the poison, Cable."

"I'm not sucking your leg!"

"You have to! To get the poison out."

"Will you shut up? Let me see."

The *whip-crack* of a bullet passing overhead got my attention firmly fixed on something else.

"Who's out there?" a voice yelled from the trailer.

"The Boy Scouts," I shouted. "Now stop shooting a minute. I got a snake-bit man here."

"Snake-bit?" The voice modulated from cantankerous to interested. "You better suck the poison out!"

"Shut up a minute," I yelled back.

Reyes gripped his leg at the knee, trying to cut off the blood flow with a hand-held tourniquet. "You think it was a copperhead? It wasn't no rattler; that's for sure. It didn't make no rattle at all."

I huddled next to Reyes and flicked on my Maglite, holding it close to his bare calf. "You moron. There's nothing there but a scratch. You probably stepped on a piece of fence post or something, and it popped you on the leg."

Reyes took a shaky breath. "You sure?"

"You'd be feeling it by now if you were bit. The neurotoxin would hurt like hell. Here, take a look."

A different Thigpen called from the trailer, "Is he dead?"

The stubby detective grunted with the effort but managed to contort himself enough to see the outside of his leg. "Well. Damn. It sure felt like a snakebite."

"So much for our stealthy approach to the den of thieves and killers up ahead."

Reyes huffed. "Huh. Been your leg, you'd-a done the same thing."

"Better not have gummed up my rifle, Reyes." I flashed my light around until I spotted the weapon a few feet away. I gave the barrel a quick check for blockage then handed him the LAR-8. I crabbed away from Reyes after patting him on the shoulder.

"Well?" Thigpen One shouted from somewhere left of the trailer. "You suck out the poison? Or what?"

At some point in the last few minutes, the brothers had separated and moved away from the Airstream. Thigpen Two shouted back from the far-right side of the trailer. "State your bidness."

"Ray and Donald Thigpen, Junior," I called out in my best cop voice. "This is Sam Cable of the Texas Rangers. Y'all are under arrest for the murder of Tarik Bhatti."

A bullet chopped weeds six inches from where I crouched. "Y'all ain't takin' us, goddamn it. Not for killin' no camel jockey."

I shifted a few feet to my left and shouted, "Give it up, boys. You got the Texas Rangers and the Gregg County Sheriff's Department out here."

"No way!" Thigpen Two said. "One'a y'all's been snake bit!"

"Enough of this bullshit," Reyes barked. "Let's just shoot these motherfuckers and go home. I'm tired of this jungle shit."

"You hear that, boys? The snake that bit my partner died. That's how mean he is. You want to go up against him?"

The breezeless night carried the very faint sound of crackling grass between me and the trailer. I squinted and moved my head around until I caught the motion of a big man running from the corner of my eye. He was headed for the parked truck.

I snugged the HK against my shoulder and ripped off a couple of short bursts, aiming wide of the running man. The muzzle flare lashed out in two yellow-orange flickering tongues. Metal popped, and safety glass shattered on the Silverado. I lit up the pickup again, just for meanness.

In the strobing muzzle flash, I noticed Thigpen One throwing up an arm and juking left, toward the trailer entrance. His brother was already at the door, and a Thigpen collision created a traffic jam in the narrow opening. Spots danced in front of my eyes, and by the time I could see reasonably well again, the brothers were inside the Airstream.

"Ray? Junior?" I shifted position again, waiting for another bullet from the house. "I got an HK G36 fully automatic weapon out here, and y'all are holed up in a tuna can. You want to see what Thigpen soup looks like?"

Reyes had worked his way around the clearing to a position almost ninety degrees away from mine. He yelled, "And I gotta... I gotta damn big rifle with lotsa bullets. I'm gonna shoot whatever the Ranger misses."

Silence from the trailer.

I took a breath and sighted high, above the Airstream's windows, and stitched a sustained burst along the top of the trailer. Damn, but it was a fine weapon to shoot. Smoke curled from the HK's muzzle as I swapped magazines. Maybe they would give me another chance to ventilate their trailer.

There came another moment of profound silence, followed by the muted sounds of two big men arguing. A thump rocked the trailer, followed by the sound of shattering dishes. Then, muffled from the inside the Airstream, came, "Stop shootin'. My brother and me give up."

One big, round Thigpen came out, followed by one round, big Thigpen. Both had their hands up. Reyes pinned them with a flashlight while I stepped up and ordered the brothers down on their knees.

"What the hell?" I asked the bearded Ray after I had him on the ground. "I thought you said we wouldn't take you alive. Why give up without a fight?"

Ray hemmed and hawed a bit.

"Tell him, Ray." His brother had a knot forming over his left cheekbone. Apparently, his brother had been forced to convince Junior to surrender.

"I made a tatticle air," Ray mumbled.

"What kind of tactical error did you make?"

"I... I left all our guns and ammo in the truck this afternoon." Ray craned his neck to give me a look that said, *Gee, ain't I a dummy?* "We were gonna take off this mornin' and head for Georgia. We didn't have nothin' in the trailer but a couple'a huntin' rifles. Five rounds each."

"We holed up," Junior spit the words at his brother, "in a refuge without any weapons." Sprawled with his cheek on the ground, he glared at his sibling. "I was for fightin' it out anyway, but Ray here..." He shook his head. "You always was a mama's boy."

Minutes later, Reyes had the cuffs on the brothers, both of them facedown in the weeds in front of their little slice of heaven in the Piney Woods of East Texas.

"I'll go bring up the truck," I said.

Reyes nodded and fired up another Marlboro. "No way I'm walking back there through the dark again. Not with the snakes and shit." Reyes rubbed his leg and looked away.

"There's a pant'er out there," Ray claimed. "I saw it, plain as day."

"A panther?" I snorted. "There aren't any panthers in Texas. That's an old wives' tale."

Using the flashlight, I made better time heading back than we had creeping up. It took me five minutes reach my SUV. The moon had come out, and the white vehicle almost glowed in the dark. It promised the relief of air conditioning, four-wheel drive, and the satisfaction of a job well done.

Bone-tired from the aftermath of adrenaline and exercise, I didn't really understand what I was looking at in the upswing of my flashlight beam. I took two more steps and froze, snapping the light onto the tire tracks in front of me. Two glowing green eyes fixed on mine, freezing my heart in my chest. The creature paused at the edge of the trail and studied me. I held my breath until it vanished into the brush.

The buzzing of night bugs and frogs pressed in from the surrounding forest, and sweat soaked my shirt collar. My good mood shriveled up and huddled in a dark corner. I sucked in a breath and let it out in a big whoosh. A shaky laugh dribbled out between my teeth. "I guess I owe Ray an apology."

A black panther. Good God.

The biggest black cat in the world had just crossed my path. Good thing I wasn't superstitious.

Chapter 2

"You know how it works, Jake. You ride with the outlaw, you die with the outlaw. Sorry, you crossed the line." – Lonesome Dove, Larry McMurtry

Jade

Jade Stone waited in line for her All-Inclusive Wanted Fugitive Escape to Mexico disguised in a baseball cap and sunglasses, carrying a new North Face backpack stuffed with everything she owned. A two-bedroom apartment condensed to one graphite-colored rucksack.

One way to downsize, she decided. *Go on the run for your life.*

She had a hundred yards left to go. The pedestrian queue at the San Ysidro border crossing moved steadily; she should be at the checkpoint in minutes. The line was longer than Jade had hoped but not as long as she'd feared. She'd ditched her car at the San Diego airport two hours ago. She should still be ahead of the pursuit.

Six lanes of vehicle traffic idled on her left. Exhaust fumes burned Jade's sinuses, and a headache was gathering strength behind her eyes. Add the pressure cooker of heat and stress, and the dull throb in her head could flare to a full-blown migraine before long.

Thousands of people flowed past the San Ysidro border station every day, crossing over to the *mercado* to buy a fifth of rum or an authentic Mexican peasant blouse—*handmade in China!*—or to fill a prescription at the *farmacia*. Few were stopped by Customs on the Mexican side, most undergoing nothing more than a cursory scan.

Getting into Mexico wasn't a problem. Getting into Mexico while fleeing a team of federal agents was a whole different level of gibbering panic.

The crowd inching toward the checkpoint consisted of Saturday-morning shoppers, with a few exceptions. A pair of college boys directly in front of her, wearing Fresno State T-shirts, talked sexual trash deliberately loudly enough for her to hear. They snuck glances at her to see if she was ready to swoon at their feet.

"...and, man, I was thinking with my little head that night, but, dude, I swear, that chick could suck start a Honda."

"Dude, I know. She loved gettin' the dick, right?"

Real studs.

Jade dug out her iPhone, hooked up the earbuds, and rolled through her playlist. What songs would help her not look like a fugitive? Bob Marley's "I Shot the Sheriff" seemed inappropriate, as did Toby Keith's "Bullets in the Gun."

I need a getaway playlist. Something catchy, that you can run to.

The line shuffled forward, snaking toward the gates. She passed under a pedestrian bridge displaying a green directional sign for the vehicles on I-5 headed into Mexico. Tall gates of tan metal loomed ahead, and an eight-foot fence to the left funneled all traffic down the path, like cattle in a chute.

Not long now. One of her daddy's stock phrases echoed in her head, like a song she could never quite get rid of. *Keep your eye on the ball.* Daddy could speak at length on any subject with authority, his Southern drawl as thick as willow bark and as soft as bayou fog. Though a great speaker, he had an unfortunate tendency to repeat several worn homilies.

She wished he could tell her how to get a good fake ID. Jade had found a wealth of information on the internet on how to build a new identity, all of which turned out to be stupidly erroneous, a link to a virus, or an enticement to part with her credit card number. In novels and movies, there was always some guy who, for a price, would hook up the hero with everything from a driver's license to an AARP card. Jade Stone didn't know a guy like that.

In books, she'd read about how people created fake IDs by visiting a cemetery and finding tombstones with the right date, kids born around the same time as the hero and dying shortly thereafter. Armed with the name, the stalwart hero could walk into the county registrar's office, pick up a birth certificate, and be on their way to a new life.

Turned out, county registrars had read the same books. With the rampant increase in identity theft, getting a copy of someone else's birth certificate was now as likely as getting a ticket to the International Space Station.

Without a fake ID, bluff and prayer seemed her only options. She'd chosen to walk across the border at San Ysidro, the busiest border crossing in the world, figuring that blending in with a big crowd would be her best bet. To further reduce scrutiny, Jade had worked hard at dulling down her appearance to her slobbish worst. Shabby jeans, a T-shirt that fit her like a tent, a baseball cap, and sunglasses, all of which combined to turn down the wattage of her looks.

Jade bore no illusions about her physical appearance; she'd received enough feedback from men and women alike, ever since high school, to doubt about how people saw her. Much of the comments involved words like *stunning, gorgeous*, and *dazzling*. One boyfriend had called her *unconsciously sensual*, at which point Jade had laughed out loud. Since it was in the middle of sex, the mood suffered a bit from her reaction. Beauty: a gift and a curse.

Jade took a casual look around. If she could act nonchalant and natural, everything would be okay. Nothing to see here but another bored tourist hopping the border with her backpack. Another gal on her day off, headed for a little afternoon shopping in the duty free—

Oh no!

Jade froze for a split instant, her heart stuttering. Cold sweat broke out under her arms. Behind her, about thirty people back, a man in a black-and-gold Hawaiian shirt, sunglasses, and a Boston Red Sox hat idled with his hands in his jeans pockets. A Bluetooth dangled from one ear, and he appeared to be studying the cars creeping along the freeway.

The same guy had been at the Arizona hotel where she'd stopped the previous night. Or at least, he *looked* like the same guy. He'd spooked her so much, she'd snuck out of the hotel and hit the road again.

Had one of Bartlett's thugs followed her the entire way from Dallas? Or had they picked up her trail somewhere along the way? Maybe it was just a weird coincidence. Maybe Mr. Hawaiian Shirt happened to be traveling the same direction she was, stopping at the same roadside motel, and waiting in line behind her to cross into Tijuana.

Yeah. Right.

Maybe she was mistaken. Maybe this was a different guy.

Jade angled her body so she could see Mr. Hawaiian Shirt from the corner of her eye. She fiddled with her phone, scrolling through the apps, while she snuck another glance at him, trying to recall the scene from the day before.

The Arizona hotel had a coffee shop decorated in plastic ferns and Formica. At ten o'clock, the place was about to close for the evening, so she ate while the waitress bussed and cleaned for the night. Jade sat where she had a good view of the front desk and picked at cold iceberg lettuce salad. The vinaigrette dressing was more vinegar than -rette, and the coffee was burned to tar, but growing up poor in Mississippi had taught her to never leave food behind.

She noticed the man when he came in because she recognized the type. She didn't have a word for the type, just a number of traits that, put together, spelled "jerk." Bartlett surrounded himself with guys just like this one. Handsome, mid-thirties, ex-jock, high-cut hair, and unblemished skin. Unbelievably smug and self-satisfied, the Jerk's only sensitivity would be in the tip of his penis.

Jade had no problem with handsome, muscular men; on the contrary, they made her heart race as hard as the next gal's. She had a problem with men who thought they were doing a woman a favor by allowing her to worship their existence. Like women should genuflect at the sunlight streaming from their ass.

Men like Bartlett. Men like the guy at the check-in desk of the Desert Inn. He looked so very much like one of Bartlett's sycophants that Jade's heart jumped into her throat, and she could barely swallow the lump of salad.

Black hair glistening with product, the man spoke with the desk clerk too low for Jade to hear. He had a thin nose with wide nostrils, and he wore a sport jacket despite the Mojave heat outside. *Not a tourist then. Somebody who wants to hide a gun, maybe?* Cops often wore sport coats—or Hawaiian shirts—to conceal the firearm on their hips.

Jade couldn't take the chance if he was following her or stopping at the same ratty motel in the desert by happenstance. She dropped a twenty on the table to cover her bill and slipped away while the black-haired man signed the check-in form.

She headed for the hallway leading to the diner's restroom, intending to hide inside the ladies' room until the man left the front desk. To her relief, the back door at the end of the hall was propped open. Jade stepped into the desert heat, spooking a little when she almost ran into the Mexican cook, who leaned against the wall, smoking a cigarette. Jade muttered an excuse, and the cook nodded and looked away.

She quick-marched to her room, grabbed her bag, and took off in her Toyota Camry, eyes on the rearview mirror. No one followed, and she was sure she'd lost the pursuers.

Until now.

As she stood in line at the border checkpoint, two dozen feet from the gated entrance to Mexico, the man in the loud shirt loafed along behind her, radiating innocence. It had to be the same guy. In all the time she'd been observing him, he had not once looked her way.

How did they find me? What did I do wrong?

An ICE officer sat in a lawn chair under an umbrella next to the fence, with her back to the highway. The Customs officer had buffalo hips and brown hair pulled into a tight bun. She monitored the pedestrians as they sweltered and sweated, shuffling toward Tijuana. She looked at everyone except Jade.

Two more officers loitered near the gates, under the word Mexico spelled out in huge block letters. They, too, seemed to be avoiding eye contact with Jade.

What are they waiting for? She was five foot five and a hundred twenty pounds when she carried a sack of groceries. If they made her, wouldn't they simply pounce on her? She'd imagined an officer flashing a badge and calmly saying, "Come with me, ma'am."

Of course, Bartlett's guy probably wanted to kill her rather than arrest her... after he tortured her for information.

You're being paranoid, Jade. So what if they don't look at you? None of these cops are interested in you. Keep your eye on the ball.

The line moved, the flow of traffic quickening as she got closer every second. Before long, she would be trapped in a funnel, Bartlett's boy behind her, two cops ahead at the gates, and one to her left by the highway fence. No way out.

Sweat blotted the back of her shirt; she transferred the backpack to her other shoulder and pulled off her cap long enough to mop her forehead with her sleeve. It was a warm day for May, and temperatures in the Southern California desert were as hot as anything she'd lived through in Dallas or Mississippi. And that nonsense about dry heat wasn't helping.

Jade had only seconds left to decide. After a few more steps, she would be committed to the attempt to cross the border. Both the flanking cops were looking at her now, their sunglasses reflecting flickers of movement as people passed. Ten or so more steps would get her through the gates and across the border. In Mexico, they frowned on extradition for potential death penalty cases.

Jade glanced back. Bartlett's guy—he couldn't really be anyone else—was watching her, as well. If she bailed right this second, she would have to go back past him. Would he do something? Make a move to arrest her? Why hadn't he already? If she got past him, maybe she could make it back to her car at the airport long-term parking.

Jade's heart thudded in her chest, and cold sweat trickled down her ribs. Her bra strap and hat band were both soaked. She shivered and stopped in her tracks.

The woman behind her bumped into her, muttering, "*Perdóneme.*"

One of the Fresno State boys said, "Are you okay, ma'am?"

The cop to the right of the gate frowned and took a step in her direction.

Jade bolted.

"Hey!" someone shouted from behind her.

The ICE officer in the chair looked surprised and struggled to get up but was too late. Jade ran past her. She registered the startled faces of the pedestrians in her peripheral vision. Another shout came from behind her, and Jade kicked it into high gear.

Mr. Hawaiian Shirt took a step like he was going to get in her way, then let her pass. People shrank to the side, their eyes and mouths open. One or two held cell phones up, panning as she passed.

In a few hundred yards, she'd be clear. Out of the trap. Living to fight another day.

Jade glanced back—and took her eye off the ball for a split second. A toddler pushing his own stroller waddled into her path. His mom shouted, her arms full of infant, one hand extended to reach him. Jade reacted too late to avoid him. She tripped and went sprawling. Before she could get up, cops were all over her.

Chapter 3

"The airplane stays up because it doesn't have time to fall." — Orville Wright

Sam

When I got home from the Thigpen arrest Saturday at eight thirty in the morning, the smell of dirty socks and stale Cheetos reminded me it was cleaning day. I made a pot of furnace-hot coffee and got busy cleaning. Guns first, then the house. Grit clogged the LAR's action.

"I'll get you for that, Reyes." Maybe I would find a harmless rat snake—they looked a lot like cottonmouths—and drop it in his car.

I motored through the day on autopilot, doing laundry and watching college basketball on TV, trying to ignore my drooping eyelids. At seven in the evening, I gave up the fight, took a shower, and hit the sack.

At that point somewhere between awake and asleep, when the mind drifts on fluffy clouds floating over oceans of nonsense, reacting to something as mundane as a ringing phone could seem more difficult than teaching a giraffe geometry. The first call went to voicemail before I figured out the ringtone wasn't part of a musical dance routine by trained squirrels. I found my cell on the bedside table and squinted at the display just as it rang again.

"'Lo?"

"Cable, it's Marshall. Were you asleep?" Captain Marshall, my boss in the Rangers, was as old as dinosaur bones and twice as hard.

"Um, no."

"Good. I need your ass down here Monday morning."

"Here? Austin?"

"No, I mean Mars. What the hell you think I mean? I've got a job needs doin', and you're the lucky bastard gets to do it. Or will be, once the paperwork gets done."

"A job?"

Marshall huffed. "Wake up, boy. They caught the skank what killed the cop in Dallas. You're going to Cally-for-nye-ay to bring her back."

California? I stopped myself from saying it out loud in the nick of time. "Isn't that a job for the DPD?"

"Would be, but the gal's parents are making noises that the cop she killed was bent. Her old man's a congressman, and he's got enough pull to get people to pay attention. The Dallas DA is gonna put through paperwork to have us do the exterdiction."

Extradition? Another question I wisely kept to myself. "Why Austin? Why can't I fly out of DFW?"

"We're usin' the company plane."

Oh, hell no. The Rangers had come into possession of a twin-engine Cessna by confiscation of drug profits in a recent bust. Some bright bulb in the governor's office, or maybe in the Department of Public Safety hierarchy, had thought we could use it in our crime-fighting arsenal. They convinced an ex-military vet and current DPS trooper to be the official pilot, and shazam! The Rangers became an airborne force.

I hated the damn rickety plastic-and-fiberglass flying coffin. It rattled like a Number Two washtub full of marbles and shook worse than a crack addict in rehab. "Jesus, boss, what did I ever do to you?"

"Cowboy up, Cable. I don't got time for your whiny shit. Get your ass down here Monday morning. *Comprende?*"

"*Si.*" I hung up and tossed the phone into the pile of sheets beside me. *Why me?*

Because a black cat the size of a German shepherd crossed your path—that's why.

I flopped back in bed and went back to sleep... after muting my phone.

Jade

JADE STONE OFFICIALLY became property of the California Department of Corrections at five o'clock Saturday evening. She'd endured arrest and handcuffing, transport to the southern division of the San Diego Police Department, and a long wait in an interview room. The interrogation lasted long enough for Jade to invoke her right to silence and request an attorney.

Then came the call to her parents in Mississippi. She explained her side of the story, and after her mom had cried herself dry and her father had yelled and cussed awhile, they agreed to find her a California lawyer.

Her intake jailer, Martinez, was a heavyset Latina with a single eyebrow sprawled across her forehead. "Oh, the gals in lockup gonna like you, *mi hermosa*."

The other deputy in the room, a washing machine-sized black woman with Hamilton on her name badge, laughed. "Maybe she play for the other team. She might like the attention. You gay?"

"No... What? *No!*" Jade straightened and struggled into the orange jumpsuit they'd handed her. "I'm not..."

"Oh, look at her turn red. I done think you embarrassed the girl, Amelia."

Hamilton escorted her to the cell, passing row after row of hard-eyed women, some lounging on their bunks, others with their hands draped through the bars. After a glance, Jade kept her eyes on the floor. The place smelled of Pine-Sol and sweat, mixed with a faint odor of human waste—both literal and figurative.

Hamilton stopped in the middle of the row of cages and spoke into her shoulder mic. The door buzzed and clanked open. Inside, a purple-haired black woman with a scarred cheek said, "Whoo, look at de angel down from heaven. What dey getchu fo? Stealin' de cookie money?"

"Behave yourself, Clarice," Hamilton said. "Angel here's in for killing a cop."

"Holy Mary, Mothah'a Gawd." Clarice swung her legs off the top bunk and slid to the floor. "C'mon in here, child. I won't bite ya."

Jade stepped into the cell and twitched when the door clanged shut behind her. Even though she'd been expecting it, the finality of that sound jolted her. Her nose tingled like it did before she started crying, so Jade willed her eyes to stay dry and took a deep, fluttery breath.

"Sleep tight, ladies." Hamilton waddled away, stopping now and again to exchange words with other inmates.

"Don't you mind her." Clarice put an arm around Jade's shoulders and guided her to the bottom bunk. "Sit a spell and get yo wind back. This yo first time?"

"To be in jail? Yes."

"Don't you worry none; jail ain't like prison. Down here we don' got the queen bitches tryin'a fuck you in da shower and whatnot. You go to full-time prison, you gots to watch out, or dey be rubbin' pussies on you mornin', noon, and night."

"What did you do to get locked up, Clarice?"

"Me? I cut dis stupid Mexican, wanted his money back affa I done my bidness wid him."

"Bidness?"

"Y'know, bidness." Clarice made a gesture with her hand in front of her mouth.

"You're a..."

"A ho. Das right, you can say it. A damn good one, too, even at sixty-two year old. Why I can still suck a peel off a potato when I want."

Jade laughed.

"Now," Clarice said, "I can find you a job in a heartbeat, you wanna come work wit' me. Men be paying you a million dollahs a night, get somma yo pussy, girl."

Seven hours later, listening to Clarice snore, Jade stared at the underside of the top bunk. She tried to let her mind drift free and finally achieved a zoned-out state of no thought, where she could float along the current and not consider the future or contemplate the present.

Somebody coughed, and a toilet flushed, jarring her back to reality—locked in a cage. Ten feet by ten feet of concrete and steel.

How did I get here? What decision put me on the path to wind up in jail? Do I have a character defect, or could I have made better life choices? Maybe if she'd turned down the invitation to go out with the handsome and chiseled—and corrupt—Dallas Police detective Tommy Grace. Or should she go all the way back to the offer to join Cleburn & Harris? Maybe that was the turning point. Or going to law school?

Jade sighed and rolled over. The thin blanket did little to warm her, and she shivered. Voices carried from somewhere faraway, too distant to make out the words. Other jail sounds—metallic clangs, coughs, grunts, and sneezes—scratched her raw nerves with dirty fingernails.

She would be tried for killing a cop. There wouldn't be any parole. No plea deals that would get her off. She would be in jail for a long time. Unless the other guys on Bartlett's crew got to her first—then she would be dead. Bartlett would kill her faster than he could slice a drive off the tee.

Don't go down without a fight, honey, she heard her daddy's voice say.

"Damn right I won't," she whispered. There was still a way out. She just had to quit feeling sorry for herself and find it.

Sam

BY MONDAY AFTERNOON, I had all the extradition paperwork in my leather satchel, and I followed my GPS out to Austin Executive Airport on the northeast side of town. When Captain Marshall sent me off, he'd said, "They want this gal something fierce up 'ere in Dallas. You fetch her back quick, hear?"

"You never explained why I'm getting this assignment."

"'Cause I want it done right." Marshall fixed me with his Clint Eastwood stare. "I know I can count on you to get 'er done without fuckin' around. And speakin' of your pecker, don't ever be alone with this woman, y'hear? She cries rape, and that's all she wrote for your career."

"Wonderful."

I found Marlon Boggs, DPS trooper turned DPS pilot, doing a walk-around of the airplane we were supposed to fly to California and back. Boggs was about my age and had an upper body big enough to bench press the damn plane. Still, the aircraft didn't look big enough to make Waco, let alone cross three states, with mountains and stuff in between. It had a long nose cone, five round portholes along the side, and twin engines with three-bladed props, and it stood on three wheels—one under the nose and two under the wings.

Shaking Boggs's hand, I asked, "Who made your plane? Revell?"

"Huh?" As if sensing my skepticism about his toy, he launched into a lecture about the airworthiness of the Cessna 421C, but he shut up when I raised a palm.

"Never mind, Marlon. Just refrain from a vertical deployment of the aircraft into the turf, and we'll both be happy."

A handsome black man with a bald head and a powerful upper body, Boggs came off as serious as funeral director and as earnest as a Jehovah's Witness.

"Don't worry, Ranger Cable. This aircraft is as safe as your grandma's Buick."

I handed him my duffel. "Mama Cable drives a 1963 Chevy Stepside powered by a 283 V-8, three on the stick, with Jesus Christ riding shotgun. We call ahead when she gets a notion to go to town so the county cops can clear the road of the innocent."

Boggs opened a clamshell door in the middle of the plane and folded out a three-rung ladder. I ducked into the fuselage and navigated between two pairs of seats—one set facing aft, one forward. Then I squeezed into the co-pilot's seat, which had more room than I expected. Even so, I racked the seat back and vowed not to touch any of the knobs, switches, dials, gauges, levers, or cupholders in my immediate vicinity.

Boggs put on earmuffs, poked this, twisted that, and pulled something else. Within minutes, we were taxiing onto the runway. He said arcane words into his microphone and jabbed what I assumed was the throttle, because we went from piddling along to zipping down the runway. The airplane vibrated and rattled its way into the air, at which point the ride didn't smooth out much at all. Marlon got it pointed west, leveled out, and engaged what I assumed was the autopilot.

"You want to take her, Ranger?"

"What? Fly the plane?" I shuddered. "Not on your life."

Boggs bared his teeth in a huge grin. "This is fun, huh?"

"Fun. Yeah. Listen, you even know where California is?"

He frowned. "Of course. Plus we have GPS and other navigational equipment. We'll have no problem reaching San Diego. The 421C has a range of fourteen hundred eighty-seven nautical miles. We will not need to refuel—"

"Stop! Just land before you see the ocean, okay."

I pulled out the documents on my soon-to-be prisoner and ignored Boggs's serious expression. Flipping open the file, I commenced to learn about this Jane Dillinger of Dallas wanted by the DPD for murder of her cop boyfriend, Thomas Paul Grace.

The Cessna shuddered through a rough pocket of air, and my ass pinched up a chunk of seat. It was going to be a long damn flight.

Chapter 4

"Flying is learning how to throw yourself at the ground and miss."
— Douglas Adams

Lee

Lee Bragg waited in the parking lot of the Brown Field Municipal Airport outside of San Diego with the windows of his dusty Chevrolet Impala rental rolled down to catch whatever breeze there was. That equaled not much and very little. Sweat stuck the black-and-gold Hawaiian shirt to his body. He leaned forward and fanned the shirt, wrinkling his nose at the stale smell of his own body. Southern California in the middle of a heat wave. *Unseasonably high temperatures. Go figure.*

Using a pair of field glasses, he focused on a white Cessna with blue trim as it settled onto the runway. He read off the tail number and compared it to one scribbled on a Holiday Inn notepad in the seat next to him. He picked up a burner phone from the center console and dialed a number from memory.

The phone was answered after two rings. "Go."

"They're here," Bragg said.

"Understood. They'll probably stay overnight, pick up the package in the morning. You know what to do."

"You got it."

"Lee?"

"Huh?"

"Don't fuck it up this time. I want that package to fail to reach its destination. Understood?"

"Hey, it's not my—"

"Understood?"

Bragg's nostrils flared, and he said yes through gritted teeth, clicked off the phone, and tossed it in the passenger seat hard enough that it bounced into the floorboard.

All this over a damn sorority girl fresh out of law school. What a sick joke. The blond Barbie doll had faked him in Arizona after he'd spotted her car in the fourth roadside motel he tried. When Lee glanced at the parking lot after he checked in, he'd nearly had a heart attack; the woman's taillights were zooming onto the desert highway and disappearing fast. He'd had to race like a scalded cat, not catching sight of her until just outside San Diego.

After she'd dumped her car at the airport, Bragg had to tail her on foot. She'd gotten on a bus and hopped public transportation all the way from San Diego International to the San Ysidro border crossing, staying in crowds all the way.

"Don't fuck up," Bartlett says. What? I'm supposed to kill her in broad daylight? "No, follow her to Mexico," Bartlett says. So I follow her, and she tries to run back *into the US!* She must have made him, was all he could figure.

Bragg cranked on the Impala and got the AC blowing, then he hit the window buttons to seal out the arid heat. At least now that the state cops from Texas had landed, he could wait in relative comfort for them to leave the terminal. After that, he could go to work.

Sam

MARLON BROUGHT THE Cessna to a stop next to a metal hangar and flipped switches. The propellers fluttered to a stop, and the silence made my ears ring.

"Good job," I said.

"Thank you, sir."

"We didn't crash once."

I followed Marlon from the cramped interior of the Cessna onto the tarmac and refrained from kissing the ground. The asphalt was baking in the afternoon sun, and a mild breeze barely moved the windsock hanging by the runway.

"Hel-*lo*," I said. "I thought San Diego was supposed to be cool year-round. Hell, this is only May."

"Heat wave," said a lanky kid wearing mechanic's overalls. Wiping his hands on a red shop rag, he came from the dark interior of the San Diego Jet Center hangar. He had rusty hair and an overbite. "Plus, you're inland a bit here. Ain't it a bitch?"

"Might as well have stayed in Texas."

The mechanic directed Marlon to the office, where he went to make arrangements for refueling and storage of the Cessna while I found the rental-car desk. The chipper Latino kid gave me a map, directions to a budget motel near the county courthouse, and a humongous key to a Ford Fusion.

Thirty-two minutes after landing, we dumped our overnight bags in the back of the Fusion, and I took the driver's seat while Marlon rode shotgun. His expression of grim determination and serious purpose hadn't changed in the six hours I'd known him.

"Here. Take a look at who we're transporting." I handed Marlon the file on Jade Stone.

"Oh, wow," he said, flipping it open. "She's pretty."

"She's also a cop killer, so don't let her looks fool you."

"Why is it always the pretty ones who go bad?"

I couldn't tell from his look whether he was trying to be funny, but I suspected not. I turned onto Otay Mesa Road and accelerated toward San Diego. "Are you always so serious, Marlon?"

"Serious?" He looked perplexed. "What do you mean, sir?"

"I mean, I think I've seen you smile one time in the last six hours."

Marlon's brows contracted. "I can be funny."

At a T-junction, I made a jog left then turned right onto 905. "When we see the judge tomorrow to get our paperwork signed, you can do all the talking. They like earnest and sincere a lot more than a wiseass."

"At Thanksgiving, when my family gets together, we tell jokes and stuff," Marlon said.

"Really?"

"Yes, sir. Wait a sec... let me think." He held up a hand. "Okay, okay. There's this guy... these two guys... They go in a restaurant, okay?"

"Two guys in a restaurant. Got it."

"And they... I mean, the waiter, he's carrying the tray from the kitchen, and he slips and falls, right? Everything crashes to the floor." Marlon illustrated with his hands, indicating that a mess went everywhere. "So everything crashes, and the waiter, he's on his ass. And these two guys, they're like tech guys, right? They're in computers and whatnot. One guy looks at the other and says, 'Oh, look, the server's crashed!'"

Brown desert flowed past the window, and the car rocked in the pressure wave from a semi flying by in the left lane. I looked at Marlon and back at the road. "The server crashed?"

"Yeah. The server. Like computer server—"

"I get it, yeah. Hey, Marlon?"

"Sir?"

"You're invited to my folks' place this Thanksgiving. You'll be the hit of the party."

"Thank you, sir. That would be an honor."

"Don't say honor until you've tried Mama Cable's sweet potato surprise." I changed the subject. "Tomorrow, we're due in court at nine a.m. to get our docs signed. Hopefully, that won't take long, but this is California, so who knows? After that, we pick up Stone at the county jail and head back to Brown Field. How long you think it'll take to get the plane ready to fly?"

"Under an hour or so to file the flight plan, check the weather, and whatnot."

"So, with any luck, we'll be back in Texas by dinnertime tomorrow, right?"

"Sounds like a plan, sir."

"Good. I want this over and done with fast."

Jade

IN THE JAIL, THE DEPUTIES distributed sack lunches around noon—one slice of unidentified meat product and a Xerox copy of a cheese slice pressed between almost-stale white bread soaked with oily mayo. A plastic package of carrot sticks and a juice box complemented the sandwich. Jade ate it all.

Before her daddy had turned his single garage into a chain of quick lube and oil change stations, Jade had earned an appreciation for eating what was put in front of her. Poke sallet was nothing but a weed to most folks, but many a time, that was all the greens her mama had to cook with. Breakfast was grits when they could get it, cornbread on good days. Lunch was more of the same, maybe with some fatback bacon or leftover fried chicken. When chicken was scarce, dinner consisted of whatever her brother, Diamond, could shoot—squirrel, rabbit, or possum. Maybe some raccoon.

Food got better as time went on, and Daddy got rich and went into politics, but Jade never forgot the feeling of going hungry. It had a way of making every meal a banquet.

"Well, it ain't much," Clarice declared, "but it sho' is nasty."

"I've eaten worse," Jade said.

"Well, I have, too, girlfren. But when I do, I gets paid fo' it. I licked *ass* had better flavor'n that sammich."

Deputy Hamilton appeared at the cell door. "Open twelve," she said into her mic. A buzz and click released the lock, and their door clanked open.

"C'mon, Angel," Hamilton said to Jade, not unkindly, "it's time for you to say goodbye to Clarice. Your ride to Texas is here."

"Go on now, girl." Clarice hopped down from her top bunk and put a hand on Jade's shoulder. "You be okay. Girl like you, nothin' bad gonna happen. God won't let it."

Jade shared a hug with Clarice, who patted her back. "I be prayin fo' you, Angel."

"Thank you," Jade whispered. She shuffled through the entrance and waited while Hamilton radioed for the cell door to be closed. Hamilton took her by the arm, and Jade allowed herself to be guided away. She glanced back at Clarice, who gave her a sunny smile and a wave.

Hamilton said, "Don't fret, honey. You should see the pair'a hunks they sent to take you back. I wouldn't kick either one outta my bed, no ma'am. Mm-mm."

The deputy buzzed through the jail door into a narrow hall with another remote-controlled door. That one hummed and clicked open, and Hamilton led Jade to an office door labeled Property Clerk, which she opened with her ID badge.

Two men made the small room feel even smaller. Like black and white chess pieces, they flanked the Dutch door leading to the property room on the opposite wall from where she entered.

The shorter one, a black man in a khaki Texas Department of Public Safety uniform, gleamed like a new car on a showroom floor. From his polished shoes, razor creases, tooled-leather belt, and handsome, poster-boy face, the uniformed trooper could've passed inspection on any parade ground. His massive upper arms strained the short-sleeve cuffs of his uniform blouse.

The other man was easily six inches taller than his companion, a blue-eyed and blond-haired contrast in male diversity. A well-worn cream Stetson complemented his strong, direct face and broad shoulders. His arrow waist and long tan jeans ended at scuffed cowboy boots. *If you combined the DNA of Bradley Cooper, Toby Keith, and George Strait in a lab,* she thought, *this is what you would get.*

His white cotton button-down shirt was poorly pressed—one sleeve had an extra crease—and he wore a high-rise holster with a cocked-and-locked .45 on one hip. A Texas Ranger star-within-a-circle badge was pinned to his chest.

Hamilton had not exaggerated. *A pair of hunks, indeed.*

"Ms. Stone?" The Ranger took a step forward and extended his hand. "I'm Sam Cable of the Texas Rangers. This is Marlon Boggs. We're here to take you back to Texas to stand trial for the murder of Thomas Grace."

Jade shook his hand without thinking about it, her mind still on autopilot. She felt the handcuff a heartbeat later and looked down to find the Ranger had snapped it over her wrist with his left hand while he held her right.

"Please extend your other hand, Ms. Stone." When he had her cuffed, he said, "You're not gonna run, are you? I'd hate to use the leg irons."

"No, sir." Jade felt about six years old, standing in front of her father's desk.

"If you behave, I'll keep you cuffed in front, where it's more comfortable. You act up, and I'll not only put the leg irons on, I'll cuff you in back, which sucks when you want to scratch your nose. *Comprende?*"

"Yes."

"Good. If you behave yourself the entire way, I promise I won't let Marlon tell you a joke."

Chapter 5

"A particularly beautiful woman is a source of terror." — Carl Jung

Sam

"I know who you are," our female prisoner said.

I looked in the rearview mirror and was struck again at the unique color of Jade Stone's eyes, which was almost no color at all. I wanted to say they were like ice, but they weren't hard or cold. Even unwashed with no makeup, her looks could stun an unwary man and leave him goggle-eyed and stupid. And I'd put Marlon Boggs in the backseat with her.

"Hey, Marlon?" I said. "How you holdin' up back there?"

"Fine, sir."

Stone had been subdued through the out-processing, answering direct questions in monosyllables, keeping her eyes down. She seemed defeated more than anything else. The San Diego people wanted Stone's coverall back, so I'd relented and uncuffed her long enough for the female deputy to escort her to the restroom to change. Stone now wore jeans and an oversize white T-shirt with a Nike swoosh and *Just Do It!* in blue.

I met her gaze in the mirror again. Being of pure heart, I failed to flinch at the eye contact. Knowing she'd killed a cop with a butcher knife helped keep my libido in check, as well.

Fresh-faced, with naturally arched brows and full lips outlining a generous mouth, Stone looked like the girl next door all the boys longed for. In a movie, she would be the tomboy who transforms into a teenage dream during a musical montage. She would come to the door on prom night, and some boy's jaw would drop so hard, he would break his chin on the floor.

I looked back at the road. *Why is it always the pretty ones who're trouble?*

"What do you think you know about me?" I asked her.

"You were in the news... When was it? Last year?" She paused, but I didn't answer. "You were framed for killing a Senate candidate. April Fortney."

"True," I said. Thinking of April Fortney made me think of Rita Goldman, FBI Agent. Gone to New York to work on some task force, fighting terrorists or spies or terroristic spies. An unexpected pang of something like nostalgia poked me under the ribs.

"So you know about being framed," Jade Stone said.

"Oh no." I glanced up. "We're not going there."

"What?"

"Let me guess: You're innocent. It's all a setup. You really didn't stab that cop in the throat with a kitchen knife—which had your prints on it—nor did you flee the scene of the crime, blah-blah-blah."

"But—"

"Uh-uh. No way, sister. All you crooks are the same. None of you ever did a thing. It's all a lie, a frame job. And you see me, the one guy in ten million who really was set up, and you think, 'Geez, maybe he'll be sympathetic and join my crusade to clear my name.'"

She winced, and I continued, "Well, bullshit, lady. Pardon my language, but that dog won't hunt. Tell it to your lawyer, because I don't give a damn."

She wiped her face on her shoulder. Great. I'd terrorized a hand-cuffed female into tears. I felt like a big man.

The sign for Brown Field came up, and I slowed, putting on my blinker. It was after one in the afternoon. Depending on how fast the Junior Airman Boggs could get the rubber bands wound up on his toy plane, we could be in Dallas in six hours or less. Figure an hour to get Miss Congeniality downtown...

"Hey, Marlon, where's a good place to eat by the Dallas County jail? With a tailwind, we could be at the table by eight."

I IDLED IN THE PRIVATE terminal lounge with our prisoner while Marlon did pilot stuff. I'd draped my windbreaker over her cuffs, so it wasn't obvious, but she drew a few stares from the males in the terminal. *Looks or handcuffs? Or maybe good-looking woman in handcuffs?*

The counter guy trundled in from the back room. He looked like the before picture in a lap band surgery commercial. A polo shirt tented over his prodigious belly, and a goatee fuzzed just below his lip. He spotted me in the lobby and said, "Is there a law enforcement convention in town, or what?"

"Not that I know of. Why?"

"Yesterday, we had an ATF guy come by. Said he was meeting another guy here." He leaned on the counter and squinted through plastic-framed glasses at my prisoner. "You okay? You want some water or something?"

"ATF?" Stone asked in a weak voice. "What did he look like?"

The counter man frowned. "Uh... I don't know. Medium height, black hair."

I said to Stone, "What do you care what the ATF guy looked like?"

Her light-gray eyes flickered to me then back to the floor. She shook her head. Her Nordic complexion had drained to ghost white.

"Come on. I promise I won't bite your head off."

Another flicker, on and off. "John Bartlett is ATF," she said in a tiny voice. "He wants me gone, out of the way. Tommy was his brother and his... They were into something together. Something crooked."

"So you're saying this Bartlett guy is the one that framed you for the murder of his brother?" I didn't bother hiding my skepticism. "He killed his own brother to set you up."

She rocked back and forth in her seat, her eyes fixed somewhere far off. "I... I—No, that's..."

Marlon poked his head into the lobby. "We're ready to go, Ranger."

I watched Stone for a few more seconds, but she was done talking. I stood and stretched. "Let's go, sister. Time to get bounced all over the air in a tiny tube of glue and balsa wood."

Marlon lifted us into a clear blue sky lit with a brilliant, eye-watering sun. I sat in the passenger compartment, in a rear-facing seat directly behind Marlon. I put Stone in the forward-looking seat diagonally across the narrow fuselage, as far away from the door as I could get her.

I stretched my legs out and reclined to the backrest's limit. The engines thrummed a healthy beat, no turbulence rocked the airframe, and Marlon said we had a strong tailwind pushing us home. My prisoner had lapsed into a thoughtful silence—not that she talked a lot anyway, but thankfully, she'd shut up about the ATF—and was staring through the porthole at the brown desert passing fifteen thousand feet below.

A peaceful trip so far, in and out without a hitch. As these things went, Jade Stone was a model prisoner. I'd taken a chance back at the terminal and uncuffed her long enough for her to go pee while I waited at the restroom door. She'd taken care of business and presented her freshly washed hands for the cuffs without a tiny bit of trouble. Except for that nonsense in the car about being framed, she'd been a joy compared to the average lunkheads I'd escorted to jail.

I shifted in my seat, looked out the window, then fiddled with the armrest. The twin-engine plane droned and vibrated happily along. The prisoner stared at her feet.

"Hey, Stone." I waited until she looked at me. "What did you mean about the ATF guy, Bartlett, being into something crooked?"

"I thought you didn't want to hear it." Her tone bordered on sarcastic.

"When that guy mentioned ATF, you looked like you ate a bad plum. Color me stupid for asking, but I'm wondering what got you so spooked."

Her mother-of-pearl eyes narrowed in suspicion. "I think I'll wait until I have my attorney present before I answer any further questions."

Women. They can hold a grudge forever, every single one. "Suit yourself. At least tell me about John Bartlett. Who is he?"

She paused long enough, I thought she wasn't going to answer me. "Bartlett is a supervisory special agent with the Dallas field office of the ATF."

"And Thomas Grace was his brother?"

"Half brother."

"And you think Bartlett's out to get you because he and his brother were into some crooked stuff."

"I know they are. Were."

"What kind of crooked stuff?" I asked, but it seemed Stone was done answering questions. She looked back out the window, giving me a chance to study her profile.

A five foot eight, she was tall for a woman and had an athlete's body: slim legs, narrow waist, and modest curves. Stone was almost a total physical opposite from Rita Goldman, who could've best been described as "cute," as long as her voice wasn't on full volume.

The corners of my lips ticked up in a smile as I wondered what Rita would think of Ms. Jade Stone. Her Bronx squawk echoed in my head, "*Oh my Gawd. Who left the toy box open? Barbie's escaped.*"

I snickered, and Stone snapped off a glare in my direction. "Sorry," I said. "Not about you. Hey, Boggs!"

When Marlon leaned his head around the partition, I asked, "Did you give the aircraft a good preflight check?"

His serious face turned almost funereal. "Of course, sir."

"Good. Thanks."

"Uh, sir? Air traffic control is pushing us a little farther north of Phoenix than I originally planned."

"What's that mean for us?"

"An extra thirty minutes. Sorry, sir. I know you wanted to be on time for dinner."

"Don't worry about it, Trooper Boggs." I leaned back and tilted my hat down over my eyes. "Wake me when we're on the way down."

Lee

"THEY'RE MOVING."

"Good signal?" Lee Bragg asked.

"Strong and true." Toby Glenn, the BATF helicopter pilot sent by Bartlett, studied the laptop screen and traced the GPS signal from the transponder Bragg had planted on the Cessna.

Late yesterday afternoon, once Bragg had finished working on the Texas DPS plane, he'd flown commercial to Phoenix and met Glenn at a motel on the outskirts of Phoenix Sky Harbor International Airport.

After sleeping eight hours, Bragg drove to biggest sporting-goods store he could find and bought enough backpacking supplies to outfit a Boy Scout troop. He charged it on his government purchasing card, which had less oversight than a church bake sale, and packed it all back to the airport motel room.

Since the Texas cops wouldn't go south from San Diego and risk crossing the border, the only route home they could take would come well within the range of BATF's Bell 407 waiting for them at Sky Harbor. Then they would have a little rendezvous with electricity and C4.

"I just thought of something," Glenn said. "That plane they're flying? It has a ceiling about ten thousand feet higher than our bird."

"Doesn't matter," Bragg told him. "All we have to do is get close enough to see the bang."

Glenn nodded. "Good enough."

"After that..." Bragg zipped his shiny new backpack closed and tested the weight. "I make sure they're all dead."

"You couldn't just shoot 'em all when they land?"

"Kill a couple of cops and a woman at a crowded airport?"

"Just saying." Glenn shrugged. "Seems like a lot of work. Lot of shit to go wrong."

"Nothing's going wrong. The fuel pump I rigged blows, the plane goes down somewhere nice and remote." Bragg patted his weapon case. "We swoop in and seal the deal."

Glenn chewed his lip and focused on the laptop. "We'd best get moving. Looks like they hit Arizona airspace."

Chapter 6

"If you can walk away from a landing, it's a good landing. If you use the airplane the next day, it's an outstanding landing." — Chuck Yeager

Sam

Thud!

The aircraft jolted, snapping me out of a light doze. "What was that?"

Marlon didn't answer, and seconds later, the left engine coughed, sputtered, and died. The right engine surged with power long enough for my heart to start beating again. It cut off with a flutter. Silence pounded my eardrums.

I met Stone's wide-eyed look. "This can't be good."

"No," she said. "What happened?"

"Marlon!" I twisted in my seat but couldn't see our pilot, though I could hear him muttering and flipping switches. "If this is a joke, it's not funny."

"Mayday, Mayday, Mayday," Marlon said in a clear, calm voice. "Albuquerque Control, November Lincoln Three-Two-Six, Cessna Four-Two-One declaring emergency. Engines out. Repeat, both engines have failed. Please advise closest airfield." He rattled off a series of numbers that I took to be our position and altitude.

A freezing hand clamped around my heart. With an act of concentrated will, I forced my fingers to release the armrests and tugged the seat belt latch. *I knew this damn thing wasn't safe. I should call Marshall and say I told you so before I die.*

That dropping elevator sensation lifted my stomach as the aircraft lost altitude. I pushed out of my seat, sparing Stone a quick glance—she looked as pale as I felt—and stuck my head and shoulders into the cockpit. "Talk to me, Marlon."

"We lost power to both engines, sir."

"How—"

He held up a hand for silence and cocked his head, listening to his headset, I assumed. "Roger that, Albuquerque. I won't make that distance. We're descending through eighteen and sinking fast. I estimate about five, maybe ten minutes, of glide time left. Please advise SAR of our current location... Yes, sir, I'll look for a soft spot. Thank you, Albuquerque. November-Lincoln Three-Two-Six out."

Marlon banked the Cessna into a gentle left turn and spoke without looking at me. "Did you catch that, Ranger? Better get strapped in."

"No. Tell me we have parachutes."

"Negative."

"What the hell happened?"

"Don't know. There was a bang, and both engines quit."

"Where are we?"

"Gila National Forest."

"The what?"

"Western New Mexico." Marlon leveled the plane after making a one-hundred-eighty-degree turn. "Huge national forest preserve. There's two or three small airstrips near Glenwood, and I'm pointed at one now, but we'll never make the distance."

Wind buffeted the Cessna. Other than the rush of air, it was eerily silent. The view from the windows showed a rugged, green wrinkled terrain with jagged rocks frosted with white.

"Is that snow?"

"Some of these peaks are over ten thousand feet."

"What's happening?" Stone called from behind me.

"We're crashing," I yelled back over my shoulder. The airplane bucked and shuddered in rough air, and my stomach twisted and whirled with the motion. *I should have flown commercial. When was the last time I called my mother?*

Marlon spoke into the microphone, reporting to air traffic control, then turned to me. "You better get strapped in, sir, and make sure Ms. Stone is too."

"You belly landed a plane before?"

"Never."

"Crashed into mountain?"

"No, sir."

"If you kill us, you're going to get a very bad review in your personnel file."

Marlon nodded. He fiddled with the controls, fighting to glide the unpowered craft in a more-or-less straight line. "I'll keep that in mind, sir. Please strap in."

I backed out of the cockpit, using the rear-facing seatbacks to keep upright as the Cessna bumped and warbled over more rough air. Mountain scenery blurred past the porthole, the trees looking close enough to touch. Hell, some of them *were* close enough to touch.

"What's happening?" Stone asked again.

"Both engines lost power." I worked at loosening the cushion from the seat across from Stone. "Marlon's going to glide us in, soft as a bunny's ass. He's done this a thousand times before."

She snorted and hunched over, her cuffs clinking when she moved. "You're full of shit, and you know it."

"Here. Put this over your face." I handed her the tan leather cushion. "Hopefully, it'll take some of the impact. Hold out your hands."

I keyed open the handcuffs, kneeling in front of her to avoid falling over. The Cessna rocked, cavorting and veering all over the sky. *Mountain updrafts? Thermals? Buffalo farts?* Something was toying with us, making Marlon growl and mutter curses from up front.

Stone rubbed her wrists and looked at me with a puzzled frown.

"You deserve a chance," I told her.

She nodded and held the cushion up to her chest while I found my own seat and inserted the metal tab into the buckle. Years of commercial flying had prepared me to properly use my seat belt in the event of a crash.

"There's a small meadow up ahead," Marlon yelled. "The slope's in the wrong direction, but I'm going to try for it!"

All I could manage was a dry-croaked, "Okay."

I gripped the armrests and closed my eyes, trying to swallow past the constriction in my throat. I needed to whizz like crazy.

"Please, God," I said to myself, "don't kill us today. I'd rather not go out like this, if it's all the same to you, but if that's your will, at least don't let me pee myself."

"Hold on," Marlon shouted. "Hold on, hold on, hold—"

Wham!

Jade

THE SEAT BELT SLAMMED Jade's stomach hard enough to knock the wind out of her. Something hit the cushion she held in front of her face, and a moment later, she realized it was her knees. The plane bounced in the air, and everything became weightless for a brief moment before—*wham!*—it hit the ground with a bone-crushing impact that slapped the cushion back into her face. Jade opened her mouth to scream but couldn't draw breath. Horrific sounds assaulted her. Cracks. Snaps. Rumbles. Squeals.

She lost the cushion on the next bounce. Images came in flashes through her watering eyes. Blinks of reality, like a broken film reel. The Ranger—Cable—bucking in his seat, hat flying from his head. Glass shards, diamond-bright, spraying the air. A coffee mug arced past her face.

The smell of hot engine and hotter plastic filled her nose. Then, even worse, the bitter, astringent odor of raw fuel seared her sinuses. Something banged, something else squealed, and the plane slewed sideways. *Wham!* Her world rolled over, as if she were traveling through a spinning barrel at a carnival funhouse. Jade blanked out, her brain refusing to process the signals from her senses.

Whump! With one last hard crunch, the plane smashed to a stop. Her whirling mind refused to accept it, though.

Jade felt like an old sock left behind after the dryer stopped. Things ticked and creaked, and wind fluttered through a gaping hole to her left where a door had been. Her ears rang from the sudden cessation of sound.

The plane lay on its belly, tilted nose down and to the left. The view outside showed gravelly soil mixed with tufted bunches of grass and a scattering of wildflowers. The smell of cedar blew in with the temperate breeze that stirred the dust eddying through the cabin. Along with it came the oily odor of kerosene, strong and biting.

"Oh my God," Jade breathed. *I'm alive.*

The Ranger groaned and lifted his head. His dazed, unfocused look wandered through the cabin until his blue eyes found her watching him. Blood stained the temple over his right eye and ran down his cheek. He blinked. "What happened?" he rasped.

"We crashed." Jade fumbled with the seat belt, her fingers shaking worse than an alcoholic's. The band around her middle where the seat belt had snagged hurt like fire. Dizziness found nausea and woke it up. She suddenly wanted to throw up. "We have to get out of here. I smell gas."

"Gas?"

"Yes, gas! Like in fire." Her belt came loose, and Jade executed a graceless tumble from her seat. Her legs trembled and didn't want to work. She stumble-crawled to the Ranger and reached for his buckle, but he waved her hands away.

"I got this." His voice sounded stronger, more clear. His daze appeared to be lifting. "Lift the metal flap..." he muttered.

A trace of smoke drifted through the air, sending Jade's heart into overdrive. The doorway from the cabin to the cockpit was compressed into a triangle, and Jade had to contort her body and crawl through it to check on the pilot.

The flight deck was a mess. Smoke seeped from the control panel, and a heavy odor of burned plastic hung in the air. No glass remained in the windows, and the nose of the plane had pancaked into a crumpled heap.

The pilot hung from his safety harness, his headphones askew, and the left side of his body buried in a tangle of wreckage. Blood covered his upper lip and splattered the front of his uniform. When Jade reached two fingers to check for a pulse, his head moved, and he moaned.

"He's still alive," she shouted over her shoulder. "We have to get him out of here. Something's burning!"

"Move," Cable ordered.

Jade slithered out of the way and crouched next to the Ranger. His eyes were clearer, and he surveyed the narrow opening with a frown. "Get out of the plane."

"But—"

"Get going," he barked. Then he caught her eyes and said in a softer voice, "Look, you'll only be in the way here. Get yourself to safety."

Jade nodded and squeezed past him, staggering along the canted aisle to the new doorway to the open sky. She glanced over her shoulder. The Ranger had his back braced against the seat behind him and planted his boots on the co-pilot's chair and doorframe. He grunted and heaved. Metal squealed and shifted a half-inch, maybe less. Cable gasped and relaxed. He glanced at her.

"Get moving." Without waiting, he shouted a wordless cry and stamped both feet against the reluctant frame. A crackle of plastic and metal shuddered through the fuselage, and the opening spread another inch, maybe two.

Smoke fogged from the cockpit more heavily, crawling across the ceiling of the aircraft and trickling through the gaping hole where Jade waited. "Cable! The plane's going up any second!"

He didn't spare her a glance this time, just barked. "Move it, sister. Don't make me come over there and throw you out."

"But—"

"Marlon's coming to Thanksgiving at my house, and that's final. Now move!" He heaved and strained against the bent frame. His body shivered as he held the pressure. With a groan, metal shifted and popped. Another inch gained.

He'll never make it.

A percussive beat had been teasing her ears for the past few seconds, but the identification of the sound had eluded her, until it popped into her head. "A helicopter!"

Search and Rescue must have noted their crash and sent a rescue chopper. Maybe the forest service or even the local sheriff's office had homed in on their crash site from some nearby helipad.

Jade ducked through the opening into the field. The Cessna had come to rest with its tail at the edge of a pine forest, its nose facing downslope, in a meadow surrounded by mountain peaks and long ridges. Skid marks and bits of debris lined up behind them, showing where they'd plowed from the lowest end of the field to the highest.

The sun settled over a peak to the west, dazzling her eyes and making them water. She blinked and shaded her face with a forearm, searching for the source of the thumping rotors. Relief and excitement vied for attention. Would they arrive in time to help Cable pull the pilot from the wreckage?

It was almost on her before she spotted it. A sleek black helicopter traversed the meadow at treetop height from her right to left. It had no markings beyond an identification number. *No, wait.* There was a small seal on one door she couldn't make out.

Jade waved her arms, and the chopper banked at the far end of the field and came back. She shielded her face from the dust storm it kicked up as it slowed to a hover fifty feet away. Through blinking, watery eyes Jade could make out two men in the front seats.

Why aren't they landing? She squinted and peered through the blowing dust at the men in the helicopter. It edged closer, and she waved it in. "Come on! What are you waiting for?"

The chopper tilted, and sunlight bathed the interior of the aircraft. The side door gaped open, and the man in the passenger compartment studied her with an intense frown. He had a thin nose and black gelled-up hair. He carried some kind of rifle propped between his knees.

Jade's arms fell to her sides, and a sense of sick hopelessness washed through her. It was the man from the border, the one who had followed her to the motel in Arizona. Mr. Hawaiian Shirt.

But... how?

It didn't matter how. Bartlett's men had followed them, either electronically or by sight... and had probably brought the plane down, come to think of it.

Jade slumped to a seat on the ground. *I survive a plane crash, only to be killed by Bartlett's goons. I should win an award for unluckiest person alive.*

Chapter 7

"There is no such thing as paranoia. Your worst fears can come true at any moment." — Hunter S. Thompson

Sam

The Cessna's cockpit was a tangled mess of busted-ass plane. The crash had squeezed the narrow, Y-shaped gap in the cockpit-cabin divider into a tiny slot. The control panel and the flight controls pinched Marlon's left side.

To get my extra-tall body up front and drag Marlon's ultra-wide shoulders out, I needed more room than I had time to make. Smoke stung my eyes. A combination of throbbing headache and the reek of aviation fuel made me dizzy. I'd pushed the cabin divider open about six inches, and I needed a good six more. It was a race to see if I would pass out before or after the plane blew up.

I braced my back against the side of my seat and planted my boots on the narrow strip of cabin divider, took a deep breath, counted to three, and *heaved*! I held the tension until my legs trembled and sweat stung the cut over my eye. "Yah!"

A tiny creak. A half-inch wider, maybe. I sagged and tried to catch my breath.

"Give it up, Ranger," Marlon gasped. His skin, normally the color of polished oak, had faded to a pale walnut and gleamed with sweat.

"Shut up, Boggs. Start getting loose from those restraints." *One. Two. Three!* "Yaaah!"

Metal squawked and groaned. The divider popped sideways, bending toward the cockpit. If I couldn't spread the opening, maybe I could knock away one side of it. I kicked it over and over with both heels, pounding the barrier farther back, smashing it against the co-pilot's seat until it stuck for good.

I paused, panting smoke into my lungs and coughing. Sweat streaked my face and burned my eyes. "You ready to go yet, Boggs?"

Marlon undid the final harness latch with a shaking hand and tried to lift himself free of the pilot's chair. He sank down with a gurgle of pain and hissed. I twisted around to get a look. His left arm was pinned between the arm of the chair and a bulge in the bulkhead.

"Hold on a sec," I told him. "I've got to kick some more, push that wall back."

Smoke rolled from under the control panel, to be torn away by fitful gusts through the broken windows. How Marlon had managed to not get shredded by flying glass was beyond me. The oily stink of burning plastic hung in the air.

Stone yelled something from outside the plane, but I didn't catch it. I twisted and torqued my body into pretzel shapes, bracing my back against the piece of cabin divider I'd previously beaten out of the way. I had to stretch my legs over Marlon, who appeared to be fading; his head lolled to the side, and his eyelids fluttered.

"Stay with me, Trooper Boggs. That's an order."

"Yessir," he slurred, barely audible.

The bowed-in section of fuselage trapping Marlon's arm was made of weaker stuff than the divider; one solid *push* was all it would take to bend it out of the way.

"C'mon, buddy." I levered up to my knees and gripped Marlon by the armpits. His head rolled to the side and bumped my chest. "I can't deadlift you, Boggs. You're gonna have to help."

His left arm was a limp rag, oozing thin snakes of crimson. It dangled while the trooper pushed off with his right. He hissed through clenched teeth. His butt came loose from the seat, and he screamed, "My leg, my leg!"

"What's wrong? Is it jammed in there?"

"No," he panted. "No... it hurts... to move." Marlon blinked his eyes clear and sucked a deep breath. "Okay, okay. Let's go."

Stone stuck her head inside the plane and yelled at me, "They're coming!"

"Who's coming?"

"The guys who want me dead!"

I craned a glance at her. Her face reflected serious, scared, and mad all at once. "One disaster at a time, sister."

She said something else, too low to hear.

"What?" I yelled over my shoulder. I settled my arms around Marlon's shirtfront, clamping my hands together across his chest from a squatting position. "You ready, big guy?"

"I said, hurry up, you stubborn ass," Stone hollered back.

"C'mon, Marlon. Heave!"

With one sustained gurgle of pain, Marlon slid loose from the seat, and I fell on my butt with the trooper on top of me. I caught my breath for a long two-second count then wrestled out from under him. Stone squatted beside me.

"I thought I told you to get out of here."

"How can I help?"

"Can you get his feet?"

I recovered my grip around the trooper's size-fifty chest while Stone slithered past us. Blood slicked my hands, and I coughed from the pall of smoke hanging in the cabin. Orange light flickered in the cockpit, and tendrils of flame crawled up the instrument panel. We were down to seconds.

Marlon had passed out, and I could see why. His left foot lay twisted in the completely wrong direction, broken at the knee or ankle. I jerked my chin and said to Stone, "Be careful with that one."

"Oh, Jesus!"

Lift with your legs, Cable. I grunted and pushed to get half-upright. My head spun, and I nearly fell again but managed to stumble backward with Marlon in tow.

Stone held the trooper's legs at the calves and kept them from bumping along the floor. Smoke shrouded her, and she coughed in ragged bursts. When she glanced up, her eyes were reddened and streaming tears.

Once I noticed hers, I realized I was doing the same thing. I'd been hacking steadily for a while, and my vision kept swimming in and out of focus, either from irritation or dizziness.

The good news was the door—or the big hole where the door used to be—was close. "Swing around," I said, and Stone nodded. I felt for the ground with my heel, found it, and ducked my head next to Marlon's. He groaned but didn't wake up.

Coming out of the smoky interior into the gusty mountain air felt like being sprung from hell. The wind whipped smoke away from the ragged portal and chilled the sweat soaking my shirt. It took me a second to realize a helicopter, not Mother Nature, was generating the breeze.

"That's them!" Stone shouted.

I squinted at the sleek aircraft hovering ten feet in the air at about the distance of an NFL Hail Mary. A guy in the passenger door sat there, not moving. I only caught a glimpse between smoke clouds. "What are they doing?"

"They want to kill me," she snapped. Her hair whipped across her face, and strong drafts plastered the T-shirt to her body. Stone held Marlon's legs and tossed her head, trying to clear the hair from her face. Together, we blundered and tripped across the stubbly field, gaining distance from the smoking wreck.

Stone's paranoia leeched into my bloodstream like the flu. Something about the way the helicopter hung there, unmoving in the late-afternoon sunlight, seemed... menacing.

I scanned the meadow, looking for a hidey-hole to protect us from any fireballs that might erupt once the fuel tanks blew. And to hide us from any boogeymen in black helicopters.

Black helicopters. Some of my neighbors have nightmares about black helicopters.

The hovering machine backed away and settled to the ground a good long sprint from the crash site. A hundred yards, maybe one hundred fifty. *A sensible precaution against explosive fuel? Or something wicked this way comes to kick our asses?*

A scattering of pines started a few steps uphill from where the Cessna's tail lay. Farther upslope, the forest grew thicker and the cover denser.

"Into the tree line!"

Stone nodded, and we made it between the first two pines before a whoosh sent orange flames shooting into the sky. Black oily smoke boiled away from the fire, and the heat warmed my face.

"That's not the tanks going," I shouted. "That's the loose fuel."

The woman was in good shape, not breathing hard, even with the crash and exertion, but the thin air was starting to bite my lungs. I huffed one ragged breath after another. *But,* I said to myself, *I'm carrying the heavy part and doing all the work; the only thing she has to do is hold his legs.*

My heels dug into loose soil, and Marlon grew heavier with every step. I likened it to humping a sack of concrete up a sandy hill while being chased by a fire-breathing dragon. The trooper's left arm drooled blood along the ground in a steady trail, dribbling from cuts along the dark skin of his forearm.

I looked over my shoulder, hunting better cover. "There! To the left." A fallen tree lay sideways to the slope, twenty yards higher. It was blocked at either end by neighboring trees, like a goal post with a fallen crossbar.

Zing! Crack! Bark exploded from the pine on my right.

I flinched and nearly fell. "They're shooting at us!"

Stone's look said, "How dumb can you be?"

I guess people really are *out to get her.*

"C'mon. Let's move it!" I repositioned myself, getting my arms around Marlon's waist and twisting him into a fireman's carry. With a grunt and a curse, I deadlifted the trooper onto my shoulder. My legs wobbled for a second, but another bullet whining by my head got me moving forward. Churning uphill, blowing like a Clydesdale, I lumbered in a drunken beeline for our makeshift bulwark.

The Cessna's fuel tanks cooked off with a dull *boom.* The blast shoved me in the back, and I tripped over the log.

"Oof!" I slapped the ground with a palm, which nearly broke the wrist on my free hand and sent a cattle prod of fiery pain into my elbow.

Marlon landed with a whump, and his head bounced off the ground. He moaned, and his eyelids fluttered.

"Shut up, ingrate," I said. "At least you didn't get blown up." A bullet chipped bark overhead. "Or shot."

Stone landed beside me, belly down with her eyes squeezed shut.

"Are you okay?" I asked.

"No."

"Are you shot?"

"No." One gray eye squinted open. "No, I'm not shot."

"What's wrong?"

She glared. "Are you kidding me?"

"Take care of Marlon while I see what I can do to discourage these boys from shooting at people."

Stone crawled to Marlon and checked his pulse with two fingers. His breathing came fast and shallow, and his complexion had lost even more color. The boy needed a hospital.

I dragged myself around so I could peek over the fallen pine and pulled my Kimber .45 from its high-rise holster. The eight rounds in the pistol and two extra magazines—twenty-two shots—was all the firepower at my disposal. Marlon had taken his utility belt off to fly the plane, and I hadn't thought to grab it when we pulled him out.

The Cessna's funeral pyre glowed orange with yellow highlights, and a greasy stink of burned plastic and gasoline boiled from it. The helicopter and its friendly fliers were hidden on the other side of the bonfire.

The shooter, whoever he was, had to have been firing nearly blind when he took those shots, which was fairly stupid. It would've been easy for him to walk up on us while we dragged Marlon from the plane and shoot a couple of magazines' worth of bullets into each of us.

Unless he wanted to miss. That thought gave me pause. *Why sabotage an aircraft's engines... because you don't want to leave any evidence of premeditated murder. Your target plane crashes, you're hanging around with a helicopter near where you think it'll come down, you swoop in, make sure everybody's dead, and clean up the scene. Oops, sorry Mrs. Cable, your son died in a tragic accident while transporting a wanted fugitive.*

But they could've gotten the drop on us and easily polished us off at their leisure. Shooting only put us on alert. That left either stupidity or poor marksmanship.

Stone had said she was being chased by the ATF, so I couldn't discount a sincere lack of mental ability. Most feds were pretty damn bright—Rita, for instance—but the ATF seemed to attract a different type of agent. *Look at Waco. Look at Operation Fast and Furious. Case closed.*

"Cable?" Stone sounded urgent.

I twisted around to find she'd made Marlon as comfortable as she could, propping his feet on a branch of the same tree we sheltered behind and bunching pine boughs under his head. She held his wounded forearm against her belly, staining her T-shirt and jeans with blood.

"What?"

"This arm needs a bandage," she said. "I can't stop the bleeding with just my hands."

The first aid kit on the plane was surely just a lump of bubbly plastic. I cast around for an alternative, but nothing leapt into my hand. "My T-shirt. That's all I have."

I shot a glance downslope. No one moved. The fire had subsided to a billowing cloud of dirty-gray smoke—the perfect screen for anybody approaching. Likewise, we were screened from a gunman coming uphill. Unless, or until, he looped wide and flanked us, we were concealed from incoming fire.

I laid the Kimber on top of the fallen pine and stripped off my cotton button-down and damp T-shirt in record time. Stone caught the white tee when I tossed it to her, followed by my pocketknife. The thought crossed my mind that I had armed a prisoner in my custody, making me an uncommonly stupid Ranger and potential corpse.

Stone started cutting bandages without sparing me a glance, even though I was bare-chested. *She must be preoccupied.* I shrugged into my once-white shirt and scanned downhill. Motion to my right flickered between the pines.

"Look alive, Stone. We've got company coming."

Chapter 8

"When trouble arises and things look bad, there is always one individual who perceives a solution and is willing to take command. Very often, that person is crazy." — Dave Barry

Bartlett

The orange Wilson basketball arced in a perfect rainbow and swished home with a satisfying *sssh-ute*. Nothing but net. Bartlett held the gooseneck pose with his shooting hand for an extended moment, dancing back a few steps before his victory fist pump. He cocked an eye at the sweat-dripping Luksa and said, "Six games to none, Dan. Give up yet?"

"Mercy, Reeder." Dan Luksa panted and sagged. "Mercy."

John Reed Bartlett grinned and chugged from a bottle of Gatorade before slapping it back down on the patio table.

The backyard of Bartlett's two-story ranch-style home featured a concrete half-court basketball layout, complete with NBA-official-distance free throw and three-point lines. Next to it, a small patio separated the court from an Olympic-sized lap pool and a six-person hot tub for lap activities of a more personal kind.

"The sun's getting low on the horizon, Danny Boy." Bartlett threw the shorter man a towel. "You ready for a beer?"

"And a shower." Luksa mopped the sweat from his face. "Six years in Houston, I still can't get used to the heat."

"Lose some of that spare tire, and it'll help."

"Easy for you to say."

Bartlett threw back his head and barked a laugh, but he secretly agreed. At fifty-nine, he had the body of a thirty-year-old. At six-two, with a hundred ninety pounds of animal muscle stretched over hard bone and tied together by leathery sinew, Bartlett wore a size-thirty-four waist and had to have his jackets tailored to fit the breadth of his shoulders.

He led the way to his patio door without looking back, knowing Luksa would follow. Men always followed Reeder Bartlett; that was how it was. How it would always be. He cut a path through the world with a strong jaw and jutting chin, taking charge of international crises and backyard cookouts alike.

The satellite phone on his kitchen counter rang as he opened the sliding door. He glanced at the display before answering. *Speaking of a crisis in the making...*

"Talk to me, Lee."

"On scramble?"

Bartlett let a snort stand for his answer. As if he would have this kind of conversation unencrypted when the geeks at the NSA could find out the color of his underwear from an open call.

"Well, the plane went down, just like I planned it..." Lee started strong then paused. Wind buffeted the phone's pickup. "No problems there."

"And?"

"It crash-landed way the hell back in the Gila National Forest. On a mountainside. I don't know which one right this sec..."

"And?"

"Pilot did a great job. I, uh, I don't know how he managed it, but he brought the plane down in one piece."

"And?"

"I've got 'em pinned down about a hundred yards up from the crash site." The bustle of wind drowned out a couple of words. "Burning to the ground as we speak, so my little bit of C4 damage won't likely be found."

"Pinned down." Bartlett caught Luksa's eye, pointed to the fridge, and made a drink-tipping gesture.

Luksa draped his towel around his neck and nodded.

"The pilot's wounded, I think."

A slow squeeze of intense irritation compressed Bartlett's jaw, and he had to force himself to relax. When leading men, sometimes it was necessary to keep calm, even though all he wanted to do was strangle them until their eyes popped out! "Talk to me, Lee. In English, *compadre*. Is the girl still alive, or what?"

"It... it looks like she may be, yes."

Bartlett thought through his next response, discarding several cutting and demeaning comments. Ridiculing one's subordinates reduced their loyalty and eroded team morale. Was it time for the Gipper, or Barry Switzer? He accepted the cold Heineken Dark Luksa handed him and took a sip before responding. "What is your action plan to resolve this situation, Mr. Bragg? You said you could handle this responsibility, and yet at the moment, it's looking a little like an egregious amount of fuck up to me. You're not a fuck-up kind of guy, Lee, so tell me you have a resolution strategy."

"Well... you said no signs of foul play, right?"

"That would be optimal."

"I had Glenn call in the crash site as six miles in the wrong direction, using fake call signs. So we got some time before Search and Rescue shows up. I thought I'd run 'em up the mountain here, away from the plane. Either the elements will get 'em, or I'll shoot 'em and drop 'em in a ravine where they'll never be found."

Bartlett waited, thinking over the idea.

"The pilot's injured," Bragg said. "Looks like they'll be dragging the pilot for a ways, so I've gotta harass 'em a bit to get 'em moving."

"Sounds complicated, Lee."

"I know, boss." Bragg sighed, and Bartlett pictured his shrug. "Look, here's what I'll do. They don't move, I'll shoot 'em all, and we'll load 'em in the chopper, carry the bodies somewhere far away, and bury 'em deep. People'll think they wandered off, got lost."

Bartlett smiled for the first time since picking up the phone. "Don't wait."

"What?"

"Don't try all that other fancy shit. Do what you just said. Kill the cunt and her bodyguards and carry them off before somebody spots the fire and shows up to investigate."

"Uh... if you're sure..."

"Damn straight, I'm sure. Excellent plan, Lee. Well-thought-out. I knew I could count on you." Bartlett tipped his beer at Luksa and winked. "Call me when it's done. Bartlett out."

Lee

LEE THUMBED OFF THE satellite phone and swallowed the ball of acid that challenged his throat. Despite all his tough talk to the helicopter pilot, Lee really didn't like the idea of killing people, especially law enforcement people who were only doing their jobs.

Ironically, in the line of duty, Bragg had never shot at anyone and had rarely drawn his weapon. Only after joining Bartlett's crew had he started killing people. All three of his victims were criminal mutts, to be sure, but their deaths would be classified as murder in the first, no matter which jurisdiction caught the case.

He looked at Glenn, who stood by the open door of the chopper, headset dangling from one hand. "You catch that?"

"Some." The wiry pilot had a mat of curly ginger hair and a naturally pale complexion. Bragg couldn't see the man's eyes through his aviator sunglasses, but he got the impression of nervousness drifting off the pilot in small tells.

"We have to bag these people, then we haul 'em off somewhere and bury 'em deep."

"What's this 'we' shit, Batman? I just fly the bird. I don't do the wet stuff."

"Yeah," Bragg snorted. "I figured. Hand me that backpack."

The clouds of smoke from the blackened Cessna had thinned to wispy streamers dancing on heat waves. The view up the mountain shimmered, a green-brown blur of trees and rocks filtered through a mirage of flickering warmth. Bragg knew pretty well where the woman and the cop had gone to ground, having spotted glimpses as they staggered under the burden of carrying the pilot.

With the black trooper down, that left one poorly armed Ranger against his Aimpoint laser-scoped M4. The sun dropped behind him, giving him favorable conditions for stalking. However, charging straight up into the Ranger's gunsights would be stupid.

"I'm gonna loop around to the right," Bragg said. "There's more cover that way, and I can flank 'em."

"Great plan," Glenn told him flatly. "While you're sneakin' through the woods, I'm lifting my hairy Irish ass out of here and waiting somewhere out of the line of fire."

Bragg sneered. "Gee, thanks."

"Give me all the dirty looks you want. Bartlett pays me to fly, not shoot or get shot at."

"Just leave your damn phone on. I don't wanna be waitin' on your lily-white ass when I call."

Bragg waited for the noise and the dust storm raised by the helicopter lifting off to make his move. He scuttled across the open meadow, keeping the body of the plane between him and the probable location of the Ranger. He made the safety of the sparse pine growth without incident then paused to take stock.

The slope rose at a moderate pitch of maybe ten degrees for a long sprint before canting at a steeper grade farther up the mountain. To his right, pines intermixed with bare patches of rocky soil went on for as far as he could see, while the meadow he'd left behind covered several acres in the opposite direction.

Trees grew closer together the higher upslope he looked, and the shadows were heavier. The last of the sun's light brightened the ridge behind him. An unseen mockingbird tweeted close by and was answered by another, farther away.

Bragg's sphincter clenched, and he winced at the sudden need to take a dump. Wouldn't that be a joy? He'd seen that movie before: guy takes a squat in the woods and gets killed by the enemy. *No, thanks.*

For a moment, he wondered how it had come to this. Shooting civilians and other LEOs to protect his criminal friends. To keep Mama Bragg's middle child out of jail. Was that how he was raised? He swallowed more stomach acid and grimaced at the burn in his chest.

He crept forward, fading from one tree to the next. Pine needles and gravel scratched underfoot, and a gusty breeze chilled the sweat on his forehead. He reached a point roughly parallel to where he believed the crash survivors had gone to ground and paused again. The forest was thick enough—he could dart from tree to tree in seconds, too fast for someone to aim and fire.

The downside of those same trees was that Bragg couldn't see more than two dozen feet ahead. He could step right on top of them before he even saw them. He settled to a knee and tuned his head like a radio antenna, listening for the rustle of cloth, the vibration of footfalls, and the sound of voices.

Fucking Bartlett. Him and his goddamn alpha dog, Vince Lombardi bullshit. If his cocky little brother hadn't let his bitch get close, none of this would have happened. Bartlett had waited too long for his brother to handle his business, and she'd shanked Tommy while Bartlett waited in the car, probably practicing his politician smile in the rearview mirror. *And now I have to clean this shit up. By killing more people.*

If Mama could only see me now. Wouldn't she be proud?

He jumped at a crackling in the brush behind him, whirled, then sighed in relief when a squirrel bounded away and corkscrewed up a tree.

He sighed. Sitting there wasn't getting the job done. As it was, they wouldn't finish until well after dark, which would make it one hell of a long day. Bragg gripped his M4 in sweaty palms and checked that the safety was off. He scooted from one cover to the next, pausing at each stop to listen hard. A shallow drainage channel cut across his path, and he hopped it in one long step, pausing by a deadfall to get his bearings.

"Looking for somebody?"

The voice behind him shocked Bragg with a jolt of pure icy, copper-tasting fear. His bowels clenched, and he flash-froze to the spot. When Bragg craned his neck for a look, the Ranger rose from a thick pile of twigs and debris in the middle of the drainage cut. He held a .45 auto in a rock-steady grip, and the eyes behind it reminded Bragg of ice chips. Bragg's finger slipped through the guard of the M4 and sought the cool steel of the trigger.

"Don't do it," the tall man said. "One twitch, and I'll blow your lights out."

"Don't... don't shoot." His voice echoed in his head.

"Drop the weapon first then get that helicopter back down here. After that, we can have a nice chat about who you're with."

Images of his immediate future flashed through Bragg's head. Arrest. Arraignment. Trial. The look on his mother's face...

"Put down the weapon, boy," the Ranger said. The tall man wasn't any older than Bragg, but his eyes narrowed. His grip tightened on the pistol. "Put it down now, or get ready to shake hands with the devil."

Bragg swallowed. He thought about his future. Thought about dropping the M4. Went for it instead.

Chapter 9

"Not until we are lost do we begin to find ourselves." — Henry David Thoreau

Sam

While I was gone, Jade Stone had removed Marlon's left shoe and split the pant leg. No bones stuck out, but his foot pointed sideways, and his ankle had swollen as big as a football. She held his leg in her lap and probed the flesh along his shin.

When I dumped the pile of BATF gear next to her, Stone glanced at it before going back to Marlon's ankle. "Is he dead?"

"Yes."

"The knee looks okay," she reported, "but I think his ankle's shattered."

"What about the arm?"

"No bones broken. Some deep cuts. I wrapped it as tight as I dared."

I nodded. Too snug, and it would cut off the circulation. Too loose, and it would keep bleeding. The strips of my once-white T-shirt tied around Marlon's forearm and bicep were dark crimson.

I dug in the pile of stuff I'd taken from the ATF agent's body and pulled out another shirt, a dark-blue jersey-style cotton pullover. "Here. Use this too."

Stone eyed the shirt then me. Her clothing and hands were splattered with blood. Crimson smudged one cheekbone where she'd absently wiped a hand across it.

I handed her the jersey before settling to the ground next to her with a graceless thump. I felt like an old man who'd tumbled down the stadium stairs and been trampled by a high school marching band. "I just shot and killed a federal law enforcement officer." I set aside the agent's tactical rifle and thumbed open the ID wallet in my hand. "Lee Bragg of the Bureau of Alcohol, Tobacco, Firearms, and Explosives. Recognize him?"

She peered at the ID card. "I ditched him at a motel in Arizona, but somehow, he followed me to the border. He wore a Hawaiian shirt then."

"He carried a satellite phone, but it takes a code to turn it on." I showed her the phone, and she shrugged. A riddle she couldn't answer any better than I could. To have help at our fingertips but no way to make the connection was frustrating. I'd tried his badge number, the birthdate on his driver's license, and a few simple number combinations. The phone mocked me in that smug way technology does the ignorant.

Stone poked the tip of my penknife through the cotton shirt and augured a hole in the armpit seam. She dug her fingers through it and tugged, ripping at the seam a piece at a time. She didn't look at me.

"At some point..." I paused for an adrenaline-aftershock yawn. "At some point, you're gonna tell me that story about why federal agents want you dead and gone. But we have bigger catfish on the stove."

Marlon groaned, and his eyelids fluttered, but he didn't wake up. His forehead gleamed with sweat, and he looked almost pasty. A goose egg had swelled over his left eyebrow. Stone waited until he settled before going back to worrying the garment into strips.

"Catfish?" she asked.

"When the helicopter took off, we only saw the one guy on the ground. No telling if there were more in the chopper. Though I doubt it. If they had more, they'd have followed Mr. Bragg in his flanking maneuver, not flown off in the chopper." A chilly gust of wind shook the trees and made me shiver. Pine needles pattered to the ground. Dank gray clouds squatted directly over my head, and it had grown darker in the few minutes since I sat down.

She nodded at me. "I only ever saw the one guy. I guess they thought that's all they needed to take care of me." Stone fashioned one sleeve of the jersey into a long strip of cloth. She scooted over to Marlon's arm and eased the strip around his bicep.

"Look, here's how I see it," I mused. "Common wisdom says stay with the wreck, don't wander off. Rescuers can find you easier. But if Bragg has friends..." I cocked an eyebrow at Stone.

"Bartlett," she confirmed.

"Then Mr. Chopper Pilot might be hauling them back here. And even with my brand-new M4 and all the equipment donated by the ATF"—I toed the backpack by my feet—"I might not be able to kick all their asses, no matter how pure my heart."

Even her scowl was pretty. Stone had split the end of her bandage into two tails, which she used to tie off the wrap. It was too dark to see if the blue shirt had soaked through, but that was the best we could do under the circumstances.

"Here." I handed her Bragg's windbreaker with the yellow ATF lettering on the back. "Lay this over him; it's the closest we have to a blanket. Then put this on." I held up a Kevlar vest, only slightly damp with blood around the collar. "It'll keep you warm and maybe stop a bullet if any come your way. Put on the rest of Bragg's shirt too."

Another gust rattled the trees, accompanied by the splat of heavy raindrops. The temperature had dropped from a moderate seventy-five to under sixty. When a rolling rumble of thunder reached us, Stone studied the gloomy clouds. "Is that what I think it is?"

"Yeah, that's catfish number two. We have no shelter, unless there's enough plane left to hide in, and it's not too hot. I got a feeling night will get pretty frigid at this elevation, especially in a storm. Let's see if Lee packed a log cabin in here." I reached for the backpack at my feet with a grunt and unzipped it. Man, I was tired. And I hurt. Getting into a plane crash and a gunfight wasn't for the weak. "Hey. We have a little food, freeze-dried... and a couple of bottles of water—thank you,

Lee—and a foil blanket. Here, use this, as well as the jacket... Water-proof matches! Yeah, baby! A compass and—*hah,* a teeny first aid kit, big enough to treat a boo-boo. Some other junk. Swiss Army knife. Bet you could've used that a few minutes ago."

"So what do we do? We shouldn't move Trooper Boggs."

I frowned at the huddled form of the stocky and muscular Boggs. His breathing was faster than it should have been, and he groaned in his sleep, small, weak little moans of compressed pain. "I sure can't move him far by myself. We need to find somewhere safe and relatively sheltered. The wreck is somewhat sheltered, but it's not safe. We need to be near water."

I popped open the first aid kit, which was about the size of a pack of cigarettes. "Here's a packet of painkillers. See if you can give him this." I handed her the pills and a water bottle. "Give him as much of the water as he'll take then drink the rest yourself."

"What about you?"

"I'm okay for now. We have another."

"You should make a funnel. See if we can catch some rainwater."

"Heh. My older brothers were the Boy Scouts of the family; they could make a funnel out of pine bark. I didn't make it past Webelo. Too busy watching movies in my room or avoiding getting gang-tackled by Matt and Luke."

"You have two brothers?"

"I had three. Luke died in Afghanistan. John's a doctor in Houston. He stayed out of the fights somehow, always off doing something on his own. Too old for the kid stuff."

Thunder rumbled, closer and louder than before, and the wind picked up. "Enough yakking. We need to make a move, find shelter. Stay here for a bit while I scout around. I'm gonna check the plane, see if we can get near it. With this weather blowing in, at least we'll be safe from bad guys for a bit. They can't fly in a storm."

"You hope."

"Yes." I groaned and forced myself upright. "Yes, I do."

Bartlett

THE SATELLITE PHONE by the bedside table went off, rousing Bartlett from a deep sleep to full wakefulness in an instant. He'd always been that way, able to awaken fully alert, much like he imagined predator cats did in the wild. Out of habit, he checked the clock before answering. After midnight.

"Is it done?" he barked.

"Uh, no, sir. That's why I'm calling."

"Who's this? Glenn?"

"Yes, sir, it's me. Glenn."

"Where's Bragg?"

A pause. "That's just it. He's been on the ground for over six hours and hasn't called in for pickup."

Six hours? Fucking idiot. He enunciated his words with care. "Glenn, you waited six hours to check in? Bragg should have been done in thirty minutes."

"Well... a storm blew in, and I figured he was maybe having some trouble."

"Some trouble."

Glenn didn't say anything, and Bartlett made note to find another helicopter pilot. Finding a pilot wasn't hard; it was finding one who could bend with the breeze, so to speak, and not ask too many questions. He sighed. A coach worked with the players he was given. "You try his phone?"

"Just now."

"And?"

Glenn swallowed, a clearly audible sound. "No answer."

Bartlett screwed his eyes shut. "You might want to lead with that next time, Glenn. All right, spilled milk. We need to move on. What's the situation on the storm?"

"The heavy stuff's over. Just rain at the moment."

Bartlett sat up in bed and swung his bare legs over the side. He switched on the lamp. The figure next to him moved and asked a sleepy question.

"All right," Bartlett said, "here's the play. Find the nearest airstrip where we can bring in a charter flight. I'll load up the rest of the boys and meet you there. We'll go in and take care of business ourselves." He paused for a thought. "What's the situation on the Search and Rescue?"

"Grounded until daylight, just like I am. They're still thinking the wreck's a couple of mountains in the wrong direction too."

"All right. Get the bird ready to fly, get yourself some rest. Once we get rolling, I expect everybody to be balls to the wall, twenty-four, seven. *Comprende?*"

"Yes, sir."

"Notify me once you have an airfield where we can rendezvous. And call me if you get word from Bragg. Bartlett out."

Stupid twit. Bartlett allowed himself a few moments to fume, then his command persona took over. He slapped the blanket-covered butt of the person next to him. "Get your snug little ass out of bed. We have work to do."

Dan Luksa peered muzzy-eyed from the sheets and moaned, "What the fuck?"

"Bragg screwed the pooch. Now we gotta roll." Bartlett bounded up and headed for the bathroom, naked. Standing in front of the toilet, he gave his johnson a tug to get the flow going and spoke through the open door. "Get on the horn and find us the fastest charter plane available. I want to be wheels up by six a.m. Then round up Ray and Reuben. Mack the Knife. Dominic and Steve-O too. Tell Dom to bring his long rifle and plenty of point-five-oh to go with it."

Bartlett shook the dew off the lily, flushed, and reached for the shower controls. Luksa bumped into the bathroom, squinted against the harsh light, and lined up at the commode, his deflated cock nestled into a ginger bush. Bartlett felt a stirring below his belly.

"When you call, tell 'em to bring their hiking gear and enough supplies to rough it for a few days. No telling how long this'll take, now that Stone's detail has a heads-up."

Bartlett tested the water and waited until Luksa flushed. "Come on, let's get in the shower. We have time to knock off another one before we gotta move. Who knows when we will again."

Chapter 10

"Don't mess with Texas women." — Anonymous
Captain Marshall

In direct violation of the state's no-smoking policy, and with deliberate premeditation, Captain Les Marshall of the Texas Rangers lit a cigarette. As a nod to the lung police, he switched on his desktop air sucker, which pulled in the smoke and blew it back out, mostly clean.

At five-eight in tall boots, Marshall was a thirty-six-year veteran lawman, as tough as duct tape and as unrelenting as poverty. He'd jailed mass murderers, serial rapists, psychopaths, sociopaths, bipolar bikers, drug-addled gangbangers, and drunken wifebeaters, all without a twitch of fear.

Until now. At that moment, he would rather have charged into hell carrying a bucket of gasoline than pick up the phone on his desk, call Sarah Jo Cable, and admit that her baby boy had gone down in a plane crash.

At seven in the morning, the office outside his door already burbled with activity. One of their own was missing, and his troops were pissed. Telephones chirped, and rough male voices barked questions with an expectation of getting some answers. People darted in and out with slips of paper—email being a time-sucking invention of the devil, in Marshall's opinion—dropping them on his desk and hurrying away. No one wanted to catch a piece of whatever brewed behind his brown eyes.

So far, the crash had avoided any press coverage, which was a blessing. That gave Marshall a little extra time to get some answers before calling Sarah Jo with the news. The phone rang when he reached for it. He snatched it up and snarled his name.

"Boss, it's Dusty. Just callin' to tell you SAR's still socked in. Weather's playin' hell up in the mountains, and can't nobody move until after the front blows through. Clouds are too low."

"Fuckin' bunch of New Mexico pussies. We got any Texas boys up there? Who's in El Paso?"

"I don't know. I'll find out."

"Do that," Marshall snapped. "Call me when you find somebody with balls."

Marshall banged the phone down and took a squinting hit on his Marlboro, pinching it between his finger and thumb. *One simple job. Go to California, pick up a prisoner, come back. How hard could it be?* Marshall ground his cigarette out and stared at the phone like it had jumped up and taken an electronic shit on his desk.

Ranger Samuel Duncan Cable. How that boy could find more trouble than ninety-nine other Rangers was beyond Marshall's comprehension. Marshall had kept an eye on the Cable boys after their daddy died, dropping in on them from time to time with fatherly advice or a fatherly butt-kicking, whichever was most needful. Their father had been a close friend of his and a tough *hombre*.

After eight years on the State Troopers and being promoted early on account of Marshall pulling some strings, Samuel Cable had spent three years in the Rangers. That boy could eat scrap iron and piss steel wire. He'd lost not one jot of the mulish hardheadedness that seemed to run through the Cable clan like pine knots in a board fence. If anybody could live through a plane crash, it would be Sam.

The lingering smoke of his latest cigarette stung Marshall's eyes and made them water. He blinked, snorted up a wad of snot, leaned over, and spit it in the trash. *Time to quit being a pussy, Marshall. Get 'er done.*

He picked up the phone and dialed Sarah Jo's number from memory.

Sam

CLOUDS OF SMOKE PUFFED up when I fed a few damp twigs into the fire, the moisture hissing away as they burned. The rain had turned to a misty drizzle, more fog than anything else, that cloaked our campsite in a cottony-gray shroud. Sounds were muted. The plop and spatter of raindrops punctuated the crack and pop of burning sticks.

At some point in the geological history of the mountains, a river had undercut the ledge of rock at our backs and created a natural overhang, not so much a cave as a notch undercut in the sandstone wall. As the water sliced deeper into the mountain, the streambed dropped, leaving this shelter for weary plane crash survivors and, by the evidence left behind, small, fuzzy rodents.

I'd found it after stumbling around in the near darkness for nearly an hour last night. After skirting the hot mess of the plane's dead carcass, I'd crossed the meadow and found a game trail that disappeared to my right. Following it led me to an outcropping of blocky stones that became a ledge that turned into a cliff. Fifteen minutes of steady hiking brought me to the notch in the rock, which I decided would have to do.

The nasty weather had kicked up to a wind-whipped sprinkle of stinging droplets by the time I made it back uphill to Boggs and Stone. Between us, Stone and I managed to get Boggs on my back, piggyback style, then I managed to stumble downhill to the campsite in leg-shivering steps. Halfway across the meadow, the rain cut loose in a real temper tantrum, and lightning fired in jagged bolts. My puny little Mini Maglite was next to useless. I retraced my steps more by feel than sight, every step crushed by Marlon's one hundred ninety pounds.

"He ain't heavy…" I gasped at one point.

"Don't say it!" Stone's voice came from the darkness beside me, weak but with feeling.

"He's just damned awkward."

Bumping the rock ledge with my right shoulder, staggering through muddy soil, dodging pine trees, rocks, and lightning strikes, I found the cut about one step before I fell on my face. Getting out of the lashing rain was such a relief, I nearly dropped Marlon.

Shivering and sniffling, I built a fire with the dry tinder of some mouse's bedding and the litter of twigs and sticks close to hand. My breath came in misting huffs, and I fumbled with the package of water-proof matches, breaking three before I got one lit. I huddled over the tiny flame as if in prayer—in a way, I was.

Twelve hours of restless sleep later, things were looking up. I tended the fire, the silver emergency blanket wrapped around my shoulders while Marlon and Stone huddled under the sleeping bag. The *shush* of a nearby fast-flowing stream promised water, and we were warm, dry, and relatively safe.

I had that post-crash stiffness from being tumbled around in a metal tube, nearly burned up, killing a man, and then hiking with a human backpack down a mountain. I was sure everyone got that from time to time. *Wonder if they make a big enough pain pill for mornings like that?*

Marlon stirred and growled, "*Ahh!* Man that hurts." His unfocused gaze wandered until he found me looking at him. "What happened?" he croaked. His eyes were bloodshot and bleary, and he looked like a freight train had run him down, backed up a hundred yards, and done it again.

"Plane fall down, go boom. Remember?" I crawled over and sat next to him—the ceiling being too low to stand higher than a crouch. I tipped a water bottle to his lips. "You wrecked it, you have to pay for it."

"I—aw, shit," he snarled when he moved. "That *really* hurts."

"You're busted up pretty good, *amigo*. And you need some pain meds."

"He needs a hospital." Stone rolled up onto an elbow and braced her head in her hand. "He's burning up with fever, and that arm is going to get infected."

Marlon shifted his eyes and found the woman next to him, under the sleeping bag. "This is not how I pictured this happening."

"Anything for a date, huh, Boggs?" I checked his forehead with my palm and found she was right.

Marlon was definitely running a fever. Pearls of clammy sweat rolled off his forehead, and he shivered, even under the bag.

I took off the silver space blanket and laid it over him. "Here, drink some more water."

"I'll give it to him." Stone took the bottle and cradled the back of Marlon's head, lifting it up high enough not to spill.

"You're not a bad nurse," I told her.

"I was pre-med before I went pre-law." A tiny half smile crimped her lip, and she met my eyes.

Damn, I wish she wouldn't do that. A wiggly squirrel bumped under my ribs whenever I saw those piercing gray eyes. Even with chapped lips, unwashed hair, and no makeup, Jade Stone could launch a thousand ships into orbit.

"What now?" she asked.

"Huh?"

"I said, 'What now?'" Stone rested Marlon's head, and he hissed in pain. She gestured at the sickly-looking trooper. "We can't exactly carry him out of here, and we can't leave him."

"And technically, you're still my prisoner, so I shouldn't wander off without you or trust you to go for help."

"Trust..." Her eyes took on a wounded look before narrowing. "*Trust* me? I'm not the one who sabotaged the plane—"

"We don't know it was sabotage." I sounded lame, even to myself.

"Don't know! What more evidence do you need? They came at us with a helicopter and a *gunman*." Stone threw off the quilted sleeping bag and doubled it over Marlon in quick, jerky movements. "How can you still believe that I'm the bad guy here?"

"I—"

"I have to go pee," she snapped then paused for added sarcasm. "Unless you don't trust me not to run away. Maybe you better cuff me again." She held out her arms, wrists together.

When I made an exasperated gesture, she stomped off into the blanket of fog and disappeared. Sounds of crackling underbrush put her moving downslope, toward the river.

Marlon's chuckle was weak. "Smooth one, Ranger."

I kept my voice flat and my face neutral. "Yeah, she wants me. I can tell."

"Obviously." Marlon's grin turned to a grimace, and he hissed. It took him a moment to speak again. "But she's right. What now?"

I studied the surrounding fog rather than looking him in the eye. "We have to hold on for rescue. You got off a Mayday before the plane went down, so I suspect as soon as this weather lifts, the birds will be out."

"What did she mean by 'gunman'?"

I explained the Lee Bragg story.

Marlon moved, causing his face to screw up in pain. "Aw, *God*... It only hurts when I breathe... *Whew*. So do you think she's on the level? The ATF guys want to shut her up for some reason?"

I pursed my lips in thought. "I don't know. Problem is, I *want* to believe her."

"Because she's pretty?"

"No," I said, though the thought had slunk around the dark corners of my mind. "I have a hard time seeing her as a cold-blooded cop killer is all."

"Stone-cold?"

"Stone..." I blinked and swiveled to look at Marlon, who smirked. "Did you just make a joke, Trooper Boggs?"

"No, sir, Ranger Cable. Humor is not in my job description." He chuckled, which led to a bout of coughing, which led to a lot of groaning and cursing. I offered him more water, but he shook his head.

When he caught his breath, he said, "Prisoner's been gone a long time. You think she fell in?"

I glanced at my watch. Either she had a remarkably full bladder, or there was more than peeing going on. *Or...*

"You think she took off?" Marlon voiced my thoughts.

My jaw clenched. "She better not. I'll kill her myself if she did. Save the ATF the trouble."

Chapter 11

B arber: "How many coffins we got?"
    Fred: "Two."
Barber: "We're gonna need at least two more, no matter how you figure. You'd better get busy, Fred."
— *High Noon*, 1952

Bartlett

Bartlett enforced mission silence on the charter flight from Houston's Hobby Airport to the tiny municipal field in the high desert, south of the Gila National Forest. The pilots were outsiders, and no matter how little they might hear from the flight deck, Bartlett refused to risk a loose lip sinking their ship.

He spent the flight with Luksa, reviewing the information they pulled up on the detail assigned to extradite Stone from California. The more he read, the less he liked it. There were several news photos of the Texas Ranger, a tall man in a cream-colored Stetson. Broad shoulders. Narrow waist. Gunslinger eyes.

"Jesus Christ," Bartlett muttered. "It's the incarnation of Gary Cooper."

Dan cocked his head to the side and squinted. "I would've said Nick Nolte, back in the nineties. When he played in *Rich Man, Poor Man*. Remember that?"

"No."

"Well... same look."

"Anyway, it's a goddamn cowboy. Probably thinks he's in *High Noon*."

His ears popped as the chartered Gulfstream began its descent. Bartlett didn't want to think about how much this little jaunt was costing him. Fuel for the ATF helicopter. Chartered jet. Food and supplies... And how long could he cover the absence of so many men from the field before the big chiefs in their leather chairs noticed? He had a lot of latitude in personnel assignments, but they also had a lot of active ATF cases that needed action. Plus, the time away from their side business would put a crimp in their revenue stream.

If Tommy had only... No use thinking about woulda-shoulda-coulda. Like a shark, he had to keep moving forward, or he would die.

Grant County Airport, outside of Silver City, boasted the only asphalt runway in the southwest corner of New Mexico. Toby Glenn, the useless bastard helicopter pilot that he was, had designated it the closest airfield to the crash site. Bartlett had approved the choice when he saw how little traffic used the landing strip. Peering through the window as the Gulfstream touched down and reversed thrust, he counted eight aircraft parked near the terminal buildings, all with wheel chocks. One dip wad hayseed in a single-engine plane piddled toward the runway. Bartlett sneered. *Probably a doctor with his toy plane, looking to die early.*

The executive jet taxied to its parking spot. Bartlett popped the buckle on his belt and was at the exit before the plane came to a full stop.

The copilot twisted in his seat and glared when Bartlett unlocked the door. "Hey! Don't do that."

Bartlett waved him off and led his men down the stairs. He spotted Glenn and strode across the tarmac, the tingling excitement of movement firing along his nerve endings. The desert wind brushed the asphalt, bringing a faint scent of alkaline soil and burned AVGAS. Broken clouds indicated the passing of the storm front and promised a warm day filled with blue sky. At least the weather had cleared.

Glenn met him at the entrance to a private airfield services company, High Desert Aviation, with a serious look and his hands in his pockets. He pulled out his right and offered a shake, which Bartlett ignored.

"Status?" Bartlett got up close and used his superior height to make the helicopter pilot take a step back.

Glenn scratched his nose and looked away, studying the desert as he spoke. "Search and Rescue here is a bunch of volunteers, old farts mostly. They geared up here yesterday, met with the forest service people, and left about an hour ago. Two helicopters and some Jeeps. I listened to the briefing, and they still think the crash is where I reported it."

"Did they make you as the guy that called it in?"

"No." Glenn snorted. "Hell, no."

The rest of Bartlett's team gathered around, and Dan said, "They're unloading our bags now. We'll be ready to roll shortly."

"Good. You boys go inside, get some coffee, take a crap, whatever you need to do. Briefing in ten. Meet by the helo."

"Roger that," Dan acknowledged, and the rest of his team filed inside, leaving Bartlett to focus on his pilot.

"What kind of time do we have? How long before they figure out they're in the wrong place?"

Glenn shrugged. "Could be days. Could be weeks. It's some pretty rough country back there, and the roads will only take you so far. The old geezers will have to backpack into the higher elevations." Glenn shrugged again, and Bartlett's fist clenched.

He had to restrain the impulse to hit the scrawny redheaded pimple right in the face.

"We could get unlucky and somebody spots the wreck from the air. They start at the crash site..." Glenn didn't shrug, but he might as well have.

Bartlett did an about-face and stalked to the black ATF helicopter. This little adventure had taken on all the earmarks of a colossal Charlie

Foxtrot. He should have seen this coming, using only Lee and Glenn the Giant Vagina to take out the woman. *If I didn't need a pilot right now, I'd take Toby Glenn out in a field somewhere and shoot him.*

He schooled his face into leadership mode. Confident. Assured. Steely gaze fixed on a horizon that others couldn't see. Doubt was like a weed; once planted in the team's psyche, cracks in performance would begin to creep in. *The troops have to believe in the captain.*

He remained aloof until the men gathered their gear and formed up around where he stood, under a drooping rotor blade, in the shadow of the Bell 407.

"Take a knee." Bartlett paused to study each face in turn.

Ray and Reuben, two Hispanics, one chubby and old, the other young and skinny. Dominic, an artist with any long gun ever made. He practiced by shooting grapefruit at five hundred yards, cards at two hundred, and nickels at one hundred. Steve, his recruiter. Tall and handsome with a blarney stone in his pocket. Mack, a deceptively quiet black man with brooding eyes and more than one razor-sharp blade hidden on his person. And his logistics guy, Dan, who gave him the tiniest of winks when Bartlett made eye contact. A great organizer and detail man. The only bad thing about Dan was the way he could act so faggy at times.

Bartlett assumed a parade rest stance—he refused to pace when speaking—and cleared his throat for maximum effect. "First, here's the sitrep. At approximately fifteen hundred thirty local, Bragg achieved partial mission success by bringing down the plane with my brother's troublesome girlfriend and her two-man police escort." He continued briefing his team on the events of the previous evening, ending with, "Bragg engaged on foot to pursue and terminate the... problem. We have since lost contact with him."

His men stirred and exchanged looks. Bartlett had given some thought to how he wanted to motivate the boys, and their reaction made him smile inwardly. "That's right. We believe our friend and teammate is dead. Killed by the girl's escort detail. I had Dan do some digging on the personnel assigned to her extradition team. Dan?"

His stocky second-in-command rose and faced the group, thinning blond hair fanned by the breeze. "There are two men on the detail, as Reeder mentioned. Marlon Boggs, the pilot and a three-year veteran of the Texas DPS. Former Army, served in the Sandbox, but nothing outstanding, good or bad, in his file. We believe he is currently injured and combat ineffective." Dan glanced at Bartlett then continued. "The other guy is different story. Samuel Cable of the Texas Rangers. You guys remember the loudmouthed black woman running for Senate? Got herself killed in a hotel room? Cable was the guy framed for it. He cleared his name but shot up some dudes in the process. This guy's no stranger to a gunfight, gentlemen."

More shuffling.

"So," Bartlett said, "Lee went up against a real player and probably lost. I accept responsibility for sending him in without researching the opposition." He paused to study his toes for a minute, his lips pressed in a grim line, then scanned the faces of his men. He liked what he saw. Jaws set. Angry eyes. "I learn from my mistakes, which is why I brought the whole team this time. This guy is good. He's sharp, and he should be considered as dangerous as a cornered wolf."

Dominic spoke up. "How sure are we the other guy's down?"

"Reasonably sure, but you're right—we can't count on it. The advantage we have is numbers." Bartlett ticked his fingers with every point: "Firepower, logistics support, and mobility. Cable and Boggs will be hampered by having to protect their prisoner, and one or both may be injured."

The midmorning sun broke through the clouds and bathed the tarmac with golden light. If Bartlett believed in signs, he would have to say that qualified. The warmth felt good. "Let's stay focused on the goal line here, boys. We need a clean victory, achieved with maximum speed. I don't have to tell you how important it is for all of us that this breach in our security is plugged, once and for all. Tommy's woman may know a lot, or a little, but any probing eyes cast in our direction are enough to bring down the operation."

Nods and grim looks all around.

"All right, gentlemen. Lock and load. Let's go hunting."

Sam

OUR PRISONER SHOWED up two seconds before I went looking for her. I settled on my heels and busied myself digging through Bragg's backpack, sparing her the smallest of nonchalant glances, as though the thought of her running away had never crossed my mind.

"Mr. Bragg didn't expect to be out in the woods long," I said. "He packed three freeze-dried meals: a chicken noodle casserole, a spaghetti with meat sauce, and a chili con carne. Ugh. I hate to think what freeze-dried chili tastes like." I looked at Stone. "Did you find the stream down there?"

"I did," she said. "And a bear."

"A bear? Seriously? What kind?"

"Big." She lowered herself next to Marlon and felt his forehead.

He tried to smile at her and almost succeeded.

I scanned the woods around us. "Where?"

"About fifty yards that way." Stone nodded her chin downslope.

"Brown and black bears are usually no problem. They'll pretty much leave you alone unless they have cubs. Grizzlies, on the other hand..."

"I'll *bear* that in mind," Marlon wheezed.

"Ouch. Break some bones, and you become a damn comedian."

"Didn't break my funny bone." Marlon chuckled then clenched his eyes closed, hissing. "Ow-ow-ow." The spasm left the trooper gasping.

Stone and I shared a helpless look, which I broke off by reading the directions on the pack of freeze-dried food. *Add to boiling water, stir.* I read it twice to make sure I got it right.

"While I was dodging bears," Stone said, "did you think up a brilliant plan to get us out of here?"

"Brilliant? Doubtful." I tucked our two empty water bottles into the backpack and inspected the M4 rifle for any gunk it might have acquired during our trek downhill. "But here's what we're gonna do anyway. First, I go get some water, and we share this tasty meal of chicken casserole. Then I'll hike back to the plane and root around for anything we can use. After that, I want to hear the story of why you're on the Top Ten Hit List for the ATF."

"Okay. And then?"

"Then I'll scout around for a more defendable place." I gestured at the rock overhead. "As cozy as this is, it's a damn death trap. Bullets hitting this sloped ceiling will zigzag all over the place and chop us to hamburger. Depending on what I find, we go to phase two."

Stone cocked an eyebrow. "Which is?"

"I'll tell you as soon as I figure it out." I stood, bent almost double to avoid hitting my head. "Right now, I'm going for water."

"Watch out for the bear."

Marlon gasped out, "I'll wait here."

"You are hysterical, Boggs. My sides are splitting." I rolled my eyes and stepped into the forest.

Chapter 12

"The last time anybody made a list of the top hundred character attributes of New Yorkers, common sense snuck in at number seventy-nine." — Douglas Adams

Captain Marshall

Janelle, Captain Marshall's admin, bustled into his office a moment after he hung up from giving Sarah Jo Cable the news about her son. Janelle laid a note on Marshall's desk. "That sounded like fun."

"Like havin' a pineapple jammed up my—sorry, Janelle. What'd you bring me?" Marshall grumped.

A stout black woman, Janelle kept more secrets than the KGB and ruled Marshall's headquarters with a kind of tough love somewhere between Aunt Bea and Chuck Norris. She could slap a man upside the head one minute then offer him hot chocolate with marshmallows the next, and he would be grateful for both.

"*Mm*-hm, I bet." She pointed to the note. "That there's the number of that lawyer you wanted. The one from California."

"And the girl's parents?"

"Right there, on the same paper."

"Oh. All right." Marshall put on his reading glasses and took a closer look. "Good."

Janelle stayed in front of his desk, her expression serious.

The captain looked over the top of his glasses. "Anything else?"

"Don't you worry none about our boy Sammie. He's gonna be okay."

Marshall sighed and tapped out the last Marlboro in his pack. "I know he's double-tough, Janelle, but a plane crash... That's a helluva equalizer."

Janelle nodded, a firm jerk of her chin that brooked no doubt. "He'll be all right—you mark my words." She swished away, having given her pronouncement. Strangely, her conviction made Marshall feel better.

He pecked out the first number on the piece of paper she'd given him, dialed it wrong, and had to do it again. Fortunately for his temper and his blood pressure, he only cussed out one flunky before getting the person he wanted.

"Angela Romano. How can I help you?"

"Ms. Romano, Captain Marshall of the Texas Rangers. I understand you represented Ms. Jade Stone after her arrest there in Cally-for-na."

"Yes," the attorney said, drawing it out. Her tone sounded guarded. "That's true."

"Ma'am, I need to ask you some questions, if you don't mind."

"Assuming it doesn't violate privilege, I'll be happy to answer them."

"Something you may not be aware of, Ms. Romano, but the plane carrying your client and her escort went down in New Mexico."

"*What?*"

Marshall gave her the details about the crash and the current status of the search, which was only just getting underway.

"That's horrible," Romano said.

"Well... it ain't good." Marshall lit the cigarette he'd been toying with and took a drag. "Thing is, reason we're involved in the first place, your client made some noise about police corruption, which ain't no shock. Half the crooks in prison say the same thing. 'Cept this one, her daddy's got some pull, and he made some calls, and here we are."

Marshall paused for another drag and let Romano fill the silence. "That's true, Captain. Ms. Stone believes she's the target of a police conspiracy."

"Care to expand on that answer?"

When Romano spoke again, it was obvious she'd chosen her words with care. "My client and a Dallas Police detective, Thomas Grace, were seeing each other socially, as you probably know. Ms. Stone began to suspect Mr. Grace of engaging in a criminal enterprise—"

"What kind of criminal enterprise?"

"She did not say." Romano cleared her throat and continued, "She did mention she believed this conspiracy involved federal law enforcement, in particular Mr. Grace's half-brother, John Reed Bartlett of the Alcohol, Tobacco, Firearms, and Explosives Bureau."

"The ATF?" Marshall sat back in his chair and stared at the acoustic tile overhead. "No shit?"

"No shit, Captain. Please understand that some of what I've just told you, I learned in a privileged conversation. I believe in this case, the safety of my client outweighs the need to protect that conversation."

"And I appreciate that. I have two men missing, and if there's anything to this conspiracy thing... well, it makes that plane crash look mighty suspicious. She have any evidence of this criminal enterprise?"

"Not that she related to me," Romano said.

"Name any names?"

"None more than I've already given you."

"What about her folks?"

"What about them?"

"You think she told them anything more?"

"You'd have to ask them, Captain. I truly don't know."

Marshall thanked the attorney and hung up. "Janelle!" When his admin poked her head in the door, Marshall said, "Look up all the public stuff you can find on John Reed Bartlett of BATF. Then get me the phone number of the Wicked Witch of the FBI."

"Who?"

"That woman who helped Sam that time." Marshall stubbed out his Marlboro and rolled his hand to get his memory flowing. "Goldstein, Goldfarb, something like that."

"Rita Goldman?"

"Yeah, her."

"Uh-huh. You know she's in New York City, right?"

"Last I heard, they had workin' phones there."

When Janelle disappeared, Marshall picked up the handset again and dialed the second number on the slip of paper. *Time to see what the parents of Ms. Jade Stone have to say about their little girl's story.* Crooked ATF agents and Dallas cops. Neither one would surprise him, since he'd arrested more than a fair share of LEOs in his time, but a conspiracy seemed far-fetched. But impossible?

Not a damn bit.

The phone rang on the other end, and he yelled out to Janelle through the open door, "And get Dolph in here pronto!"

Sam

NO BEAR APPEARED, WHICH I found oddly disappointing. Stone may have been yanking my chain about it, but more likely, the critter heard all our human commotion and wandered off to do bear business elsewhere.

Both narrow and shallow, the stream ran fast and hard, as if shot from a fire hose. Had I wanted, I could've jumped across it or waded it without much effort. Slick muck and wet rocks bordered the rushing creek.

The fog muted sounds and held the temperature somewhere in the low sixties. Not cold enough to give me shivers but too cold to run around in wet clothes, so I was very careful where I put my feet. The

water chilled my hand when I dipped the empty plastic bottles in to fill
them.

Marlon had passed out again by the time I got back. He tossed and
moaned in shivery, agitated bursts, and sweat soaked the collar of his
uniform blouse.

Stone had cut the other sleeve from the ATF guy's jersey and fashioned it into strips. She was busy wrapping them around Marlon's upper arm when I loomed over her.

"His ankle's in a bad way." Her anxious look left me feeling even
more helpless than before. "I can't imagine the pain he's in."

"He's a tough son of a bitch—that's for sure."

I poured the water into the miniature camp pan—it could be dis-
assembled into a cook set, complete with knife, fork, plate, and skillet—and set it directly on the coals. My stomach rumbled when I
shook the freeze-dried meal to settle the contents. Never before had re-
constituted chicken casserole sounded so good. I checked the ingredi-
ents: chicken, mushroom, pimentos, nonfat dry milk, celery, corn oil...
hydrolyzed corn gluten... autolyzed yeast extract... *Yum.*

While I waited for the water to boil, I scouted around the campsite
for some saplings. I had half a mind to rig a stretcher out of the sleeping
bag and a couple of long poles and carry Marlon out of here between
us. I found one likely candidate and commenced to whittling at its base
with Bragg's Swiss Army knife. Stone found me, and I explained my
plan.

"Could work," she said, glancing at Marlon. "It'll hurt like hell."

"It'll hurt like hell, him just laying still."

"True."

"Like you said, he's in a bad way. If we don't get him off this mountain soon, he'll likely die." Fresh pine sap made my hand sticky where
I chipped away at the sapling's trunk. "Our other choice would be to
send you for help. I leave you here, the bad guys could get both of you."

"You trust me enough for that?"

I took my time answering, pushing and pulling the tree to work the notch I'd cut into a splintery mess. "*Trust* is a big word. Let's say I *believe* you have some bad folks after your ass. Bad enough they can take down a plane. Bad enough they have—had—a crooked ATF agent on their payroll."

The mist had lightened while I worked, and I could see almost all the way to the stream. Behind us, the rock cliff rose above the trees, big sandstone blocks stacked together. I shoved the sapling with my boot and pushed it over with a crackle of springy wood.

Stone watched me with her hands in the back pockets of her stained blue jeans. She wore Bragg's dark-blue jersey with cut-off sleeves over the bulky Kevlar vest, her hair needed a currycomb more than a brush, and streaks of blood and dirt served as makeup. *If you threw mud on the Venus de Milo, would it be it any less beautiful?*

"Are you okay?" Stone's eyebrows pulled together in a frown.

"Huh? Me?" I went back to playing Paul Bunyan, digging at the tough little strands of pine with my knife. "Yeah, sure. Ah, anyway, trust. Why don't you tell me why these guys are after your ass? Out to kill you, that is."

Stone found a chunk of flat rock, and I tried not to watch her rear end as she brushed off the leaves and twigs before sitting down. I failed.

She crossed her arms over her knees and rested her chin on them. "Are you sure you want to hear this? You sounded pretty adamant in the car that I was full of shit."

"Circumstances have changed," I told her.

A wry smile. "That, they have."

I cut my sapling loose at the base and commenced stripping and whittling the branches off. "And Jade Stone. Tell me about that. Your parents have a sense of humor?"

"Hah! You'd think, wouldn't you? I have an older sister named Ruby, a brother, Diamond, and a little sister, Gem."

"Gem Stone. Seriously?"

"Daddy liked his rocks. What can I say?"

"All right, Jade Stone, how'd you get to be number one on the hit parade?"

She scratched her nose and stared at the ground in front of her. "Tommy Grace and I started dating last fall. He'd made detective in the summer, and I'd been hired at Cleburn & Harris not long after. Tommy and his brother, Reeder Bartlett, wanted some business filings done, and the law firm assigned me. That's how we met."

Warmth crept into the day as the sun rose higher in the sky, and the mist had lifted to a layer of low clouds obscuring the surrounding peaks. I fought a pesky limb that didn't want to give up its attachment, and sweat burned my eyes from the effort. "Wasn't it... what? A violation of ethics, or some such, to date a client?"

She had a self-deprecating way of smiling, crimping her lips down at the corners. "It was definitely tiptoeing along the line. But Tommy could be sweet and charming and funny, and he had all these great cop stories..." She shrugged. "I didn't date much in college—too busy, I guess. I suppose you could say I was naïve, and I missed seeing Tommy for what he was."

"Crooked, you mean?"

"Like a pretzel." She sniffed and wiped her nose on the jersey's hem, clearing her throat. "I figured out later, the business filings I was handling? Tommy and his brother were setting up shell corporations to hide their illegal income. The corporations invested in money-laundering fronts like bars and dry cleaners. Car washes. All places you can hide funds. And man, they were raking it in too."

I finished stripping my pole and set about trimming it to a ten-foot length. More sap gummed my hands. Around me, the forest sounds blended into peaceful background music. In other circumstances, there was nowhere else I would rather be than in a secluded forest with a pretty girl. Right then, all I wanted was to get Marlon and Jade off that mountain without any of us dying along the way.

"How much?" I asked.

"Almost a hundred grand a month. When I asked Tommy about it, he said Reeder had family money from his father. Tommy and Reeder share a mother but have different fathers. Tommy was the youngest."

"So what happened?"

"Hm?"

"How did Tommy wind up dead and you on the run?"

"Well, I was naïve but not stupid, so—"

A heavy beat of rotors echoed along the valley, direction and distance impossible to determine. Stone and I froze, ears cocked. The *thumpa-thumpa-thumpa* grew closer, and I scanned the low clouds.

"Is it them?" Stone's eyes were wide, and she hunched forward on the perch.

"I don't know." I located the direction, somewhere higher and to my right. "But it sounds like they're right where the plane went down. Wait here with Marlon while I go take a look."

Chapter 13

"I've noticed when you get to disliking folks they ain't around long neither." – Lone Waite, *The Outlaw Josey Wales*.

Bartlett

When the Bell 407 touched down near the burned-out hulk of the Cessna, Bartlett yanked open the door and vaulted to the ground. Running in a crouch, he cleared the rotor arc then took a knee by the wreckage. His men fanned out and set up a perimeter, scanning the area through tactical scopes on their automatic weapons while the helicopter kicked up sand and pea gravel.

Broken clouds left patchy shadows drifting across the meadow, and mist in the higher elevations seemed to dissipate as he watched. Soon, Bartlett reckoned, the sun would be out, creating annoying shadows among the trees. *But what can hide them can hide us, as well.* He took a deep breath of pine-scented air overlaid by the reek of burned plastic and bared his teeth in a predator's grin. *Perfect day for a hunt.*

"Dominic," Bartlett yelled.

His sniper hustled over and dropped to a knee beside him. Dominic Lazzari came from Italian ancestors, but Bartlett suspected an Irishman had snuck into Mama Lazzari's bed. Dominic's sandy hair and boyish face gave him a collegiate all-American exterior that concealed an ice-cold core. One would never know by looking at him that he had forty-seven confirmed kills in Iraq, two official kills as an ATF agent, and two more of the unofficial variety.

"Where do you want to set up, Dom?"

The sniper scratched the thin stubble on his chin and scrunched his face. "All these trees... being this close makes no sense with the .50-cal. Which way do you think they'll head?"

"Closest town's west of here. I don't know if they're aware of that."

Dominic pointed with his chin to a bald, rocky crest a mile or more to the west. "Probably that ridge then. If they head toward me, they'll come right into my lap. Got to warn you, boss, I may or may not see 'em through these trees."

"Don't worry about it." Bartlett slapped his sniper on the shoulder. "Take that pussy Glenn and park the chopper over that way. You and he are overwatch while the rest of us run these characters to ground. All right? Good man."

Dominic nodded and loped back to the helicopter. A minute later, the bird lifted off in a cloud of whipping dust, banked, and climbed away. In the quiet that followed, Bartlett keyed his sleeve-mounted microphone and spoke to the remaining team members.

"All right, boys. Our last intel says they went uphill. Lee circled right and attempted a flanking maneuver. I want Reuben, Ray, and Mack to go right, try to find out what happened to Lee. If you locate our, uh, *suspects*"—due to the remote possibility of his radio signal being overheard, Bartlett changed the word from *targets* at the last second—"you are to observe and report. Wait for backup before engaging. Steve, you, me, and Dan will circle left and investigate upslope from that direction. Classic pincer movement. Questions?"

Nobody said anything, so Bartlett gave the order to move out. "And keep your eyes peeled, gentlemen. We've already lost one man. Let's not lose any more."

Captain Marshall

CAPTAIN MARSHALL'S butt was hardwired to eject him from a seated position every ten minutes. He paced behind his desk like a badger poked with a sharp stick. Movement, any movement, was required. He craved getting somewhere and doing something, not sitting on his ass, watching the damn phone not ring. More than once, he reached for his key ring, intending to drive to New Mexico and mount up in search of his missing people. That dirty bitch Responsibility kept him nailed in place, though.

"You wanted to see me?" said a talking bear standing in his office doorway, holding a half-eaten hoagie and a forty-four-ounce soft drink.

"Dolph! Get in here and close the door."

If Columbo had a country cousin, he would be Adolph Ahlberg. Six feet of potato sack stuffed into tan polyester slacks and a cream sport coat, Dolph had been Rangering since Davy Crockett died in a hail of gunfire. His "Aw shucks" manner lulled people into talking themselves right up the scaffold and putting their necks through the noose. They would often shake his hand and thank him for pulling the lever.

He toed the door shut, walked to the desk, and aimed his butt at a visitor's chair. Holding his cup out so as not to spill his drink, he settled in the seat with a sigh, like the walk from his desk had taxed his spirit. A yellow necktie struggled to hold his collar together.

"What's up, you old coot?" Dolph bit a hunk out of his sandwich.

Marshall filled in his lead investigator on everything he had so far, including the conjecture about Agent Bartlett of the ATF. "I can't reach the girl's parents. According to the housekeeper, they're on a plane from Biloxi to Tucson. Headed from there to New Mexico to join the search."

"What do you want me to do?"

"Hold your dick and whistle Dixie! What do you think I want you to do? Dig into this Bartlett guy and his dead brother. You know every fed south of the Mason-Dixon line. Call 'em up, feel 'em up, kiss 'em, and buy 'em dinner—I don't care. But get—"

Janelle knocked and stuck her head in the door. "Rita Goldman, line two."

Marshall stabbed the button for speakerphone and barked, "Goldman, izzat you?"

"What the fuck?" Rita's Bronx voice assaulted the Captain's Texas ears. "I leave for like a minute, and you guys lose a guy big as Cable? A plane crash? You gotta be fuckin' kidding me."

"Well—"

"Cable din't die in some plane crash. I know that for shooah."

"We don't know. I—"

"Whazzat big dumb cowboy got his ass inna this time?"

"Will you shut the hell up?" Marshall barked.

A few seconds of silence blessed the room. "Sorry, Captain. I don't play well with others."

"I do recall that, yes." Marshall gave her the same facts he'd fed Dolph a few minutes earlier. "Their plane going down after this gal gripes about bad cops is makin' my scrotum itch."

"That's the lice." Dolph finished his sandwich and wadded up the paper wrapper.

Rita said, "Do you know how many people claim the cops set 'em up?"

Marshall leaned over the phone, propped on his fists. He felt a hundred years older than a man nearing his sixty-eighth birthday. "I know. But runnin' this down... I'd rather be doing somethin' more than playing tiddlywinks. Know what I mean?"

"Whaddya want me to do?" Rita asked. "I can drop what I'm on and get to New Mexico today, but I'll tell ya now—I'm not any good in the woods, with the snakes and whatnot."

"No, I need something else. You're the financial wizard, right? Jab a federal anal probe in this guy Bartlett's bank records, property, assets, all that financial stuff. Do everything you can without triggering any paperwork. Work your United States government mojo. Let's see if there's any fire to this smoke. *Comprende?*"

"Shooah. And..." Rita cleared her throat but didn't say anything else.

Marshall's patience ran out after six seconds. "And what?"

She cleared her throat again. "Call me if you hear anything. About, y'know, Cable and those guys. I like the big lummox. I don't wanna go to his funeral."

"You'll be the first—no, the second, right after Sam's mama."

Marshall punched the disconnect button and glared at Dolph, who slurped the ice at the bottom of his soda. "Your butt stuck to that chair?"

"Don't get your panties in a twist." Dolph lumbered from the room, and Marshall sat back at his desk.

He fished another pack of cigarettes from the center drawer, scattering paper clips and pens along the way. *You better not be dead, Sam Cable, you big, ugly son of a bitch. Sarah Jo and Goldman. I don't want those two pissed at me.*

Sam

"SIX GUYS GOT OFF THE helicopter," I reported to Stone when I retraced my steps to our camp. "Armed up the yin-yang and dressed like secret-agent commandos."

"So, not the good guys then."

"No, I suspect not. Another one got back on the chopper and left. The rest went uphill, away from us, so we have a few minutes while they scout up that way. The rain probably destroyed our tracks. Still and all, I think we need to remove our asses from the area and get the hell off this mountain."

Stone had finished making the chicken casserole; a good-sized portion remained in the skillet by the fire. My stomach rumbled. "Have you eaten?"

"A few bites." She busied herself shoving our bits of gear into the backpack. "I tried to get Marlon to eat, but he's passed out, if not completely comatose."

"Okay. Problem for later. Fetch me the pole I cut, would you?" I scarfed the casserole, scraping the pan for every last drop.

Stone dragged the sapling back, and I finished cutting the end off.

"I wanted two of these, but one will have to do. You ever see those movies where they strap a captive to a pole and cart him off to the cook pot?"

She nodded.

"That's what we're doing here, except we're gonna use the sleeping bag instead of ropes to hang him off the pole."

Between us, we managed to zip Marlon into the bag, all the way up past his head, leaving the flap open so he could breathe. I cut a hole in the bottom corner by his feet, near where the zipper started, and threaded the pole through the bag. I missed my mark a little and poked Marlon's bad arm. He uttered a weak groan but didn't wake up.

"Sorry, buddy," I muttered and pushed the pole out past his head. "Stone, grab that and straighten it out... That's it."

"Will his head hang down?"

"Maybe a little, if he slips out any more." I pursed my lips and cocked my head. "We'll go down with him pointed feet-first and turn around going uphill. Keep the open side pointed up as much as possible."

"That won't be hard if you carry that end. What are you? Six-twelve?"

"And made of steel. You ready?"

"Can I do my nails first?"

She was game, I had to give her that. Chased by rogue government agents, plane-wrecked, and lost in the mountains with a wounded man, she could still crack jokes.

"Pack the skillet, and hand me the backpack. I'll kill the fire. We'll stop by the creek on the way down and refill the water bottles."

I scattered the last burning sticks with the toe of my boot, stepped on the embers, and kicked sand over the smoking remains. I shouldered the M4 and the backpack. Stone crouched by her end of the carry pole, so I gripped the end next to Marlon's head.

"Ready? On three." At her nod, I chanted, "One, two, *three.*"

With a grunt, we lifted the Marlon-pouch onto our shoulders. The pine sapling bowed in the middle but not enough to make me think it would break. "Go," I urged. Since I was crouched in the narrow end of the cave in a near squat, I waddled more than walked until we cleared the opening.

The first ten steps were... interesting. The footing tended to be loose and covered in tripping hazards. I slid and slipped with every step. The weighted bag swayed, adding a balancing component to the challenge of walking. After twenty steps, a slow burn started in my calves, and by the time we reached the stream, I was breathing hard and my back wanted to knot up with a cramp.

"Wait up," I grunted.

We eased Marlon to the ground, and I noticed Stone huffing and puffing a little, as well. She rolled her carrying shoulder and gave me a wry look.

"He ain't heavy," she said. "He's—"

"Don't say it."

Behind us, our scuffing and sliding had left a trail a blind man in a dark room could follow. Ahead of us, the slope led gradually downward as far as I could see, and beyond that lay another ridge. We would have to climb that to see what lay beyond.

I don't even know if we're heading toward civilization or away from it. We could be a mile from help and not even know it.

I refilled the water bottles and handed them to Stone to pack away rather than unstrapping the pack, then I drank my fill of the cold running stream. The water could be as full of parasites as Congress, but I suspected I would be dead or rescued long before I got sick from drinking bad water.

I looked at Stone. "Ready?"

"Waiting on you, big fella."

"Okay, on three."

We lifted our brother and started downhill.

Chapter 14

"There is no hunting like the hunting of man, and those who have hunted armed men long enough and liked it, never care for anything else thereafter." — Ernest Hemingway

Dominic

Dominic Lazzari cradled the Barrett XM500 rifle system and trekked upward through a rock-walled channel, the toes of his Vibram-soled boots digging into the sandy soil. Glenn labored far behind, huffing in the thin mountain air. *That guy wouldn't last ten minutes in the Hindu Kush.* This hill was a speed bump compared to the Wakhan Mountains.

Lazzari had never expected he would enjoy the solitude of the high mountains or be as comfortable in the back country as he was. The army, with their typical lack of logic, had placed the kid from the teeming docks, pizzerias, and tenements of Boston's North End in the Tenth Mountain Division and made him a sniper.

As a cherry in the Tenth, Lazzari had learned the motto "We don't do mountains" wasn't true in his case. He and his *amici* had frequently deployed to the mountains west of Kabul, at altitudes above five thousand meters, where Lazzari learned to reach out and touch distant targets with copper-jacketed projectiles while shivering in a snow-shrouded hole. He'd learned how to creep, sneak, and hide better than an Apache and how to judge wind, temperature, and barometric pressure better than a weatherman.

The XM500 he carried weighed more than a toddler and extended four feet from butt to muzzle. Using a bullpup design—box magazine behind the trigger—his XM employed a BORS integrated ballistic computer mounted on a Leupold M1 scope and fired 12.7x99 NATO rounds, capable of killing anything up to and including a T. rex. The Laser Tech rangefinder in his vest pocket would provide accurate measurements at well over a thousand meters. These tools, along with countless hours of practice, took all the guesswork out of killing people across multiple zip codes.

The gulley petered out, rock walls giving way as he climbed, until the sniper emerged onto a tabletop of reddish sandstone. The slab on the right shoulder of the unnamed mountain peak angled upward at a moderate slope until it reached the bluff a hundred yards ahead. To his right, the shelf sloped away until it merged with the tops of tall pine trees and disappeared. On the left, a near-vertical cliff vaulted another two hundred feet higher.

Lazzari belly-crawled the last ten yards to see over the lip of the crest. A valley yawned below, a long straight drop before the rock ended in a talus slope and transitioned to a tree-studded forest. At the base of the valley, a tinsel ribbon peeked through the trees. *A stream*, Lazzari decided, *or small river, reflecting the sun.*

The sniper studied the rise across the valley. More humped at the top than peaked, the mountain was covered in forest all the way to the crown. The side facing Lazzari dropped to a wide meadow, where he found the Cessna crash site, and fell to a shorn-away section of bare bluff. From there, forested slope flowed down a series of angular ridges until it leveled out at the stream.

When Toby Glenn's scuffling, panting, and cursing announced the pilot's arrival at the base of the shelf, Lazzari spared him a glance and said, "Keep the noise down."

The red-faced Glenn shot him the finger but settled on his heels and worked at catching his breath. Lazzari arched his back and peeled off his pack. He retrieved his binoculars from an inside pouch and went back to scanning the opposite hill, using the crash site as a starting point.

Lazzari keyed the microphone on his lapel. "Eagle to Six, come in."

"Six here." Bartlett's voice crackled in his earbud, loud enough to hurt.

Lazzari adjusted the volume. "In position."

"Roger that. Any movement?"

"Nothing yet." Lazzari panned the binoculars left to right, working methodically from the crash site toward the crest then back down.

"We found our missing asset. Dead and stripped."

Shit. Lee Bragg was a good guy. It had to be the Ranger, what's his face, Cable. "Uh, roger that. Eagle out."

Whoever this jackass Cable was, Lazzari wanted him dead. Bartlett had said to kill Jade Stone, no matter what, but Lazzari would be damned if he let the guy who'd smoked Bragg walk out of these mountains free and—

Wait.

Lazzari arrested his binoculars in mid-sweep and swung back to where a flash of color had twitched across his vision. Almost to the base of the mountain, a tiny break in the trees opened up, and there, sitting down like they were having a picnic, two people hunched next to a blanket-wrapped form.

The view jittered around until Lazzari settled the binoculars and took a deep, steadying breath. He focused on the figures, more than eight hundred yards away, and studied them for a long moment before exhaling in a long sigh. "Got you, fuckers."

Sam

STONE PICKED THE TRAIL, and she did a good job of it, avoiding thick undergrowth and low-hanging limbs, and generally finding the easiest path. Easy didn't make it straight, however. We traveled three steps sideways for every one down, so I found it difficult to judge the distance we'd covered. Every foot gained was a victory accomplished by sweaty, hot, cursing hard work.

Jade staggered, and her left leg buckled. "Uh!" she grunted, dropping to a knee and taking the front end of the carry pole with her. I saw her falling and lowered my end in time to keep Marlon from spilling down the hill. He stirred but didn't wake.

"What's wrong?" I sat on my heels and flexed stiff fingers. My body felt compressed, as if I'd been squat-lifting a Holstein, and sweat burned my eyes.

"Cramp," Stone said. Dripping wet hair stuck to her cheek.

"My fault," I told her. "I should have called a halt sooner. Don't try to be a hero, okay? You need to stop, just say so."

"I need to stop." She massaged her calf with both hands, and I managed not to ask if I could help rub it.

We were in a small clearing, a rocky field no bigger than my living room. Wind sifted through the trees, a mix of pine and fir, plus some I couldn't identify, with leaves instead of needles. The morning mist had burned away, leaving a postcard sky with the exact right number of perfect puff-ball clouds, a light breeze, and a mild temperature.

"Beautiful day for a hike," I remarked.

Stone grunted but didn't look up. She stretched her leg out straight and used her fingertips to pull back the tip of her running shoe.

"How's the calf?"

"Getting better." Stone shook out the leg then repeated the stretch with her right. "Nothing a hot soak in a big tub wouldn't cure."

I glanced at my watch and grimaced. Less than an hour since we'd started, and already I felt like an empty tube of toothpaste, all squeezed out and twisted in a knot. We would never get down this hill, let alone up the other one, if we didn't start making better time.

While Stone worked on her calves, I studied our backtrail. Nothing bigger than a squirrel moved on the slope behind us. *How long until the crooked feds figure out which way to look? An hour? Ten minutes?* I had no way to know. The first indication of pursuit might be a bullet in the back.

Stone stretched her hamstrings, fingertips to toes, chest pressed against her thighs. She studied me, head turned to the side. Her gray eyes were hooded and unreadable. "They'll find us, won't they?"

"Yep, I reckon so. Unless we catch a break and find a trail out of here."

"What are the odds of that?" Her eyes flicked to Marlon. "Shooting off in a random direction like we are?"

"It's not completely random," I argued. "Before we crunched into a mountain, Marlon said the closest airfield was to the west, which is thataway." I pointed downslope. "My hope is we cut a trail at the bottom of this hill, and it leads us out of here without having to climb the ridge directly in front of us."

Stone shaded her eyes and studied the mountainside across from us. The slope was steep and rough, capped by a bald and rocky summit suitable for mountain goats, lizards, and bad-tempered, man-eating rattlesnakes. Stone said, "Yes. Trail at the bottom. Definitely."

"We better—"

Light flickered from the ridge across the valley, on and off so quick that I almost missed it, like a bit of metal or glass reflecting the sun for an instant.

"Grab the pole!" I scrabbled for my end, which danced away from my grasping fingers.

"What?" Stone rolled to her feet and reached for the carry pole in one smooth athletic movement. "What's wrong?"

"Just *move*," I snarled. I never heard the actual shot, but the flat smack of a bullet slapping the ground punctuated my sentence. Mud and rock exploded two feet from my hand, pelting me with debris. The shockwave slugged me in the chest. "Damn! Go, go, go!"

The shooter had to be half a mile away, firing a big-bore rifle with enough punch to blow a rabbit-sized hole in the ground. *A Barrett .50, at least.*

At that range, the report of the rifle was lost in the distance, but the supersonic bullet made a flat *crack* as it passed. The sound of a passing bullet never failed to knot my intestines tighter than wet shoelaces.

Crack!

I ducked reflexively as we heaved Marlon aloft and stagger-stepped down the muddy slope. I missed seeing where the second shot landed. "Get under the trees!"

Crack!

The round hit a rock near my feet, striking sparks and peppering my leg with burning fragments. It hit with the force of an artillery shell. I stumbled but stayed upright, shouting at Stone to keep moving. Marlon swayed in his cocoon, and I prayed he stayed unconscious. No telling what the jostling and bumping would be doing to his broken body.

Crack!

A massive round shook a tree to my left. Pine needles pattered to the ground. Then we were under the trees, and the shooting stopped.

"Hold up."

We took cover under the thick branches of a cedar and lowered Marlon gently.

I tried to catch my shaky breath. "You okay?"

She nodded without looking up, bent over, hands on knees and doing some gasping of her own. We hadn't run far, but the exertion of carrying Marlon down a slippery incline while under fire from a high-powered rifle had taxed both of us.

When I could breathe normally again, I said, "I think they found us."

Stone pinned me with a glare. "Hello, Mr. Obvious."

"That's Ranger Obvious, ma'am."

"You're bleeding."

I followed her eyes and found she was right. Dots of blood speckled my jeans where either rock shards or bullet fragments had peppered my lower legs. Recognition made them sting like a mound of fire ants had crawled up my calves. "Just a flesh wound, ma'am."

Her eyes scrunched up in disbelief. "Are you kidding me?"

"Heh. I always wanted to say that."

"We need to dress those wounds."

"With what?" I challenged her hard look with one of my own. "Besides, we gotta move. That sniper spotted us and no doubt called in his buddies. They'll be down on us like we owe 'em money."

She flashed a smile that tickled something in my chest then grabbed her end of the pole. "On three. One, two, *three*."

"Jesus, Marlon," I gasped when I had my end of the carry pole on my shoulder. "You're going on a diet when this is over."

"C'mon, you big pussy," Jade Stone said. "Let's get off this hill."

Dominic

"I THINK YOU MISSED," Glenn said.

Lazzari ground his teeth and adjusted his cheek against the rifle's stock. "Shut up while I look."

He spent a solid ten minutes seeking movement, but the trees were too dense. He used a curse he'd learned from his Alabama-born drill sergeant. "Shit fire and save the matches."

"What?"

"Never mind," he told the pilot and keyed his mic. "Eagle to Six."

"Go for Six." The response was so fast, Bartlett must have had his finger on the transmit button.

"Subjects are approximately three kilometers west of your position. Downslope. Repeat. Downslope."

In the short pause, Lazzari pictured Bartlett cursing. Going uphill instead of down had been his decision, and Bartlett hated making bad decisions. He tended to take it out on others.

"Be advised," Lazzari said, "one wounded, carried in a sling. The other subjects are ambulatory."

"Acknowledged," came the terse response. "Was that you shooting?"

"Ten-four. Negative results." Lazzari felt Glenn's eyes boring a hole in his temple but refused to acknowledge the look.

"Understood. Track and report. Six out." By Bartlett's tone, Lazzari figured he would be in for a one-on-one bitch-out session when the project was over. And he would deserve it, too, after that performance.

He switched from his rifle scope to binoculars. Based on their last known direction, Stone and Cable were headed to the stream at the bottom of the valley. *But which way would they go after that?*

He must have muttered that last bit aloud without realizing it, because Glenn startled him by replying, "Their best bet would be north."

"Why so?"

"South of here's nothing but a bunch of box canyons and dead ends. Some old boarded-over mines, maybe." Glenn shrugged. "There's a trail to the north that cuts back west, toward Glenwood."

"And how do you know this?"

"I studied the topo maps. It's why I sent the search party to the south of here. Rugged country with lots of cul-de-sacs."

Lazzari nodded and refocused on the slope where the Ranger and Jade Stone had disappeared. Bartlett and the other guys would make good time coming downhill. They would be up Cable's ass in under an hour, so the Ranger and the woman would have to get a move on.

Carrying a wounded man, no doubt they would *not* come up and over the mountain he and Glenn occupied. That climb would be hard enough for an unencumbered person with all the right gear.

If they followed the streambed in either direction, they would have to come out from under the trees sooner or later—long stretches of the water course lay open and exposed, which would put them under his sights for a much-needed payback shot.

When he'd marked the big Ranger with his Laser Tech, the distance read out as 816 meters. Hitting a target at that range took a great deal of skill and a little bit of luck. Lazzari knew he shouldn't blame himself for missing a shot like that while shooting downhill, which played all kinds of hell with bullet drop calculations, but it rankled nonetheless. He'd rushed the first round, eager for the kill. Missing twice more, even though the targets were moving, rubbed salt in his already-wounded pride. In Lazzari's mind, killing the Ranger and Stone had gone from a *chore* to a *mission*, and he wouldn't rest until he got satisfaction.

Lazzari watched through his binoculars and chewed on ways he could get what he wanted.

Chapter 15

"New York is the only city in the world where you can get deliberately run down on the sidewalk by a pedestrian." — Russell Baker

Rita

Late-afternoon sun sliced diagonal strips through the brick buildings of Midtown Manhattan, two blocks west of Central Park. A wreck on the Joe DiMaggio had backed up traffic on 59th past Saint Luke's, forging it into solid lines of braying Yellow Cabs, delivery trucks, and cursing, angry drivers.

Rita Goldman took advantage of her official vehicle permit and parked on a yellow line near the hospital's outpatient entrance, behind a row of ambulances. Late for her meeting with her retired BATF contact, she left her government-issue green Taurus and quick-stepped through a bustling flow of backpack-toting college students and medical people in pastel scrubs.

Everybody has their uniform. She smirked. *Even me.* Hers was a steel-gray Theory pantsuit, accompanied by a plum blouse and a tailored jacket over the Sig Sauer P226 in a shoulder rig. The sensible Michael Kors loafers with a silver buckle weren't her favorites, but they were good for walking. Sam used to bust her chops about her clothes, saying they cost more than the GDP of a small European nation. "Whadda you know about it?" she would respond. "Your idea of 'dressed up' is a shirt without holes."

You better be all right, you big doofus.

Rita nearly ran into the back of a hulking Jamaican in a toboggan and a muscle shirt, jolting to a stop at the corner of 59th and Amsterdam. She crossed with the crowd, ducking and weaving through taller and slower people, her city-street tap dance steps in high gear. At five feet and a biscuit, as Sam would say, frizzy hair bobbing, Rita slipped through foot traffic without a ripple. She crossed 58th on the Don't Walk, earning a honk from a suit in a Jaguar, and found the deli where Phil Wessel had said he would meet her.

She found him defending a tiny table among a crowd of milling students who besieged the narrow eatery, laughing, laptopping, and texting. He was a gray rock in a sea of pebbles.

"Hey," she said. "Sorry I'm late."

He waved her off and pointed to a paper cup with a plastic lid. "I got you a coffee. You still take it black?"

"Mm." Rita sipped from the cup, leaving a red lipstick imprint. "Just right. So how long you been at John Jay? Two years?"

"'Bout that." After retiring from the ATF, Phil Wessel had taken a teaching post at the Criminal Justice College. Rita had heard his classes were packed every session.

Wessel reminded Rita of an aging Wyatt Earp: graying handlebar mustache and shooter's eyes, wary and piercing under salty brows. His broad shoulders strained a corduroy jacket, and his open-collared denim shirt revealed a few stray chest hairs.

Sam would like this guy. She banished thoughts of Sam and said, "You know I love to chitchat and make small talk—"

Wessel snorted. "I know you better than that."

"But I'm in a hurry." She leaned closer, meeting his green-eyed stare with her best no-bullshit look. "Talk to me about John Bartlett."

Wessel blinked, and his lip curled in a sneer. "Reeder? What's that prick up to?"

"I don't know," Rita admitted. "I'm fishing."

"If you're fishing for Reeder Bartlett, you better have some heavy tackle."

Rita filled Wessel in on the situation—Bartlett's brother Tommy getting killed, the accused murderer's allegations of corruption, the plane crash, and the missing people. She paused to sip coffee. "Look, you retired from the ATF, but you were there—what? Twenty-five years?"

"Closer to thirty."

"Thirty years. So if anybody knows anything..." Rita shrugged and waited.

Wessel leaned back in his chair, bumping a girl with hair dyed ultra-black and a nose ring. He apologized when she looked up, but Rita doubted the girl heard him through her earbuds.

He scooted forward and crossed his arms on the table. Frowning, he said to the top of his coffee cup, "The Bureau... the ATF, I mean... is staffed with some really, really great guys." He tapped a finger into the table to emphasize his point. "Good men and women, underpaid, fighting the good fight against everything from the fucking cartels to the nutjob Branch Davidian types."

"Yeah, that worked out well."

Steel sparks flashed in Wessel's eyes, and his face clouded up. "I was there. Fresh out of the academy. I lost a friend to those assholes. Easy enough for Monday-morning quarterbacks to nitpick and tell us how we botched everything up. I don't care what anybody says, that Koresh was screwing little girls and using God as a cover story."

"Whoa, sorry." Rita showed her palms. "I overstepped. I apologize."

The fire faded to embers, and Wessel seemed to shrink into himself. With another brush-off wave, he said, "Ancient history. My kids don't remember it, and my grandkids never heard of the Branch Davidian, and that's fine with me."

A student Wessel knew stopped at their table and exchanged handshakes with him. Rita waited, remembering the first time she'd met Wessel, when he came to Quantico to teach a class on explosives while she was at the academy. After class, she spent a long afternoon in a coffee shop much like this one, debating the finer points of fruit of the poisonous tree and the ethics of using torture to gain information from a suspect about an imminent bomb attack. Rita had taken the pro-torture position.

When his student left, Wessel said, "You wanted to know about Reeder Bartlett."

"The man's a ghost on paper," Rita admitted. "I haven't had this much trouble running a person's background financials since they assigned me to find al-Zawahiri's money trail."

"Doesn't surprise me." Wessel rubbed a hand down his face. He looked tired, somehow having grown older in the space of a few minutes. "First of all, you need to understand, I don't like the man." Wessel drew a long breath. "You know as well as I, law enforcement attracts a lot of alpha-male personalities."

Rita snorted. "You're tellin' me."

"Well, Reeder's the alpha's alpha. He works hard to be the most aggressive, the strongest leader, the most... powerful person in *any* setting. If he played Chutes and Ladders with a four-year-old, he'd play to win, and if he lost, he'd get even." Wessel paused. "Have you seen him? A picture?" At her nod, he continued. "Then you know he looks like a guy who just stepped off a movie screen. He hits the gym more than anybody else, like it's a contest to see who can stay fittest."

She toyed with her empty paper cup and waited. Wessel had more to say, and she figured keeping quiet would prompt the rest.

"So what you've got," Wessel said, "is a super-aggressive, super-powerful, charismatic guy in charge of a bunch of testosterone-fueled younger agents looking for a role model, a mentor, a... leader of the pack. They follow him around like he's the new messiah. I wouldn't be surprised if John Reed Bartlett had a God complex on top of everything else. And..." Wessel shifted in his seat and looked around.

Rita waited him out.

"Look, this is just rumor, okay?"

"Okay, no problem," Rita said. "All this is background for me. I'm only trying to get a handle on the guy."

"There's a rumor floating around that Reeder's a butt pirate."

"A what?"

"A homosexual."

Rita sat back, momentarily at a loss for words. "Oookay."

"I know, I know, not exactly unique, this day and age, right? But he's not *gay*, if you know what I mean."

"No, not really."

"It's like... it's like he loves himself so much, he's having sex with guys as a way to make love to himself." Wessel shrugged ruefully. "Or I don't know, maybe he just likes to screw guys."

Rita shifted gears. "The big question is, do you think he could be dirty?"

"Anybody could be dirty," Wessel told her. "But Reeder? Yeah, without a doubt. The guy lives at the center of his own universe, and the normal rules don't apply to him. I tell you what, though..."

Rita cocked an eyebrow. "What?"

"If Bartlett's gone bad, he's gone bad in a big way. We're not talking chump change with this guy. And if you go after him, Rita, be prepared for a fight. Reeder was at Waco, too, and what impressed him the most was how Koresh took everybody down with him at the end. He said he admired someone who could play all-in with people's lives like that."

Rita thanked him and left. Tightness constricted her chest as she merged into the stream of pedestrians and double-timed it back to her car.

Her phone jangled at the same moment she cranked the ignition on her Bureau-issued car. When she recognized the Texas area code, her heart bumped into overdrive. She had to take a long, deep breath before she could trust her voice enough to answer. "Goldman."

"Rita Goldman? That you?" Texas twang, male voice, but nobody she knew.

"This is Goldman. Who's this?"

"Dolph Ahlberg. Rangers. I work for Cap Marshall?"

"Okay. And?" *Have they found Sam? Is this the notification detail?*

"Cap gave me your number."

"That's good. What can I do for you?" *Goddamn Texans. Take forever to get to a point.*

"Cap said I should call you, tell you what I found out. About Bartlett?"

"Dolph..." Rita took another breath, seconds away from a detonation of gigaton proportions. People always said she had to work on her temper. "What about the fucking plane? Any word on Cable?" *People also gripe about my language, but fuck that.*

"The plane? No. Nothing yet."

Rita relaxed her grip on the phone and rolled her neck to pop the tension loose. "So talk to me. Whatcha got?"

"Well, the only address I could find on this Bartlett guy's a PO box at one o' those pack 'n ship stores, you know? So I went there, and I, uh, leaned a little on the counter guy, who gave up the name of the renter. Of the box?"

"Gotcha. Keep going." *Before I expire here, Dolph.*

"Well, it don't belong to a person at all. It was rented under a company name. Sugarland Enterprises."

"Huh." Rita let the thought simmer for a moment. "So Bartlett's somehow tied to a company called Sugarland Enterprises. Good. That gives me a place to start. Thanks, Dolph, I—"

"That ain't all."

"Go on." *Holy fuck, write me a letter, send it by Pony Express; it'd be faster.*

"I did a county records search on Sugarland and found one property zoned residential. It's a lakefront lot in one o' those expensive, high-tone communities? Ten damn acres of prime property. I went out there and knocked on the door, but nobody's home. The neighbors said Bartlett owns the place."

"So we have a real address for the guy. Good."

"Not just an address," Dolph drawled. "Address valued at one-point-two million dollars, accordin' to the tax assessor's office. Now, I don't know 'bout New Yawk City, but down here, that's more house than an honest lawman can afford."

Rita whistled. "Oh my Gawd. So Bartlett *is* dirty."

"As dirty as a used diaper in a Wal-Mart dumpster." She heard Dolph's grin at the other end of the phone. "I got a bunch of other stuff on Sugarland, but Cap says you're the prize-winnin' heifer at gettin' to the bottom of money doin's, so I attached everything to an email, but I don't have your email address. You want me to send it to you?"

"You bet your fuckin' pickup truck I do." Rita relayed her email address. "Call me back when you hear about Sam."

"Yes, ma'am, you got it."

Rita ended the call. "Finally, something I can get my hands on."

Maybe the accused murderer was right and Bartlett and his brother were bent. If she could prove Bartlett was crooked, it would establish his motive to shut the woman up. Bringing down the plane carrying her back to Texas would be a stretch, but the guy was with the Bureau of Alcohol, Tobacco, Firearms, and *Explosives*. It stood to reason his people would know how to blow shit up. If she could attach Bartlett to the plane wreck somehow...

Rita hadn't known Sam Cable long. A super-tall, broad-shouldered cowboy with a twangy drawl and Boy Scout personality was totally not her type. When the giant Ranger had been stuck in a jam, she'd helped clear his name, then they'd gone their separate ways. But...

Something about him had stuck with her, and when she'd heard he went down in a plane crash, her chest had felt crushed by a giant weight. She decided not to think too much about how hard the news had hit her. However, a nagging unease had settled over her and wouldn't go away.

And if my pal Sam's dead, maybe I can attach Bartlett's alpha-male balls to a battery and find out what he knows about what happened.

Chapter 16

"Opportunity, Motivation, Rationalization." — Dr. David Cressey, describing the three components of the Fraud Triangle

Fuentes

BATF Agent Raymond Fuentes stood apart from the circle around Bartlett. When he heard Lazzari's report, a lead overcoat of dread knotted his stomach. The woman and the Texas cops were down the hill and getting away. They were alive and armed.

He'd been at it for thirteen years, and not a day passed that he didn't think, *Is today the day? Is this the day we get caught?* Thirteen years of riding the tiger, waiting for the one mistake, one slip, that would allow the beast to turn and eat his balls for breakfast. And this situation appeared to be a perfect storm—out of control and threatening to engulf their little boat, with him three years short of his retirement.

When they'd found Bragg's body, Fuentes had taken one glance and walked away, his throat flexing to hold back the vomit. Crows or vultures had been at the man's eyes, leaving nothing but empty pits staring at the sky. The image would come back to him late at night, just like the others, assuming the alcohol didn't do its job and the nightmare circus came to town for an extended stay.

He'd wandered away from the group, stooped over, as if looking for signs like some chunky Mexican tracker in a bad cowboy movie. *De gringos? They went that way, señor.* Then he could sit back and eat his tortilla and watch the bad guys ride away. Except he was one of the bad guys now.

Static hissed, then Bartlett's voice came over the radio in Fuentes's ear, echoed by the man himself. "Track and report." Twenty feet away, Reeder stood with the circle around Bragg's body. "Six out." Bartlett's command tone resonated through the pine trees. "All right, men. We need to haul ass down this hill, *postiehastie*. Spread out as you go; cover the entire base of the mountain, from left to right. Mack, you anchor the right and, Fuentes... Where's Fuentes? Fuentes!" Bartlett spotted him leaning against a tree, hands on knees for support. "Look at that jelly-roll gut, just a-quivering. You're gettin' out of shape, old man. Need to hit the gym more. Take far left, okay?"

Without waiting for a response, Bartlett turned and put a hand on Reuben Naranjo's shoulder. "Reuben, you and Dan carry Lee here to the crash site as you move downhill. We'll get Glenn to fly over and load his body up so we can take the boy home."

"What are we gonna do with Lee?" Naranjo asked. The kid remind-ed Fuentes of a younger version of himself, except Naranjo was whip-cord thin and as eager as a puppy. "I mean, how're we gonna say he died?"

Reeder shook his head, portraying a world-weary, infinite sadness. An old general, his manner said, confiding in a trusted underling.

Fuentes rolled his eyes. *Gotta hand it to him. The man can put on a show.*

"I haven't thought that through yet, Reuben. Maybe we can pin it on the woman somehow, before everything's said and done. I just know we can't leave him here for the wolves, now can we?"

"No, sir." Naranjo stood taller under Bartlett's steely gaze.

"Good man. Knew I could count on you." With that, Bartlett waved his arm forward. "Let's move out, girls. We're burnin' daylight while the pricks who killed Tommy and Lee are getting away."

Fuentes levered himself off the tree with a grunt, shouldered his ri-fle, and did the same thing he'd been doing for thirteen years now: fol-lowed Bartlett's orders.

A breeze stirred the pines and chilled the sweat on Fuentes's body. He shivered at the ice-cold touch and picked up his pace.

Sam

TEN MINUTES AFTER THE sniper fired on us, we stumbled upon an arroyo that slashed the side of the mountain, draining runoff from higher elevations. Years of rain had washed through the cut, exposing the rock bed and flushing away a good bit of dirt and debris. Water trickled down the middle in a narrow stream.

Stone picked her way down the side and glanced back at me. "Do you want to fill our water bottles?"

"No, hold up." To my left, the arroyo created a nice flat, downhill trail that probably went to the base of the mountain. "I mean, yes, I do want to fill the water bottles, but also we're going to follow this stream for a while."

Her eyebrows came together in a frown.

"We walk on the rock," I said. "Leave no footprints that way." A blind man could jog along the elephant tracks we'd left in the wet clay soil behind us. Bartlett's guys would be on us like hound dogs on a dinner roll.

We settled Marlon next to the rivulet of running water, lowering him gently to the ground as if the bag were packed with explosives. He stirred but didn't wake. Blood had soaked a red patch near his shoulder.

How much longer can he make it with all this jostling around? The answer came back as fast as I thought of the question: *Longer than if I leave him here.*

Stone filled the water bottles while I dug my toes in the muddy bank of the arroyo and scraped the opposite slope to make it appear as though we'd continued our arrow-straight run to the bottom. I climbed the side and left more scuffed-up prints pointed due west. I tried to leave the impression of two people with a pole-mounted state trooper, out for a stroll.

I walked backward to the creek and came to a stop next to Stone, who studied my trailblazing with a critical eye.

"They'll figure it out," she said, "once the tracks disappear on the other side."

"Let's hope they're in a hurry." I winked, slipping on my game face. "You ready?"

She straightened and winced, taking up her end of the pole without a complaint. I only knew one woman I would rather have with me in a fight, a little hard-ass Yankee named Goldman. If we lived through this, I decided Jade Stone would become the second. The woman had a tractor-trailer load of grit.

"Let me lead this time." My skin itched with the need to move, and move fast. I could almost feel the hot breath of our pursuers warming the back of my neck, and burdened with one half of an injured trooper, I wanted to be ready to shoot fast.

I carried the rifle by its pistol grip, the fire selector set to burst, the safety most definitely off, and the bolt closed. Exactly the wrong way to carry the Colt M4 R0920 in field conditions with unsure footing. I rationalized that my odds of a negligent discharge were statistically smaller than, say, having a plane crash. *At least with me in the lead, if I do have an ND, I won't shoot Jade or Marlon by accident.*

"Watch where you put your feet," I ordered. We stepped off in sync, the carry pole creaking with Marlon's weight. "Try not to leave tracks."

"Duh. Ranger Obvious strikes again."

"Y'know, you remind me of someone. Your daddy ever stop by New York in his younger days?"

Fuentes

RAY DUCKED UNDER A tree limb. Water drizzled off the leaves and splattered his back, trailing chilly fingers down his neck. He was wet, he was sore, his head hurt, and all he wanted to do was curl up on his sofa and go to sleep.

"But no, here I am, in the *pinche bosque*, hunting a *pinche puta*, getting water down my *pinche* neck." He slipped, nearly fell on his butt, and banged the stock of his Browning Safari .30-06 on a rock when it slipped off his shoulder. When he stuck out a hand to check his fall, a stab of pain tweaked his wrist.

"Goddamn it!" Fuentes muttered a long string of heartfelt curses in two languages. The Browning Safari, captured in one of their off-book raids and never turned in, had a new divot in its walnut stock, near the cheek rest. He felt lucky the damn rifle hadn't gone off and blown a hole clear through his head.

Fuentes caught his breath and checked the area, looking for anybody and anything unusual. He saw trees. Trees and rocks and blue sky. Nature. Birds and shit.

Fuentes hawked and spit. He hated the goddamn forest. Hated hiking. His wife, Carla, always wanted to go camping. "Let's pack up the kids, go to the state park. Get some fresh air." The boys could sleep in a separate tent, she would say. As if.

"What, and take them away from their Xbox?" he would ask, making an exaggerated face of terror. "They'll die." She would roll her eyes and drop the subject, knowing he would go camping the minute they put up a McDonald's and a Holiday Inn at the state park.

He started downhill again, watching where he put his feet, one heavy step at a time. His stomach burned from acid, and he had trouble catching his breath. Too much stress, his doctor had said. *Well, no shit, doc. Thanks for the newsflash. Why don't you try being a cop and a crook at the same time, see how you do with managing stress? Try being part of an ongoing criminal organization that you keep secret from your wife and kids and see what happens to your blood pressure.*

A brown bird—quail, maybe—burst from cover near his feet and trilled away in a whirlwind of feathers. Fuentes leapt back, startled out of his own skin. "Shit! *Pinche párajo!*"

How did I get here? Another thought that came every day, sometimes two or three times a day. With it came the response, *Because Bartlett bought you, that's how.*

In the academy, he'd taken the required classes. Ethics. How to avoid "compromising positions" and how to stay clean while undercover. But nothing could train a man for that *moment*, the split second when it all came down to yes or no. His brain disconnects, and he could screw up a whole life in one second. Can't take it back. No do-overs.

Fucked, in other words.

He'd stood alone in the back room of a gunrunner's crib, with a guy he admired. The raid team was in the other room, cuffing the suspect, laughing, and coming down off the adrenaline high. They hadn't come to the back room yet; they hadn't seen what was right in front of him.

Piled on the table were bricks of cash. Green money in hundred-dollar bills, wrapped and banded. Stacks and stacks and stacks. Money nobody knew about. Nobody knew how much was there. The gunrunner, he wasn't going to tell.

His mentor and training officer, a bull-necked powerhouse named John Bartlett, picked up two bricks and shoved one down his shirt, the lump hidden by his bulky vest. He handed Fuentes the other one. "Call it a bonus. We earned it."

He hesitated, then his hand reached out and took the money.

Fuentes remembered how that brick burned against his chest. Everyone he'd seen that day, he was sure, knew he had a wad of illegal cash. Stolen cash. He'd avoided their eyes and left early.

A ten-thousand-dollar brick. It'd lasted about a month before he pissed it all away. He'd sold his soul to John Bartlett on an installment plan. Bartlett had read the despair in his eyes the second time Fuentes pocketed a stack of cash. He had smirked and clapped Fuentes on the shoulder, as though congratulating him on giving in and accepting his fate.

Thirteen years later, on a New Mexico mountain, Fuentes put one tired foot in front of the other, sliding a little, swatting at the spiderwebs, snagging his pants on briars, and pulling them free with muscle-taxing effort. He was convinced the weight of those years counted double against his time on the earth.

He stopped in a patch of sunlight, letting it warm his face. A conviction overcame him, seeming to pour over him with the sun's rays.

After this... After we get this pinche *lawyer bitch and the cops and bury the bodies where they'll never be found... After this, I'm done. Fuck Bartlett, and fuck the money. No more ongoing criminal organization. Bartlett will understand if I take a medical and retire early. Maybe I'll learn to play Xbox.*

Feeling better than he had in a month, as if making the decision had let the sunshine into his heart and burned away the dread, Fuentes moved a little faster. *Sooner I get this over, the sooner I can get out of the* pinche bosque *and tell Reeder I'm done.*

Sam

WITH THE EXCEPTION of having to detour around a fallen tree, the streambed provided firmer footing and a better trail than anything we'd experienced so far. We didn't speak unless the situation required it and, even then, only in whispers. I had no idea how much of a lead we had or if the sniper could catch glimpses of us and report our position, but giving it away for free by talking out loud seemed counterproductive.

By the elevation and inclination, I estimated we were very close to the base of the mountain. The arroyo had widened out to the size of an alley, overhung and shaded by trees lining the banks.

A black snake coiled by the water's edge spooked into motion at our approach. It reminded me of my midnight ride with Fernandez not so long ago and kidding him about the habits of cottonmouths. This one slid off into the brush instead of offering a challenge.

My stomach growled, and I checked the time, surprised to see three o'clock had come and gone. The position of the sun indicated several hours of daylight remained. If we could hole up somewhere until night, catch an hour's rest, maybe we could sneak out of the forest in the dark. Ninja porters, carrying a wounded samurai.

The brush on the left bank ahead of me rattled, and I froze, almost on the exact spot the snake had vacated. Before I could think *snake's big brother*, a man stumbled out of the brush. He held the walnut-stock of a hunting rifle in a two-handed grip.

Our eyes met, and I wasn't sure who was more surprised. What felt like a long moment of pregnant silence passed in a split second. Being off balance and shouldering a heavy pole forced me to try a one-handed hipshot with an M4—something Rambo might try in the movie, but in the real world, it almost always guaranteed failure. I swung left.

Too slow.

The Hispanic man—an older, chubby guy, but *fast*—recovered and twisted at the hip. The muzzle of his big-bore hunting rifle lined up with my midsection before I could bring the M4 to bear. In a Western quick-draw competition, he would've won.

Time congealed into an abstract concept. His trigger finger went white as he squeezed.

Chapter 17

"To carry a gun safely while hunting... keep the safety in the 'on' position while carrying a firearm. Only change the position of the safety to fire when you are ready to shoot." — Texas Department of Public Safety website

Fuentes

Fuentes pushed through a narrow gap in the brush, eyes fixed on the trickle of water in the streambed, and there stood the Ranger and the woman, close enough to see beads of sweat on the tall man's face. He couldn't believe it at first.

I got you, pendejo*!*

The Browning Safari wasn't designed for close-quarters combat, and the .30-06 would shoot low at that range. Fuentes compensated automatically, shifting his aim point to the Ranger's throat. His combat awareness tracked his opponent's movement, sensing more than seeing the M4 muzzle arc, knowing he had time for one well-aimed shot.

Make it count.

Fuentes steadied the rifle on target and *squeezed* the trigger—and felt the resistance, the lack of trigger motion, that told the experienced shooter he'd made a terrible mistake. The Browning's safety rested forward of the trigger guard, a simple rocker switch that took less than a second to disengage. A second Fuentes didn't have.

A jackhammer blow hit his left thigh, followed an instant later by a punch under his ribs and another in his right shoulder. The world gyrated. He saw the blue sky framed by sparkling green leaves...

Sam

TWO THOUGHTS OCCURRED, back-to-back. *I can't believe I hit him* was followed closely by *Damn, that was loud.* Every bad guy in the forest would triangulate on the reports and come running. On the other end of the pole, Stone's eyes reminded me of Mom's best china saucers.

"You okay?"

"Huh?" Her focus snapped back to me. "Yeah, I'm okay."

"All right then. Can you run?"

Her eyebrows came together. "What?"

"They're coming." I kept one eye on the downed BATF agent. He wasn't dead; one hand moved, brushing the ground as if looking for something. Dark-red blood soaked his upper thigh from hip to knee. I wished I had time to scavenge his supplies. "We need to haul ass. Can you run?"

"Do I have a choice?"

"We could hang around for this guy's friends."

She resettled the carry pole on her shoulder. "Let's run."

At various points in my life, I'd regretted the choice of cowboy boots as my footwear, none more so than I did right then. Whenever I got on Goldman about her Mono Ballnicks, or whatever they were, she would fire back at me that I was just as bad. "Look at you!" She would point at my scuffed Luccheses. "You don't wear those for comfort. It's all about your cowboy image."

In that, she was wrong. Boots *are* comfortable, *and* I enjoyed the feel and the look... just not when jogging over broken ground, carrying a backpack, a rifle, and a wounded man.

Marlon swayed and bounced, oscillating so much, his weight threw us off balance and threatened to spill us. The carry pole creaked and bowed with every bouncing step. Within a hundred yards, the breath sawed in and out of my throat, and my calves burned from strain. At two hundred, my vision tunneled and darkened at the edges.

At two-twenty, I held up a hand and called a halt, and by silent mutual consent, we lowered Marlon and set the pole aside. "This... isn't working."

Stone knelt as if in prayer, hands on her thighs, head down. Sweat dripped from her hair and dotted the ground. Panting, she nodded.

Bent at the waist, I rested my hands on my knees and sucked air until my vision cleared. It took me a long moment to realize Marlon's eyes were squinted open.

"What?" Marlon's voice sounded strained and weak.

"Rest easy, buddy," I told him between gasps for air. "We'll be home in no time."

Marlon mumbled something, and I leaned closer.

"I said," he whispered. His eyes closed again. "Bullshit."

"Have some faith, amigo." I lowered the backpack to the ground and rooted around in it for a water bottle, which I handed to Stone. "See if you can get him to drink something."

"What are we going to do about..." She jerked her head, indicating the men behind us.

I hefted the M4. "I'm going to slow 'em down a little. Here." Tucked in the small of my back was the pistol I'd taken off Bragg. I held it out to Stone, butt first. "You know how to shoot?"

She accepted the gun without hesitation, dropped the magazine, and cycled the action, catching the live round as it fell out. "Glock 17C, 9mm Parabellum, recoil reduction slots, seventeen-round magazine, plus one in the chamber, trigger safety." In seconds, Stone had the magazine back in and the extra round chambered. She tried an innocent look, but a tiny curl of her lips gave her away. "I grew up in Mississippi. Daddy has more guns than the National Guard."

"Well, all right then." Where we'd stopped, the stream curved in a gentle S, leaving an undercut bank that offered slim protection from anyone coming up behind us. I pointed it out to Stone. "You can take cover there. Hold the fort while I head back and discourage pursuit."

The slender woman regarded me with her unsettling gray eyes. Under her damp, sweat-matted hair, smudged and drawn face, and battered and borrowed clothes, Stone had a core of tempered and case-hardened steel.

I nodded and left her, thinking how I'd handed my prisoner a firearm and had turned my back on her. A minor case of chronic butt-pucker infected me until I scooted out of pistol range. No bullet punched me in the back, so the prognosis looked good... for the moment. And the moment was all that counted. I would have to wait and see what happened later, when it was time for her to go back to jail.

Luksa

"WHERE'D THOSE SHOTS come from?" Bartlett's voice crackled in Dan Luksa's ear. "Report."

A gabble of voices cut off any communication. Luksa waited for a quiet space and keyed his mic. "Six, this is Two. From my left, to the, uh, to the south."

Bartlett came back immediately. "Who was out there? Eight? Eight, report."

Ray, Dan thought. *Ray Fuentes had the far left of the line.* That made Dan Luksa the next closest to the firing.

Luksa gripped his MP5 in damp palms and charted the route he needed to take to maintain maximum cover. A stand of thicker trees below him indicated a stream. If he cocked his head just right, he could make out the trickle of water over rocks. Between him and the stream, an obstacle course of evergreen and deciduous trees offered a lot of good cover.

Bartlett called twice more for Fuentes to respond then said, "All units, all units. Converge to the south. Eagle One, shift south. Maximum speed, people. Let's group up and proceed in overwatch pattern, two by two. They're close. Get after 'em."

Luksa leaped forward, bounding from tree to tree. To his right, Naranjo would be racing to meet up with him. When they joined, they could cover each other, one running while his partner watched, weapon ready.

He slid to a stop behind a thick oak and wiped sweat from his eyes. Behind him, Naranjo churned through the forest, no pretense of stealth. Luksa waited for the younger man to form up before he moved any farther. Fuentes's silence meant he was either dead or incapacitated, which meant the Texas Ranger had taken out another of their guys. Like his file indicated, Cable could fight.

He fumbled with a water bottle, unscrewing the cap with shaky fingers. Sitting under the protective branches of a massive oak tree suddenly seemed like a very good idea. Stalling until the rest of the guys came up would be even better, but he couldn't do that with Reeder Bartlett looking over his shoulder. Disappointing Reeder would have consequences, not the least of which was being kicked out of his bed. No, he would have to move as soon as Reuben joined up.

I hope Naranjo finds Cable first.

Sam

IN OUR RUN ALONG THE gulley, we had bypassed a tumble of boulders, detouring to the side rather than trying to pick our way down. On first pass, the thought had crossed my mind that it would be a good place lie in wait. I jogged there to see if my memory matched reality.

It turned out better than I'd expected. Two enormous rocks abutted the right side of the stream, creating a natural V shape—"cleavage" was how I'd first thought of it—forming a handy shooter's rest. I lay flat on a cold, damp boulder and scooted forward, resting the M4's forestock in the gap. The sunlight slanted through the trees, casting long shadows to the right. I took deep breaths and let them out in long exhalations. My heart rate slowed.

Upstream, nothing human moved. A jay flitted to the water and drank, tipping his head back to swallow. His bird buddies twittered and tweeted. I had a great view, well over seventy yards before the next bend meandered in a slow right turn.

I had shot the dark-haired agent not far on the other side of that bend. I couldn't see the man. I hoped he wasn't dead; a wounded man would tie up more of their resources. Plus, I didn't like killing people. They came to visit on sleepless nights.

And shooting federal agents? Good Lord. How did it come to this? We'd been moving too fast for Stone to tell the rest of her story about why these guys wanted her dead. She'd told me about dating the cop, who'd later turned up as a knife block, with her fingerprints on the handle. She'd said Tommy and Bartlett were up to no good. Had she threatened to report them? Did she kill Tommy in self-defense, or did they plant the evidence on her? If she had knowledge of a criminal enterprise, why was she running for the border? It would make more sense to turn herself in and seek protection. Something didn't add up.

The blue jay by the stream bolted in a flutter of wings. Two more took flight from the far side of the bend. I cradled the rifle in my shoulder and peered through the Aimpoint sight. I took a deep breath. Let it out.

Waited.

Luksa

LUKSA SAW THE DOWNED man before Naranjo. He held a fist up to hold the other in place, then he pointed to Fuentes. Naranjo nodded. At Luksa's signal, he scuttled forward in a crouch and flopped next to Fuentes. Scanning the area, Naranjo covered Luksa as he rushed up next to the downed agent.

"Anything?"

"Nothing." Reuben shook his head, keeping his focus over the iron sights of his SIG M400. "Check on Ray."

Luksa examined their teammate and winced at the blood soaking the man's upper left leg. The normally dark-complexioned Fuentes looked gray and ashy. His chest lurched in sporadic, dragging heaves. Fuentes focused on Luksa.

"Where else you hit, man?" Luksa unsheathed his hunting knife and sliced his friend's pant leg with long rips. His hands, to his surprise, remained steady.

Fuentes's lips moved, but no words came out. He slapped a clumsy hand against his chest.

"Shit," Luksa said. "Reuben, come here. Press that wound, there. Lots of pressure, man." The hole in Fuentes's leg pulsed thick dollops of blood with the slow beat of the agent's heart. "I think he nicked the femoral."

Luksa sliced open Fuentes's shirt rather than fool with the buttons. His lips compressed in a grim line. A small trickle of red leaked from a blue-tinged hole in Fuentes's solar plexus. The tissue surrounding it was purplish with subcutaneous blood. "He's bleeding internally, Reuben."

"Shit. Goddamn it! Can Glenn lift him out of here?"

"You see anywhere to land? We'd have to carry him back up to the meadow. Ray doesn't have that long."

Fuentes grunted and scrabbled at Luksa's canvas hunting jacket with a clawed right hand.

"I'm sorry, buddy," Luksa said. He caught the stray hand in his own. Genuine sympathy tinted his voice. He liked Ray—the two of them had been around from the beginning. With Bartlett. "You're done, my friend. Don't worry about Carla and the boys. I'll make sure they're taken care of."

The air leaked from his friend's lungs as the light went out of his eyes. Luksa held his hand and waited for Fuentes's stare to go quiet and still, focused on a point none of the living could see.

"Fuck," Naranjo snapped. "This shit sucks. I'm gonna kill that cocksucking son of a bitch bastard. Cover me!"

"Wait—"

Ignoring Luksa, Naranjo scrambled to his knees and vaulted over Fuentes's body. He dodged from cover to cover, moving along the side of the arroyo with an athletic grace that Luksa admired.

With a groan, he pushed to his feet and followed the young agent, sprinting to keep Reuben in sight.

He keyed his mic as he ran. "Six, this is Two. Copy?"

"Go ahead, Two." Bartlett's voice came over radio strained and harsh. It sounded like he was running.

"Eight is down. KIA. Repeat, Eight is KIA. Two and Four in pursuit of subjects."

The silence lasted so long, Luksa nearly keyed his mic again. The radio crackled, and Bartlett said, "Two, you and Four hold position and wait for the rest of the team. Understood? Hold and wait. We're feeding targets to this asshole one at a time. Copy?"

"Hold and wait, roger that." Luksa paused at the bend in the stream. "Hey, Reuben," he shouted, "You hear—"

An automatic weapon kicked off a three-round burst—*crack-crack-crack!*—and Luksa hit the dirt so hard, air burst from his lungs. Gritty soil coated his tongue. He hunched behind the protective screen of pumpkin-sized stones and checked his body for bullet holes.

None.

"Jesus, that was close." Luksa stole a glance downstream, or he tried to. The bend in the gulley restricted his view to a few yards. To see farther, he would have to crawl from behind his rocks and poke his head around the bend. Where the shots came from.

Well, fuck that.

"Reuben!" he called out. "Reuben, you okay?"

Luksa counted off ten seconds in his head before a voice lifted from the woods downstream in a Texas twang as sharp as barbed wire, hollow and echoing under the trees.

"Reuben's gone home to meet Jesus. The welcome mat is out if you want to join him."

Chapter 18

"Good luck is when opportunity meets preparation, while bad luck is when lack of preparation meets reality" — Eliyahu Goldratt

Sam

I switched the firing selector from burst to single shot. Only fourteen rounds left in the M4, and Bragg hadn't brought any extra magazines. At this rate, I would run out of bullets before Bartlett ran out of henchmen... unless they all made it as easy as the last two guys. So far, I'd burned up an entire forest of lucky trees. The guys chasing us were overanxious or overconfident, but I couldn't count on that lasting much longer. They'd been stung hard, and a cooler head would take charge and organize a more coordinated pursuit now that they had our position marked.

I said a prayer of thanks to Saint Rambo for my wild hipshot and another for sending the man they called Reuben barreling right at me with the situational awareness of a turnip. I let him get close enough that I could see the red veins in the whites of his eyes. I almost felt sorry for him. But I wanted his gear.

Reuben was sprawled less than ten yards away. All it would take was a couple of seconds to jump up, run to the other side of my rock fortress, and cross a few measly feet of open ground. *Reach down, grab the backpack and rifle, and scoot back. Twenty, thirty seconds, max.*

But if Reuben's buddies attacked at the wrong moment, they would catch me with my butt hanging in the breeze.

Will they, or won't they? And how can I find out?

"Hey," I called out. "You still there?"

After a long pause, the guy who'd called for Reuben said, "Yeah, I'm here."

I noted the singular pronoun. Only one guy? Where were the others? Maybe I had a chance to keep this guy talking and not shooting.

"You mind telling me why y'all want to kill Jade Stone?" The second after I threw out the question, I started a slow crawl forward, M4 leading the way.

"You're in law enforcement," the guy said. "You know what they do to cops in jail?"

"Uh-huh." I had to be careful and not yak too much. If he listened closely, he might take note that I'd changed positions.

"Then you know why."

I kept quiet and snaked through the gap between the boulders. My shirt clung to my back, soaked with sweat. Grit crunched under my elbows and knees when I moved, more felt than heard. I stared so hard at the bend in the arroyo, I thought I would burn a hole through the dirt.

Ten yards turned to eight... then six.

"Your name's Cable, right?"

The guy's voice spooked me, and I froze for a second. I was off the rock and into the sandy soil by the stream, almost to the halfway point. If they caught me now... well, in Rita Goldman's words, I would be "fucked more than twin sisters at an Appalachia family reunion."

"Yep," I ventured. When nothing happened, I resumed my slow crawl toward the unfortunate Reuben. And his pretty rifle.

"You don't have to die here, y'know."

"How so?" I knelt by the body. Young guy, late twenties, Hispanic with a strong Indian influence, Reuben had a tomahawk nose, clear skin, and a strong jaw. He stared at the dirt and leaked blood from his mouth.

"Our little band of brothers makes a lot of money." Reuben's buddy didn't seem too distraught over the loss of his friend. His voice carried clear and strong, more conversational, like we were two guys out for a day in the woods. I secured the dead agent's Glock behind my belt at the back while the guy blabbed away. "You make—what? Fifty, sixty K a year? Risking your ass twenty-four, seven for a dishwasher's money? Where's the sense in that?"

"You tryin' to recruit me now?" I had the backpack's left shoulder strap off, but the right was pinned under his body. I leaned across the dead agent and caught a whiff of stale sweat, blood, and human waste.

"Why not, man? We could use a guy like you."

"Like me?"

"You know," Mr. Recruitment said. "You're a tough guy, good in a fight. Good enough to take down a couple of federal agents. Shot up all those mobsters last year."

I jerked the strap loose, and a fastener scratched on the rocks. I froze, holding my breath. Nothing stirred by the riverbank, and apparently, the guy liked his own voice too much to listen for signs of movement. I let him blather on while I shouldered Reuben's pack and crawled toward his rifle, which had stuck, muzzle down, in the loose soil next to the stream.

"I mean, think about it." He sounded like a salesman, into his pitch and pushing hard. *Sign here, please. Press hard—you're making three copies. And that'll be one soul, thank you very much.* "You gotta lot to live for, man. You're outnumbered, outgunned... it's only a matter of time before... you know..."

Sand drizzled from the barrel of Reuben's gun when I pulled it free. Maybe it all cleared; maybe it didn't. I couldn't trust the weapon until I could check the bore myself.

I scooted back to my redoubt, hauling my loot like the Grinch coming back from Whoville. I climbed the boulders and settled behind the V notch.

"I don't know. Why should I join you guys?" I called to the Recruiter for Crooked Cops. "Looks to me like I'm winning."

Luksa

WHEN REEDER BARTLETT and Mack McKenzie jogged in from the north, Luksa waved a warning. Both men panted, dripping sweat. Reeder was red-faced and glaring, and Mack was scowling. He had three degrees of scowl. One: Not happy. Two: pissed. And three: "I'm going to rip your head off, shit down your neck, burn your body, and piss on the ashes." At the moment, Mack's look rated a high One, maybe low-Two glower.

Crouched for the approach, Reeder huffed to a stop next to Luksa and settled on one knee. Mack veered left and hunkered by Ray Fuentes's lifeless body.

"Scenic route?" Luksa asked with a lifted eyebrow.

Reeder waggled his head. "Fuck, no." He sounded disgusted and out of breath. "The trail hit a dead end... Had to backtrack... about a mile, find another way. Whew! No fun." He puffed his cheeks and blew. "Situation?"

"Fucked. Ray's dead, Reuben's down, probably dead. The guy—the Ranger—is holed up around this bend. Looks like he's digging in for a fight."

"How do you know that?" Reeder kept his voice soft, blue eyes burning plutonium fuel.

Luksa pointed at the swollen spot on his cheek. "See this? I poked my head out and nearly caught a bullet. It hit a rock near my face, blew chips everywhere."

"Poor *bay*-bee."

"Screw you, Reeder."

"You wish," the older man murmured with a twinkle in his eye.

Luksa couldn't help the tiny smile that broke out at Reeder's playful tone. Bartlett was patronizing him, no doubt, but the man's charm got to him more than he'd expected it to.

Reeder keyed his mic. "Six to Eagle."

"Eagle, go." Lazzari's voice came back with a hash of static.

"Subs headed south. Repeat, south. Keep an eyeball peeled."

A double click indicated acknowledgement.

"So what are we going to do?" Luksa glanced back in the direction of Ray's body. "I mean, three federal agents dead. How're we going to explain that?"

Reeder nodded and scratched at a faint dew of snowy beard stubble on his cheeks. He raised his voice to include Mack. "Been thinking on that. Remember those two smokes from Sunnyside, Nyquil and Jimma-maya-something... Hey, Mack, how do you say those gangsta names?"

Mack's stare was deader than Ray's. "Fuck and You."

"Naqueil and Jemahya," Luksa supplied.

"Yeah, them." Reeder sat with his back to the arroyo's slope and dug out a bottle of water. "Always bitching about the product, the delivery—speaking of which, Donny's bringing some more cigarettes over to the warehouse tonight; we need to move those out soon. Gettin' full." He took a healthy swig from the bottle.

Luksa kept a wary eye on the surroundings and noted Mack doing the same. Reeder might seem unconcerned, but Luksa wouldn't put it past the Ranger to sneak up and blast them all where they sat.

"Anyway," Reeder continued, "we take Ray and Reuben and Lee back with us. Have to get 'em past the charter pilot somehow. Then we pick up Nyquil and Jemima, take 'em all out to the bayou, and stage a scene. Big shoot-out, everybody dead. By the time they're found, forensics will be fucked because of the water."

A chill soaked into Luksa. "Is that what happens to the rest of us when we get killed? We rot in the swamp?"

"Don't worry." Reeder slapped him on the knee, showing horse teeth in a big grin. "Gators and coons'll eat you up before you rot."

"Jesus, Reeder." He looked at Mack for support, but the black man brooded, crouched motionless. Whatever he thought, he kept it locked behind an unreadable expression.

"Enough of the girl talk," Reeder ordered in his command voice. He swigged the last of his water and put the bottle away. "Let's get this prick and finish the mission. Mack, flank wide left. Dan, take right. I'll keep him occupied while you guys move into position." He swatted at a whining gnat. "I'm tired of this jungle adventure."

"Roger that," Mack rumbled.

Luksa nodded. A shot of acid bubbled up, and he grimaced.

"Click twice when you're in position," Reeder said. "I'll give the go order, but don't wait. If you get a good shot, take it." Hefting his MP5 sub gun, Bartlett grinned with all his teeth again. "Kill 'em quick, boys, and we'll be home for breakfast."

Sam

A SERIES OF MUTED POPS echoed behind me, sounding like an overgrown woodpecker with a steel beak. I picked up the pace, hopping from boulder to rock, avoiding the damp soil of the streambed. It wouldn't take them long to figure out I had retreated, leaving Reuben's empty M400 poking through some brush piled in my V-notch fort. I'd stripped the ammo before leaving it behind. When they did take the position, they would come on fast but hopefully not as fast as before.

The sun touched the top of the mountain to my right. Already, deep shadows filled the sheltered spots, and golden tinting colored the sunlit ones. In another hour, we would have the cover of night.

Vee are children of zee night! The bad Dracula voice spoke in my head, making me smile even while I sucked wind, panting like a front-porch hound. I ignored my hurting feet, cramping calves, burning thighs, and all the other aches and pains.

I recognized the bend in the river where I'd left Jade and Marlon. I slowed to a fast walk, thinking we should have arranged a duress code word before I left, in case one of us had a gun to our head.

"Hey, Stone, don't shoot! It's me, Ranger Obvious."

She didn't answer, and a sick feeling twisted my stomach. Did the bad guys get around me? Or the sniper? Did he find an angle from a new position? Or did she run off?

"Jade Stone, sing out." I pitched my voice to carry no farther—I hoped—than where I'd left Marlon and the woman.

Nothing.

I angled wide right, bringing the M4 to my cheek and panning the riverbank as I moved. I saw Marlon first, or at least the bag he was in, a blue-nylon tortilla rolled around a stick.

I stumbled and nearly fell; stress or hunger was making me dizzy. I clamped down on it, blinked the sweat away, and slid forward until I reached Marlon. Pain fogged his eyes, which fixed on me with a stupid-groggy expression.

I scanned a complete arc before crouching next to him. "Dude, where's Jade?"

He thought about the answer for a long time, long enough that I repeated the question. He focused on me and whispered so low, I had to read his cracked lips to understand. "Jade?"

"Jade Stone, our prisoner. Where is she, buddy?"

He swallowed hard and in a stronger voice said, "She took off."

Well. Hell.

Chapter 19

"What you northerners never appreciate... is that Texas is so big that you can live your life within its limits and never give a damn about what anyone in Boston or San Francisco thinks." — James Michener, *Texas*

Dolph

Behind the wheel of his parked dove-gray Silverado, Dolph Ahlberg sipped from a paper cup of coffee and pulled a face. The java came from a chain with more locations than an outhouse had flies, and everybody except Dolph seemed to like the burned taste of their product. He bought the coffee in exchange for using the shop's Wi-Fi and didn't have the will to finish it or the wastefulness to throw it out. So he drank it like a kid taking medicine.

And sweated.

Not a breeze stirred, and the humidity approached the density of sea water. Muddy clouds covered the sky and held the heat like an electric blanket, and every breath felt like he was being waterboarded.

He answered his cell phone when it jangled a tune. "Yo?"

"Ahlberg, are you still in Houston?" Rita Goldman's squawky Bronx voice violated his ear, and he held the phone farther away to minimize the damage. *Who could live with a woman like this? Her voice alone would cause instant erectile deflation.*

"Ahlberg, you hear me? You there?"

"Yep."

"Listen." She read off an address on Mosley Street and asked, "Do you know where that is? I looked it up, and it's down by Hobby Airport. You know where Hobby is?"

"Yep."

"Can you find the address?"

"Yep."

"There's a warehouse there, belongs to the same company owns Bartlett's property?"

"I know."

"We need to—Wait. You know? Whaddya mean you know?"

"I been sitting on it for the last hour."

"You..."

"Y'all ain't the only one can use the inter-webs. I did a property record search in the county records database, and I—"

"Well lookit Sherlock-fuckin-Holmes. So what's there?"

Dolph's lip twitched in a smile. "Warehouse." He exaggerated his drawl on purpose, making it sound like *warrr-house.*

Muffled swearing followed as Goldman covered the mouthpiece. In a long-suffering tone, the FBI agent said, "Is that all? Are there, like—I don't know, maybe clues and shit?"

"What we got is this." Dolph shifted in his seat and killed the dregs of his awful coffee. He set the cup in the center console holder. He paused as a blue-and-orange Southwest Airlines jet screamed overhead. "Two lines of small buildings, perpendicklar to the street. Down the middle runs a mostly paved alley. I'm parked across the street, in front of a closed-up auto shop. The war'house buildin's look like they got kicked out of Mogadishu for being too shitty for the construction codes. The Sugarland Enterprises unit—the one Bartlett owns, in other words—is mostly bluish, ugly, with a streak of snot gray on the front where the paint come off. All the other units got rusty padlocks on the roll-up doors, except for Bartlett's, which has got this shiny new, high-grade steel lock with a protected shank."

"Protected shank..." Goldman mused in a distracted way.

"Yep, the shank's covered to keep people from cuttin' her open with bolt cutters."

"I know what 'protected shank' means," she growled. "Can you see inside?"

"Nope. No windows."

"We get a warrant?"

"Based on what?"

Goldman huffed in frustration. During the silence, Dolph pictured the woman's teeth grinding protected-shank steel locks into metallic flakes.

A black Escalade with chrome spinners boomed from his right, bass thumping in his chest as it passed, rolling south on Mosley. Dolph retrieved a palm-sized pair of binoculars with a built-in camera from the seat beside him and made a note of the license plate.

In a subdued tone, Goldman asked, "Any word? About... you know?"

"Hun, we got nothing on Sam—" Dolph straightened and leaned forward. "Hold on."

"What? What is it?"

A dark-green Jeep Cherokee slowed at the entrance to the row of warehouses and turned into the alley. It stopped at Bartlett's unit, right side tight against the building, the rear bumper a few feet past the roll-up door. The taillights flickered, red-white-red, then died.

A slender man, maybe late-twenties, hopped from the driver's seat and bounced around the tailgate, moving like a man in a hurry to be somewhere else. He marched to the warehouse door.

"Rita, darlin'," Dolph drawled, "buy yourself a lottery ticket, because today's your lucky day."

"Wha—"

Dolph hung up and tucked the phone in his shirt pocket without looking, eyes focused through the dinky pair of binoculars.

The young man bent over to work the lock then tugged. Dolph heard his grunt from across the street. The door rattled up and tried to slide back. The guy shoved it higher and held it until it stayed up.

Dolph reckoned the Jeep's driver to be about six feet tall. Caucasian, athletic but not a muscle head. Dark-brown hair, stiffened with gel and spiked up. He dressed like he was on the way home from a low-level office job: polo shirt and slacks with loafers.

Dolph framed the shot and clicked the camera's shutter button once, twice, then a third time, getting three solid pictures of the guy's face as he turned back to the Jeep. The driver popped the lift gate, revealing a full load of plain brown cardboard boxes. Dolph took pictures of those, including some action shots of the guy dragging the first box out and carrying it to the warehouse.

"Let's go see what you're haulin', boy." He fired up the Silverado and dropped it into gear. "If it's your mama's Tupperware, I'm gonna look mighty stupid."

His heart jitterbugged the way it always did when the action got rolling. To Dolph, the moment he nailed some sack-of-shit felon's scrawny balls to a fencepost gave him the same jolt as touching a hot-wire fence. Or like the buzz that zapped his heart when a three-pound lunker hit the crankbait and bent his rod double. His wife would never know it, but he liked that feeling better than Saturday-night sex.

He roared across Mosley without looking, trusting his peripheral vision and Jesus to keep him safe. The Chevy bounced on its springs cresting the road. Stooped under the Jeep's lift gate, the driver froze solid, slack-jawed and goggle-eyed, holding a second carton.

Dolph screeched to a stop, his off-hand mirror almost touching the Jeep's left side, blocking the driver's door from opening. The kid might run, but he wouldn't be driving away.

"Keep your hands where I can see them," Dolph ordered. His top speed was somewhere between an amble and a mosey, so it took Dolph a few seconds to climb out of the truck and round the back. By the time he made it, the Jeep's driver had put the box back in the cargo compartment and moved to block him, palm out like a traffic cop.

"Who the fuck are you, and what are you doing here?" On closer inspection, the driver was definitely in his late-twenties, with delicate features and wire-framed glasses. Still a kid, in Dolph's opinion, but not as young as he'd first assumed. The polo shirt he wore had a BATF crest over the left breast, which the wearer confirmed by saying, "I'm with the federal government."

Dolph moved in close, causing the younger man to back up a step. He hooked his thumbs in his belt so the kid could get a look at the star he wore and the bone-handled .45 automatic on his hip. "The federal gubberment," Dolph drawled. "Where's my welfare money, then?"

"Huh? Hey!"

In the blink of eye, Dolph snagged the ID card hanging from the kid's belt. It was on a retractable lanyard, which unreeled when Dolph brought it up close to his face. "Adams, Don. That your name, boy?"

"Yes, it is. Give me that back."

Dolph let go, causing the badge to snap back into place. "Don Adams, huh? With the feds? You get a lot of shit about being Agent Eighty-Six?"

Adams's brows knitted together. "What the hell are you talking about?"

"*Get Smart?* TV show? Nothing? Generation thing, I imagine." Dolph stepped around the confused-looking Adams and ambled to the open warehouse door. "ID says you're a civilian employee of the Bee-Ay-Tee-and-Eff. What you do for my brethren law enforcement officers?"

"Look, you can't be in here." Adams scrambled to get between Dolph and the open door. He reached for the pull chain hanging beside the track and gave it a tug. The door didn't budge. Adams looked around and found Dolph holding the door up with one beefy hand.

Stacks and stacks of cardboard boxes filled the interior of the metal building, which could hold a semitrailer's worth of goods. A strong smell of fresh tobacco filled his nose. One of the boxes close to the entrance had the flaps laid back.

"What's in here?" Dolph reached his free hand into the box, having to stretch a little to hold the door at the same time. Cellophane crinkled under his probing fingers, and he picked up one of the small packets.

"Hey, you can't touch that!" Adams bounded forward to clamp Dolph's forearm in a panicky grip, though the Ranger barely noticed the restraint. Like a dog leashed to the bumper of a pickup, Adams was coming along whether he wanted to or not.

"Marlboros?" Dolph examined the pack of cigarettes with a raised eyebrow. "There's no tax stamp on here."

"That's evidence," Adams told him. He had a blustery, obnoxious attitude that put Dolph's teeth on edge. Two minutes, and he already wanted to slap the kid's face.

"Evidence, huh?"

"Yeah, look here, Sheriff—"

"Ranger."

"This is a federal evidence locker, and you have no right to interfere with it." Adams fixed Dolph with a stern look. "You've probably already tainted chain of custody by touching that pack."

"Where's the evidence tag?"

"The what?"

"Evidence tag. You know, that thing what labels evidence and has a case number and all? What do you do for the ATF, anywho?"

"I, ah, computers." Adams shook his head and blinked. "IT."

"Why don't that surprise me none?" Dolph tossed the pack of cigarettes back in the box where he'd found it. "All these boxes have cigarettes in them?"

"Yeah, I—look, you shouldn't be here." The BATF employee reached for the chain again and held it, as if expecting the Ranger to wander off. His bluster had blown away like so much smoke.

"You should clean off your glasses." Dolph stood in the threshold, one hand propping open the roll-up door, as placid as a Longhorn steer chewing his cud. "They're getting kind of fogged up. Humidity, I expect."

"Listen, dude," Adams whined, "you really don't want the kind of heat my boss can bring, you know? He's like... like a ton of badass. Why don't you let me pack up here, and I won't say anything."

"Your boss happen to be a feller named John Bartlett?"

"I—no, ah, it's somebody else." The IT geek looked everywhere except at Dolph.

"I know some folks over at the ATF." Dolph fished his phone out and made a production of scrolling through his contacts. "Why don't I just give my old pals a call and see why they're storing illegal cigarettes in a warehouse owned by Sugarland Enterprises?"

Adams folded faster than a lawn chair, sinking to the concrete floor and putting his head between his knees. Dolph wasn't sure, but he thought the kid might be crying.

"Ah, shit" was all he said.

Dolph ambled over and sank to a knee beside the dejected Adams and patted him with a hand the size of a catcher's mitt. "Donnie, my son, I expect you feel like you're in a world of trouble right about now," he said in his best Andy Griffith manner. "In fact, I bet you feel like you're in a whole universe of trouble. From here to the Milky Way, nothing but trouble."

The air in the alley moved in the tiniest of breezes. To Dolph, it felt more like standing in the open mouth of a giant while he exhaled hot, moist, smelly breath all over him. He wanted back in the air conditioning, but he had to exercise some patience with the computer guy.

"I won't kid you, boy," Dolph continued. "You're in a leaky boat on an ocean of shit, and you're sinkin' fast. We suspect your boss may have killed a couple of law enforcement officers—friends of mine, in fact—which would make you an accomplice. You know what they do to cop killers in Texas, boy?"

Adams sniffed. He buried his face in the crook of his arm, glasses held to the side, dangling from an earpiece.

"The needle ain't a pretty way to go, Don. I ain't lyin' about that." Dolph let the IT geek stew in his own sweat and fear for a long count of sixty. "You know," he said in a speculative way, "there might be something you can do, get yourself outta this here mess."

Adams looked up. His eyes were only slightly redder than his flushed face. At that moment, he reminded Dolph of when he told his son, at twelve years old, his dog had been run over by a car.

"What?" Adams whimpered. "I'll do anything. I can't go to jail. I'll *die.*"

Gotcha, you little shit. Hooked, reeled, and boated. Dolph smiled. "Why don't you tell me about John Bartlett."

Chapter 20

"Get Kyle and Dusty over here. And keep your eyes open! I'm runnin' out of deputies." — Sheriff Cobb, *Silverado*

Sam

"Gone? What do you mean, 'gone'?" I looked around as if I expected Jade Stone to pop out of a bush and yell, *Surprise*!

Trees. Stream.

Rocks.

But no Stone.

When I asked Marlon where Jade was again, he mumbled something about his mama making him a peanut butter sandwich. Trooper Boggs had left the building. I squatted and held the back of my hand against his forehead. Warm but not flaming.

"Well, buddy, I sure figured that woman wrong," I told him. "I never expected her to rabbit."

Maybe she just went to take a leak again; women could be finicky about peeing in the woods. About peeing in general, in fact.

I stayed by Marlon and took another, longer, look around the vicinity. The river chuckled, and the wind whispered. No prisoner appeared. No bear with a full tummy wandered by.

I had bought some time with my rear-guard action; how much was anybody's guess, though. Not enough, for sure. The baddies would be leapfrogging their way along our back trail with the eagerness of teenagers on a first date. "Damn you, Stone."

Captain Marshall's voice pounded in my head. *"You gave the prisoner a what?"*

"A gun."

"And you left her unguarded?"
"Well... Trooper Boggs was there."
Jesus wept a river, it'd be better if they killed me here and now.

Marlon weighed two hundred pounds, easy. Carrying him by myself, I might get half a mile before the *federales* caught up with us. I needed a place to fort up, make a final stand.

I patted Marlon on his good shoulder. "Wait here."

"I don't like playin' piano," he whined. His eyes were closed, and I hoped he was dreaming about better times. Piano lessons? I'd have to ask him about that later.

Downstream, the arroyo spread out, its banks transitioning into an expanse of gravelly soil before sloping upward to the tree line on my left. On the right, broken rock walls jutted into the forest, covered by shadows as the sun sank behind the ridge. The stream widened and slowed from a gurgling tumble to a lazy drift. A pine needle rotated atop the green water like a lost compass pointer.

I paused long enough to splash water on my face and take a couple of palmed sips. My legs sang the chorus to "I Ain't Marchin' Anymore" when I straightened, and vertigo fuzzed the edges of my vision.

The rocky embankment offered better concealment. The stream abutted the cliff, so I wouldn't leave tracks going that way. If I could find a defendable place close enough to pack Marlon on my shoulder and hike to it, I could lay up and give them a good fight. I splashed through the shallow water along the stony face, looking for a crack big enough to hide in.

"Jade Stone, you rotten..." I used a word my mother would not be proud of. "I'm going to get through this, and when I do, I'm going to hunt your ass down and stake you to an anthill."

I kept glancing over my shoulder, checking on Marlon and keeping an eye out for rogue BATF agents, so the person stepping from the rocks in front of me failed to register for a split second.

"Gah!" I snapped the rifle to my shoulder and had nine-tenths of the slack out of the trigger before my foggy brain caught up to my reflexes. "Jesus, Stone," I breathed, lowering the weapon and *very carefully* letting my finger relax. "Where have you been?"

"Finding a place to hide." Her reaction to nearly being shot? A small widening of the eyes. She waited, ankle-deep in chilly water, one hand braced against the rock, head cocked to the side. "Why? Miss me?"

"Not at this range. Let's get Marlon. I don't know how long we have before your pals show up." I started back the way I came, hiding the relief I felt at seeing her again. "What do you mean, 'a place to hide'?"

Jade sloshed up next to me. "There's a split in the rocks back there. It leads to a ledge, which is a bitch to climb, by the way. You have to fight through some brush, but up against the next rise is an old mineshaft covered over with timber. It's hard to see until you're right up on it, and nobody would look twice once they see the mess you have to climb through to get there."

"So why'd you go? Through the mess, I mean." I glanced sideways at her, gauging her reaction. Her bare arms were scratched with red welts, supporting her story of fighting through the undergrowth.

"I'd already climbed the ledge." She shrugged. "I thought I'd find a trail at the base of the ridge."

When she said nothing else, I decided to drop it. We needed to move Marlon and get the hell out of sight. The pressure of waiting for the pursuit to show up weighed on me with the same sick dread as sitting in a dentist's chair, watching the long needle loom closer to that joint in my jaw.

Besides, she'd come back. Did it really matter why she'd disappeared?

Stone cut her gaze at me. She must have seen something in my expression. "What's the matter, big guy? Think I ran away?"

"Not for a second." I moved in front and slung the rifle opposite Reuben's backpack. I snagged Bragg's pack from the ground and hooked that over my shoulder, as well.

We picked up the ends of Marlon's carry pole and hefted him into place without a hitch. Practice, practice, practice.

"Let's not piddle around," I told Stone. "No telling how long until they figure out the back door's open."

"Try to keep up this time." Stone threw the pole over her shoulder.

We slogged back into the stream and along the slab-sided rock face, to the point where I'd seen Jade emerge. Behind us, birds flitted through the trees and along the waterway but not in an agitated or startled way. Still, the itch between my shoulder blades swelled to a full-on skin-crawling rash, from neck to butt. Like a bunch of spiders with fat hairy legs would feel.

With an abrupt right turn, Stone led us into a gap in the rocks. We climbed out of the water and onto a rugged trail. The footing underneath was rough and uneven, and my shoulders brushed the sides of the narrow channel.

Stone's harsh breathing echoed my own. The long hike down the mountain, spiked with gut-clenching terror and moments of deadly peril, had taken their toll on both of us. We scuffed and scrambled, panting along the cut, for a solid fifty yards or more, weaving through tight turns and climbing fallen slabs and rubble.

I lost track of time, working to put one foot ahead of the other and keep the wounded trooper from banging against the rock walls. I tried to think of something witty to lighten the tension, but my tank of funny had run dry.

Stone stopped moving, and I jarred to a halt. When I looked up, "You've got to be kidding me" was all I could say.

The cut ended at another ledge where two massive rock formations came together. The path had widened enough two people could stand side by side. We faced a flat, head-high wall. Beyond it, the slope angled upward into the forest and the thick undergrowth Stone had reported.

"I told you it would suck," Stone said.

"Now who's Ranger Obvious?"

I looked back the way we'd come, and my throat tightened. To say our backs were against the wall would be an understatement. On the bad side, if the rogue feds came this way, all they would have to do was poke their guns around the last bend in the trail and cut loose a magazine or two of blind fire. We would be chopped into bite-size pieces.

On the good side, if we could get Marlon on top of this little obstacle, we'd be in a pretty good position to guard our rear. No one, short of Superman, could mount the wall in the face of some full metal jacket discouragement.

"How'd you get up there the first time?"

Stone pointed to a wobbly stack of rocks piled against the base of the barrier. "I improvised."

"All right, let's think about this a minute."

We lowered Marlon to the ground. He moaned and said something about doing an oil change on the Camaro.

"I'll climb up first—"

"We'll have to prop Marlon against the wall."

"I was about to say that. I'll have to drag him up by the shoulders while you lift from below—"

"And keep the pressure off his bad leg."

"And keep the pressure off his bad leg."

I looked at her, and she did that upside-down smile thing, where the edges of her lips crimped down. On anyone else it would be a smirk, but she made it cute.

I matched her smile and said, "Let's do this thing."

For the first time since the Cessna lost power, I felt like we had a good chance to get out of the woods alive. Climb this pesky little barricade, find a cave to hide in until we lost the federal pricks, then hike out on our own.

Easy.

Rita's voice squawked in my head. *"Don't jinx it, you big doofus."*

"Shut up, Rita."

Stone cocked her head and frowned. "What? Who's Rita?"

"Nothing. Talking to myself. Let's get Marlon situated."

Lifting the trooper into a leaning position against the rock face turned out easier than I'd feared. We used the pine pole as a brace and propped Marlon up like a sack of laundry tied to a stick. Stone wrapped her arms around him to keep him from sinking into the bag and pressing against his broken leg.

"Ready?" I asked.

"Ten minutes ago."

I tested the stack of stepping stones with one foot, achieved a sense of balance, and grabbed the top of the wall with both hands. Just one big chin-up, right? Nothing to it.

"*Huhn!*" I pushed off with my right foot.

Too hard.

The rickety pile of rocks gave out before I had a good grip on the ledge. The weight of the equipment on my back pulled me away from the wall. I clawed the sandy grit and found no purchase.

"Aw, shit!"

"Look out," Stone urged.

There's a point in every fall when a person knows gravity's going to win. To avoid landing on Marlon, I twisted right as I went down. Like a plucked guitar string, something twanged in my knee.

I hit the ground hard, taking the fall on my left side, slamming my hip and hand into the granite. Electric, white-hot pain lanced through my wrist and up my forearm. My knee went cold. I grunted with the freight-train impact of the fall, air bursting from my lungs.

My head bounced off the ground. Light flashed in darkness. Gear clattered—*the rifle!*—and in the calm split second before all the pain hit, I cringed, knowing I had broken my best weapon.

Luksa

THE METALLIC *ping* echoed, dissipated, and was lost. Luksa froze. *Where'd that come from?*

Sounds bounced all around out here in the fuzzy end of nowhere, making a single noise difficult to pinpoint. Luksa crouched by the stream and scanned a complete three sixty, taking in all the input his senses would allow.

Somewhere to his left, Bartlett ghosted through the forest, fading in and out along the edge of the trees. Mack advanced along a parallel axis in the higher elevations to Bartlett's left. Luksa had the most exposed position, down near the stream. The sound—though faint and hard to locate—didn't strike Luksa as coming through the trees, more like the sound of metal on rock.

He keyed his mic and whispered, "I heard something. Metallic. You guys drop anything?"

"No," Mack said, and a second later, Reeder said the same and barked, "Location?"

"Unknown. Stand by."

Deep shadow covered the western bank, the sun having dropped behind the ridge. Luksa strained his eyes, scanning the darkness for any hint of something out of place. He was content to settle in and check every square inch before he moved. Ray and Reuben had set the example of what not to do, and damned if he would ignore the lesson.

A pair of frogs sang to each other, and something flopped in the water. Luksa caught the reflection of the spreading ripples from the middle of the stream. A fish. He flinched when a dark shape swooshed by his head—either a bat or an owl—and dipped away. Directly across the water, a darker shape materialized against the shadowed cliff when he focused on it. A gap? Or his eyes playing tricks on him?

"I have movement. Front," Mack rumbled.

Luksa winced at the voice, loud in his ear after the stillness.

"Report," Bartlett ordered.

"Unknown movement at my twelve, approximately your ten o'clock. Engaging."

Luksa's heart hammered a staccato beat. Excitement, coupled with relief that Mack was the one who'd found the Ranger and his friends first, rushed through his chest. He guessed Mack's direction and took off at a slow jog, concentrating on solid footholds until he left the gravel streambed. With luck, they would wrap this thing up in a few minutes and be on their way.

The *pop-pop-pop* of semi-auto fire bounced from the mountainside, and Luksa slowed to a walk. If he timed it right, he would get even luckier and find Reeder and Mack had taken care of everything. Luksa slipped into the forest and followed the sound of gunfire.

Chapter 21

"I am determined to sustain myself as long as possible and die like a soldier who never forgets what is due to his own honour and that of his country—Victory or Death." — William Barret Travis

Rita

In seat 29F on American 1171, LaGuardia to El Paso, Rita Goldman stewed. She toyed with her silent phone as the Boeing 737 idled in a long line of departing flights and debated badge-whipping the flight attendant with her FBI credentials. She wanted to call Dolph Ahlberg again, despite FAA nannies and their stupid rules. Seriously, how many delicate instruments would they need, creeping along the tarmac, waiting their turn to take off? One cell call wouldn't cause a mid-taxiway collision. *Could it?*

The engines spooled up, and the aircraft moved another six inches toward escape then stopped.

"Nervous?" The guy crammed in the middle seat—six pounds of sausage in a five-pound can—eyed the way she fidgeted with her cell.

"No." Rita slipped the phone into an inside pocket of her blazer. "My friend probably died in a plane crash, and I'm going to hunt for his dead body."

"Oh, I, uh..." The man flushed, and his eyes darted away, seeking escape from her glare.

"Read your *Skymall*, 'kay?"

"Yeah, sure."

Rita went back to watching the ground crawl past the distorted lens of the porthole. Four hours to Dallas, then she could call Dolph again.

Maybe he would have a lead on Bartlett they could follow, figure out what the crooked prick was up to. Not that it would help find Cable.

You big, stupid jerk. Why can't I think of anything else besides you dead in a plane crash? Why is my stomach all in knots? It's not like we even dated.

Heat built behind her eyes, and Rita bit a knuckle to hold on to her emotions. A boo-hoo party would be an admission of defeat, and Rita Goldman didn't back down, didn't back up, and never quit.

Since she learned of the crash, Rita'd been running on adrenaline and determination. Pursuing leads on Bartlett had felt a lot like forward progress, but in reality, it had sidetracked her from thinking too much about Sam Cable, broken and bleeding in a pile of twisted wreckage.

Images in a continuing nightmare of ghoulish scenarios played across her mind whenever she lost focus. Cable, burned beyond recognition. Cable, bleeding out his life while she drank a latte and searched for clues on a rogue federal agent. Lifeless blue eyes—

In the middle of a record search, she'd banged the laptop closed, grabbed her go-bag, and headed for the airport. On the way, she called her boss to tell him she was taking PTO then called Marshall.

"I'm going to New Mexico," she announced when the Ranger captain answered. "I can't sit around anymore."

"I'm already on my way. Meet me in El Paso."

Two hours later, Rita had a flight to the Texas-New Mexico border city, connecting through Dallas. She would hook up with Marshall, rent a car, and make the two-plus-hour drive to the command post for the search in Silver City, New Mexico. With any luck, they would make it by three or four in the morning and be in the Gila National Forest by dawn.

The plane rolled forward, and a *ping* announced they were next in line for takeoff.

"Finally."

I'm coming, Cowboy. Don't be dead.

Sam

WHEN A RANGER FALLS in a forest, can you hear him scream?

I squeezed my eyes shut and clamped down on the shout of pain that wanted to burst from my chest. Held it. And held it some more. Held it so hard, I couldn't breathe.

Stone moved to come help me; Marlon slumped against the rock wall. I held her back with a raised hand, unable to speak.

Darkness receded, or vision returned, I wasn't sure which. I drew a shaky breath and let the nerve endings loose to go find all the bad places where I hurt.

Shoulder, check. Arm, wrist, hand, triple check. Knee? Holy mother of all checks. A frozen sun wrapped my knee and sent flares of icy fire shooting out in all directions.

"Fuck," I hissed. "That hurts."

"Hah," Stone popped out a dry laugh. She held Marlon pinned in his rough-used sleeping bag. The trooper's head lolled to one side, resting on her shoulder. "That's the first time I've heard you use an f-bomb."

"And you wouldn't hear it now," I gritted out, "if my mother was anywhere near. She's grim death on foul language and rude behavior."

I sat up and put my back against the wall of the cut. First things first. I ignored the distress flares bursting from my knee and fumbled the M4 around to get a look at it. I popped the magazine and cycled the bolt, dropping the expelled round into my lap. I checked for grit in the receiver, dry-snapped the trigger, and took a look down the muzzle. I managed not to cry for joy when I found all the moving parts still worked.

The only bad news came when I took a look through the Aimpoint sight. The optics were spiderwebbed with cracks. "Could be worse," I told Stone. "Iron sights will have to do."

"If you're through playing with your gun, I could use a—"

"Shh!" I held up a finger in warning.

The cracking of gunfire rattled in the not-too-distant forest. A jumble of quick shots, a pause, then four more rapped out. A longer pause, followed by a single shot.

"That sounded like one weapon," I said. "One shooter, no return fire."

"At least it wasn't pointed at us." Stone shuffled into a better position.

Marlon groaned, and his eyelids fluttered. "For now," he said with a scratchy, weak voice.

"Yeah." I sized up the short ledge we had to mount to get out of this box. My knee screamed for attention, and I flexed the hand that had borne the brunt of my fall. It ached, and I had a nice road rash oozing droplets of blood, but all the mechanical bits seemed to work.

My brother Luke, the leader of the Cable boys and a self-professed tactical genius even before he became a Spec Ops soldier, had always found complicated ways to get into trouble. His favorite phrase once we were deep in the shit: work the problem.

Problem one, stand up. Keeping my right leg stiff, I shifted, crabbed, rolled, and pushed my way upright. Success.

Problem two, get up the freaking ledge, this time without falling. I hopped over and stacked the rifle and backpacks next to Stone. "Wait here."

"God, you're hysterical." Deep lines of exhaustion cut into her face. Sweat dripped from her hair, and a droplet clung to her nose.

"You still have the pistol I gave you?"

She nodded.

"Good. Save the last bullet for yourself."

Stone rolled her eyes, but a tiny smile crimped the corners of her lips. "Stop fooling around, jackass. Marlon's getting heavy, brother or not."

"I can help," Marlon grumbled. For the moment, his eyes seemed clear, though too bright and watery.

"About time you woke up, sleepyhead. Hold still and try not to put pressure on your leg."

"You too."

"All right." I gripped the shelf and settled my left foot on the rock cairn while keeping my bad leg off the ground as much as I could. Every time I joggled the knee, hot knives stabbed the joint. If a woman weren't close by, I probably would've cried. "One time for all the marbles. Huhh!"

I shoved and pushed up until I could flop, face-first, over the rim, both legs dangling. Taking a deep breath—because the next part was going to hurt—I squirmed and twisted until I could swing my left leg up first, followed by the everlasting-damnation-hurting right.

"Jesus wept," I hissed. I laid my cheek on the ground, and dust puffed when I blew out a breath. Sweat and grit burned my eyes until I blinked them away. "Come on, Sam. No time to rest. Now comes the hard part."

"What are you saying?" Stone rasped.

"Nothing, dear." I scooched into a position—semi-kneeling, semi-standing, one leg stuck out straight—where I could grip Marlon's sleeping bag at the shoulders.

"Ready?"

"No, Sam, I'd rather stand here another hour."

"Nag, nag, nag. Okay, on three. One, two, *three*!" I pulled, she pushed, and Marlon grunted in protest. His right arm flailed for purchase on the ledge. No telling how much damage this was doing to his already-torn-up body, but I didn't see any good choices. "C'mon, son. Up!"

I dragged Marlon with me, more a matter of me falling backward than anything else. He wound up in my lap, grumbling in a sleepy-bear way. But he was on top of the ledge.

Stone passed up the rifle and the backpacks when I could maneuver back to the lip. I caught her hand and gave her a boost up, as well.

We lay side by side next to Marlon, panting. The last little bit of daylight painted the mountaintop behind us. Night bugs were singing, and a frog croaked his love song.

"How's your leg?" Stone murmured.

"Shrieking in excruciating pain. Thanks for asking."

"Mine too," Marlon said.

"Can you walk?" Stone asked me.

"Can you carry both of us?"

"No."

"Then I guess I have to."

"The cave's not far." Jade rolled to her feet and brushed her butt with both hands. "Let's go."

I remained prone. "You really are a nag. You know that?"

Her teeth flashed in the darkness. She picked up the rifle and both packs. "Stop checking out my ass and get up, Ranger Obvious. Marlon doesn't have time for your hormones."

My witty comeback died for lack of wit.

I struggled upright and tested my right foot on the ground. The good news was I didn't fall down. The bad news... Well, to borrow a sentiment from Forrest Gump, that was all I wanted to say about that.

"Get me out of this bag," Marlon said. "I can hobble along."

"Easier for you to stay put for the moment," I told him.

Taking up the carry pole, I bit my lip and lifted when Jade did. Sweat ran down my face, and I wanted to throw up the lining of my stomach. Then we started walking. Shuffle-step-hopping was a better description. But I managed not to whimper.

We made it to the slope, which led into a brush-choked screen of trees. Beyond that, according to Stone, a hideout waited. A place we could pause and gather our strength until we hiked out of the mountains.

A fiery knife stabbed me in the knee, and I buckled.

Hike out? Who am I kidding?

Like Marlon, the only way I was getting off this mountain was prone.

Bartlett

BARTLETT REVELED IN the burn of his powerful leg muscles driving him—no, *propelling* him up the slope. Times like this, he felt like a force of nature: unstoppable, implacable, and utterly without mercy.

The quasi-light as the sun dropped away made the footing treacherous and the path vague. Nightfall would be soon. When hunters prowled and prey died squealing. Bartlett grinned at his own fancy.

Based on the sound of firing, Mack had found the woman and her guards and eliminated the threat. Better to say, shot the bitch who'd killed Tommy. Good. They could write Mission Accomplished on this little fiasco, chalk it to the win column, and take their men home for... disposal.

He slowed to a walk and keyed his radio. "Three, report."

"Up here," Mack called out in the clear, not bothering with the radio. His voice came from the trees higher and to Bartlett's right. "It's all clear."

Bartlett cut between a pair of low-hanging limbs and climbed along a rock spur until he reached Mack's position.

In dark tac gear, the hulking form of his subordinate blended into the forest, as invisible as a black hole in space. He knelt by an unmoving human form on the ground. Farther along the narrow deer trail, another body sprawled in a twisted heap.

Bartlett took one look. "It's not them."

"No shit," Mack grunted. "What gave it up? The white hair and plaid shirts or the fact they're both men?"

"Jesus Christ, Mack. You shot a pair of hikers?"

"Not just hikers." A dark finger pointed out the radio lodged in the rocks next to the closest man. "Search and Rescue."

Bartlett felt like an elevator had dropped from under him. Two civilians dead with no explanation complicated the mission to the point of absurdity. For the first time in his life, the thought that he might not get away with something crossed his mind. Only a fourth-quarter touchdown or last-inning home run would save him this time. "The shot clock is winding down."

Mack's eyes gleamed. "What?"

Luksa's voice crackled in Bartlett's earbud. "Six? Six, this is Two. Position?"

"Stay where you're at, Two." Luksa would be less help than a blind man at a shooting gallery. He was such a pussy, he would probably go directly into menstruation when he saw the dead bodies of the two SAR people. If Luksa wasn't so... creative in bed, Bartlett would've moved him out of the organization years ago. One way or the other.

Mack rumbled, "What now, boss?"

"Oh, you shoot fucking civilians, and suddenly I'm boss again, that it? Shut up and let me think." Bartlett retrieved his water and drank a hefty slug.

Night handicapped tracking Stone's group. Stumbling around in the darkness after live game would be suicidal and stupid. Not only could they walk into the muzzle of the Ranger's gun, but they could very likely wander right past their quarry without seeing them. Any tracks or trace evidence would be invisible.

No, better to fort up for the night, make camp while they still could. Everyone had single-person camp stoves, sleeping bags, and freeze-dried food. Getting through the night wouldn't be a problem.

Bartlett chewed a lip. A gnat whined in his ear, and he brushed it away. Mack remained as impassive as a boulder.

Bottom line, they had a day, maybe half a day, to bring this to a head. If they couldn't wrap up all the loose ends and be gone before, say, fifteen hundred hours tomorrow, then Bartlett would cut loose his two pals and head for the coast. In his bag, he carried a complete set of fake docs, along with credit cards, a passport, and the keys to a forty-foot Beneteau Oceanis Clipper.

In his head, he carried the account numbers and PINs for three investment accounts chock-full of laundered, clean, safe cash. Two-point-two million, last he'd checked. Enough for a nice run to the Caribbean and points south.

Tommy, you dumbass. Why'd you have to get involved with the lawyer?

Bartlett pulled himself out of his funk. No need to get all hysterical and weepy because of a little setback. Plan B wasn't a bad option. Besides, he could probably find a tanned, muscular cabin boy to keep everything trimmed out. Win-win.

"We need to get rid of these bodies," Bartlett ordered, back in control. "Destroy their electronics, find a deep hole, and toss 'em in."

"In the dark?"

"The fuck, Mack? You shoot it, you clean it. That's the rule." He keyed his radio. "Six to Two, come in."

"Two."

"Find a defensible position. We need to set up camp and get some chow. Can't see shit in the dark."

"What was all that shooting?"

"Three got attacked by a man-eating squirrel. Six out."

He ignored Mack's hairy-eyeball stare and toed the cooling body of the old duffer in his plaid CPO jacket. A citizen volunteer, no doubt. A dentist or retired lawyer, playing golf and doing good deeds by looking for people lost in the woods.

"Search and Rescue people this close means we don't have long."

"Ya think?" Mack snorted.

"But they can't operate at night any better than we can." Bartlett clapped his subordinate on the shoulder. "We'll get up first thing tomorrow and run these cunts down. Promise you that, brother." Bartlett swigged more water, swished it around, and spit to the side. "Promise you that."

Chapter 22

"**B**ecause brothers don't let each other wander in the dark alone."
— Jolene Perry

Sam

The mineshaft was right where Stone said it would be. A narrow channel led to a rough rectangular opening cut into the side of the mountain. Old-growth forest and dried brush concealed the entrance until we were right up on it. A plank door, eaten around the edges with wood rot, lay like a doormat at the entrance.

"I pulled... the door off," Jade panted. "So I don't think... there's any bears inside."

"Good." I hated to think what a puny .223 round would do against a bear—any bear, brown, black, grizzly, koala, or teddy. I had no faith in any rifle cartridge smaller than .30, and these high-velocity .22s didn't come close.

I limped into the shaft behind Jade. The knee had begun to cooperate as we moved uphill, and I could put more weight on it. Flexing was out of the question. We continued another ten yards into the darkness—and by "darkness," I meant the mother of all Dark-Ness. The phrase *six feet up a well-digger's ass* came to mind.

"Far enough," I said, and Jade agreed. We settled Marlon, and I collapsed next to him.

Night pulled a curtain across the entrance, lighter blackness compared to the utter blackness farther down the shaft. A musty draft, as if the earth exhaled, puffed from deep in the mine, bringing with it the odor of rotting timbers and old bones. Or maybe I imagined that last part.

"Anybody want to hear a ghost story?"

Jade's disembodied chuckle echoed. "No."

"Hand me the backpacks, would you?"

By the hooded light of my Mini Maglite, I examined the contents of the pack I'd recovered from the agent by the stream. The .223 had no problem bringing him down, but then, I'd put three in his chest at spitting distance. I found an ID case on top.

"Reuben Naranjo," I read. "Know him?"

"Uh-huh. Young guy. Followed Bartlett around like a puppy; always looking to get the boss to notice him."

"Well, he died trying to make an impression." I rooted deeper in the bag. "Oh, ho. What do we have here? Thank you, Reuben."

"What?"

"A one-burner camp stove, with a propane bottle attached. No cold supper tonight. And more freeze-dried crap. You like turkey tetrazzini? Or beef stew?"

"I'd eat the ass out of a dead horse right now."

A breeze shifted the trees, and leaves whispered. Something skittered near the mine opening, and I switched off the light until I was sure nothing wicked this way wandered. After a count of thirty, I went back to searching.

"Another sleeping bag. A compass. Two water bottles, both empty. A map! Bless you, Reuben." Something down in a corner crinkled under my fingers, and I tugged loose a small baggie containing what we law enforcement types liked to call "a leafy green substance," a pipe, and a Bic lighter. "Well, lookie here. It seems Reuben the ATF agent liked to smokey a little dopey."

"Yes!"

I turned the light on Jade, who seemed very happy for someone stuck in a cave. "What? You feel like getting high?"

"Painkiller," Jade prompted. "We can give it to Marlon. Make a tea or something?"

"Hey!" Marlon's voice wavered. "I don't do dope."

"Shut up, Marlon. Good idea." I rooted around until I found our water bottles. One was completely empty; the other contained about a cup. "Need water. Feel like a hike back to the stream?"

"No, but I will anyway." Jade sighed and scrubbed both hands in her shaggy hair. She'd peeled down to her damp T-shirt, which clung to her body in interesting ways when she lifted her arms. I focused the light onto the camp stove and read the directions. Twice.

"Take a look at Marlon," I suggested. "I'll get some marijuana tea brewing."

"Sure."

Jade wrestled with the zipper on Marlon's bag—it had twisted and snarled during our nature walk—while I fired up the stove and set our last cup of water to heating. Never imagined I'd be making a teapot of, well, pot tea.

The blue flame illuminated the mineshaft with a surreal, film-noir look. Rough-hewn sandstone walls closed in from both sides and the low ceiling. Deeper in the shaft, I made out the first support timbers, which really looked more like lack-of-support timbers at their current stage of decay. No way I was going any farther down this particular shaft. I would fight it out, hand-to-hand, with all the crooked feds and pissed-off bears in New Mexico before I ventured deeper into the Pit of Doom.

Everybody had their own anxieties, closets full of personal monsters. Being buried alive in the dark took up a good chunk of mine, wedged on a shelf between being trapped in a sinking submarine and dealing with health insurance screwups.

I shivered.

Jade made a distressed noise, and I shuffled next to her.

"Oh, hell," I said. Marlon's left leg had swollen to three times its normal size, looking like an over-stuffed sausage in his uniform slacks.

I never knew polyester could stretch that much. The bandages around his arm were stiff, but no fresh blood had leaked through.

He groaned and shifted. Marlon's eyes were open and focused, but reddened, and a stout reek of old sweat and coppery blood rose from his body in waves.

"We need to split the seam on these pants," Jade murmured. "And rewrap the bandages on his arm."

"Agreed." I handed her the tiny flashlight. "Go get some water. Carefully. Take your pistol and be as quiet as a mouse. I'd go, but climbing up and down that ledge would be too much for my knee right now. I'll take care of Trooper Boggs. We'll figure something out when you get back."

She sniffed and nodded before scooting away. I waited while she collected the water bottles, stuffed them in Bragg's empty pack, and crabbed toward the door. She paused at the entry, and I could just make out the white oval of her face when she looked back.

"Be careful," I urged. "Watch out for Bartlett's crew. It would be stupid to get caught now, after all this."

"Okay," she whispered and disappeared.

I split the seam on Marlon's pants, wincing at the swollen flesh underneath, then cut strips from Bragg's old shirt, fashioned more bandages, and wrapped those around his upper arm. Boggs watched me without saying anything, a sheen of sweat dampening his face.

I fiddled with the flame on the stove. The water stubbornly refused to boil while I watched, so I concentrated on laying out our meager equipment and otherwise piddling around the campsite, straightening this and arranging that. I refused to think about there being only one extra sleeping bag.

When I looked back at Marlon, his eyes were locked on mine, and his throat worked.

"Help." His voice, when it came, had a dry rasp and little sound. Poor guy. He probably had some deathbed confession he wanted to make, or he wanted to ask me to look after his mama or tell his friends how he tried.

I leaned closer. "What is it, buddy? What do you want?"

"Sam," he husked. "I need to piss like crazy."

Jade

RETRACING THEIR ROUTE toward the creek, Jade made the trip in short bursts: a few steps forward, stop and listen, then a few more. She kept low and moved when the wind blew, hoping to mask her sound with the rustling of the trees. Pausing at the ledge where Sam had fallen, she listened hard.

An owl queried her presence. Night bugs sang in harmony with frogs. A few stars flickered on, pinpoints in a blue-black sky. Scents of pine trees, water, and her own unwashed body competed for her attention. What she wouldn't give for a hot shower, followed by a soak in a deep, soapy tub. A glass of wine. A velvet robe. Firm bed with a dozen pillows and one of her grandma's quilts.

"Wish in one hand, spit in the other." Another of Daddy's favorite sayings. *While I'm at it, I may as well wish for a tall Texan to share that big four-poster.*

Sam Cable. Jesus, could things get any more complicated? She had to develop a crush on the man assigned to take her to jail. He and Marlon both were a pair of the best men she'd ever met. Real Good Guys, capital letters intended. "Keepers," her mama would've called them.

Jade let herself down the ledge, lowering her body in a reverse chin-up until her feet touched the ground. Enough light filtered through the trees, she rarely needed the palm-sized flashlight. The bulb had yellowed as the battery drained; she didn't want it to run out at the wrong time or for Reeder—or, worse yet, Mack—to spot it. That one was the polar opposite of Good Guy. Would things have worked out differently had she met Sam before she hooked up with Tommy?

With the oncoming night, the temperature had dropped like a bad cell connection: suddenly and without warning. Jade shivered, wishing she'd put the flak vest back on, or at least the extra shirt she'd worn all day. What had possessed her to take it off in the first place?

Jade grinned and crept toward the sound of running water, sneaking forward in rolling steps, heel-to-toe, to avoid bringing her weight down on loose twigs. *Admit it,* she thought to herself. *You wanted to show off the girls, catch the big hombre's eye. Worked too.*

Not that she needed any reassurance of the Ranger's interest. The attraction felt as inexorable as planetary motion, gravity tugging her insides and dragging her closer to the heat of a fiery sun. She had sensed Ranger Cable becoming aware of the growing attraction, as well. The big man's eyes lingered more and more frequently, and he'd lost the stern resolve of a law officer toward a criminal.

Jade had been aware of male interest since she was twelve, and rarely had she returned it, which included Tommy Grace. She'd rejected the high school boys who came sniffing around her ass like dogs in heat, and most of the boys in college and law school. Her first time had been clumsy, awkward, and messy, an act completed to check off a box on her to-do list. The rare recurrence of the act of sex had been more to seal a deal than for any emotional need on her part. Her thing with Tommy Grace had been strictly business.

Jade found the stream by stepping in it; the water's edge was hidden in shadow. She waded into the deeper, faster-moving flow, reasoning it would be cleaner and contain fewer parasites. The chilly water soaked her legs up to the knees, and she clamped her jaws to keep her teeth from chattering.

The burbling water masked sounds; she could hear nothing over it. Jade strained her eyes, trying to pick up any hint of human presence, and sniffed the air like a wary deer. *After all,* she reasoned, *wasn't Bambi's mother shot while taking a drink?*

Jade filled a water bottle, drank, then refilled and capped it. She put it away before filling the rest.

Taking care not to slosh, Jade slipped out of the water and followed the now-familiar path leading to the ledge. Her feet squished like icy-cold fish stuffed in soaked paper bags. It was hard to tell what felt worse, the aches and pains of the day's hard travel or her freezing feet.

Resting in a dank mineshaft had never sounded so good. She looked forward to getting back. *Who knows, maybe I can get Sam to warm my feet for me.*

And then what? Jade asked herself. She'd never been in this situation before, actually liking a guy and wanting to get to know him better. What would happen if she had to choose between going to jail or shooting the Ranger and running?

No answer appeared.

She found the ledge and, after rebuilding the rock cairn, shinnied over the edge with a jaw-clenching effort. Jade lay on her back and stared at the star-dotted sky. A meteor zipped across her field of view, so fast that she thought for a second she'd imagined it.

Ranger Sam Cable. A guy she would really like to know a lot better. A guy who, in a different life, she could see being a keeper. Interesting to see how a relationship with somebody she actually liked might turn out. It was too bad, really.

Sam

"WHAT DO YOU MEAN, YOU have to piss?"

"You know... piss. Take a leak. Urinate."

Marlon looked at me, and I looked at Marlon. His hurt-puppy eyes worked on my conscience while I considered the... logistics of how two guys with one working leg apiece could achieve urination in a pitch-black cave.

"Can you roll to the side?"

"I can't piss on my side, Sam. C'mon, help me up."

"Wait for Stone to get back."

"I—I can't do it in front of a woman!"

"It's dark; she'll never see a thing."

"No way. Uh-uh. I can't."

"Jesus, Marlon. Seriously?"

His eyes answered my question.

"Oh hell. Come on." I sighed.

Struggling and groping in ways I never thought I would grope another man, we made it into a hunched, somewhat upright position, Marlon's good right leg against my good left. His left arm dangled uselessly as we tottered together like drunken sailors on a three-day leave.

"Okay," I panted. We wound up facing away from the entrance. "Let's go that way. Deeper into the cave." Right where I'd just said I didn't want to go.

"'Kay."

We stumble-hopped about two dozen feet from camp.

"Far enough?" I gasped. Hunching over to keep level with the shorter man was testing me in new and interesting ways.

"Sure."

"Okay, go ahead."

A pause.

"I can't unzip my pants," Marlon complained. "My arm's busted."

"What? Well, I'm not doing it for you."

"Hold on. Wait..."

"What're you...?"

"I'm trying to... Fuck. Goddamn it, this hurts."

"Stop, stop, stop," I commanded. "You're gonna fall."

We panted in the darkness. Ghosts of long-dead miners laughed at us.

"All right, stand still," I said. "Don't move. I'll get the zipper, but I'll be damned if I'll hold your dick for you."

"Why don't you bear hug me from behind? Then I can use my good arm."

"Good idea." We completed a complex transition worthy of a Broadway choreographer. "How's that?"

"Working... on it." The rasp of a zipper came to my ears, followed by, "Ahh, Jesus, that's better." The splatter of mission success went on for a long time. It sounded like Marlon urinated the contents of the Missouri River. I hoped the flood didn't fill up the mine.

"Okay, Sam, thanks. Let me zip up."

Yellow light clicked on behind us. "Should I leave you boys alone for a little while longer?"

Chapter 23

"A lovely nook of forest scenery, or a grand rock, like a beautiful woman, depends for much of its attractiveness upon the attendance sense of freedom from whatever is low; upon a sense of purity and of romance." – PT Barnum

Sam

"Help me get him back to camp," I told Jade.

By the time we settled Marlon on his sleeping bag, the water was boiling on the camp stove. I dribbled in a pinch of dried pot leaves, thought about it a second, then threw in another pinch. *If a little is good...*

"Is that...?" Marlon grumbled.

"Herbal tea."

"Yeah, right."

"Trust me; this will be good for you." I looked at Jade, who'd taken off her shoes and socks and was drying her feet with the last of our rags. Her jeans were soaked to the knee. "Any trouble?"

She shook her head. "No."

"I'm going to put the door back up. It'll hide our light and maybe keep out skunks and bears. Sasquatch. Things like that."

"Knock yourself out." She chafed her feet without looking up.

Jade seemed out of sorts after her trip to the creek, but I imagined she was about worn out. I mean, who wouldn't be? Even I, Man of Steel, could've used a solid eight hours of sack time and a good dozen meals.

I limped to the mine entrance and levered the plank door off the ground, employing dumb muscle and awkward swearing. Best I could do was lean it against the original timber doorframe, which blocked about three-quarters of the opening, leaving most of the gap at the top.

Good enough.

I tottered back, one hand on the wall for support. "Done," I reported.

"Mm-hmm." Jade held Marlon's head in her lap, feeding him the marijuana brew in tiny sips.

"How's that taste, Marlon?"

The trooper lifted his hand in a weak thumbs-up gesture. His eyes drooped, and he looked on the verge of passing out again.

I flopped next to the camp stove in a graceless lump and retrieved our other cook pot from Naranjo's pack. "Water?"

Jade pointed with her chin to the bottles propped against her shoes. Her mouth was pressed in a thin line.

"What's wrong?" I asked.

"Nothing."

Oh, hell.

One lesson I'd learned early in life: when a woman uses that tone and says, "Nothing," it means, "Something, but I'm not in the mood to tell you all the ways you screwed up and ruined my life right now, so leave me alone, or I'll start at the beginning of time and detail your major and minor faults, one by one." Loosely translated.

I rolled my eyes—where she couldn't see me; I wasn't completely stupid—and busied myself with a delicious packet of freeze-dried turkey tetrazzini. Ripping open the foil released an aroma that set my stomach growling and my mouth watering.

"Oh, man," Marlon croaked, "that smells good."

"Getting the munchies?"

Feeding the three of us took both meals from Naranjo's pack. We still had two of the trail packs from Bragg's supplies, so we wouldn't starve anytime soon, though I suspected we would be pretty hungry before the trip was through.

Marlon faded into a drugged stupor after a few bites, then Jade and I ate the rest. During the meal, she communicated the basics but nothing more. Our water bottles were empty by the time we finished eating, drinking, and washing up.

"I should probably go get some more," she said but made no move to get up.

"Take a break, rest up. You earned it."

I turned off the one-burner stove, and its blue glow died, leaving us in thick, musty darkness. Sounds were muted, nature's volume turned to the lowest setting. I stretched out on the open sleeping bag, keeping my right leg straight. The knee had swollen tight enough to stretch my jeans, and it throbbed with a dull ache, punctuated with stabbing pains.

I wonder how much pot tea is left.

"Shit," Jade said, "I can't see a thing." She clicked on the light long enough to crawl next to me and lie on the other side of the bag, leaving a few miles of space between us. An invisible, chilly barrier, as strong as a brick wall. When she turned off the flashlight, the after-image glowed on my retinas.

I let my mind drift loose...

"What now?" Jade murmured.

"Hm?"

"Do we wait for rescue or try to hike out of here?"

Her question echoed the one that had buzzed around the back of my mind since we'd made it to the cave. Mineshaft. Deep, dark hole in the ground. I shivered.

"Sam?" Her voice had taken on a softer tone, less rigid than before. Jade shifted, and her weight settled closer to me. I sensed her with paranormal clarity. Her heat, her scent, her... body. "Sam?"

"I heard you." I cleared my throat. "It's obvious we—and I stress *we*—aren't walking out of here. I can't carry my half the load with a bum knee."

"Stay here then?"

"No," I sighed. "I don't think Marlon can wait that long. He might lose the leg as it is. It looks... bad."

"So that leaves..."

"You, yes. You're going to have to hike out of here on your own."

Jade moved again, and her fingers, feather-light, touched my arm. Her voice, when it came from the dark, whispered so softly, I had to strain to hear her. "Do you trust me to do that?"

"I think we're beyond that, Jade Stone. You're either a good guy or..."

"Or what?"

"Let's say it this way." I paused for a second to find the words I wanted. "I don't think you're going to run, but if you do, I expect you'll send help in the right direction. And if you're innocent, you don't need to run. Bartlett and his crew are finished."

"And if I run anyway?"

"Hm?"

Somehow she'd gotten closer without me noticing. Her warm breath tickled my ear when she spoke. "What if I decide it's too much? What if I run anyway? Will you come find me then?"

Her fingers trailed lazy circles on my bicep, leaving tingling goose bumps behind. An image of Rita popped into my mind for some reason. I'd briefly thought she might have some interest in me, but when she went back to New York, that pretty much killed that thought. Besides, she was so not my type. It would never work with her.

"Count on it, Jade," I vowed. My words came out hoarse and rough, so I coughed and said, "Count on it."

The back of her hand brushed my face, and I nearly rolled over and took her in my arms. Whatever had been bugging her before must have dissipated; I had a feeling she would welcome the advance. However, there was still the whole prisoner-custodian thing holding me back. Until the matter of her legal status was resolved, getting involved felt... wrong.

Plus, Marlon needed our help, not our making out.

"Listen," I said. "There's a map in the backpack. I took a look while you were filling the water bottles, and I think I know where we are. This mountain ridge we're on runs from the northwest to the southeast. If you could work your way back northwest, you'd cut across a stream called Mogollon Creek. Maybe a ten-mile hike. Turn left, follow the creek, and Highway 180 is fifteen to twenty miles further on from there."

"A thirty-mile hike?"

"Wait, it gets worse." I sat up and fumbled in the dark until I found the pack and the map inside it. "Turn on your light for a second... Jeez, that's bright."

I blinked to clear my over-exposed eyes. "See, here's about where I think you'd hit 180." I showed her the spot with a grimy finger. "Unless you can flag down a car, you'll have another ten-mile walk to Glenwood. Make it there, and you're home free."

"Free," she mused. "Sounds good."

"So look," I pointed out, "the bad part is Bartlett's guys are around here somewhere, maybe camped on the north-south arroyo we came down this afternoon. To get to Mogollon, you'd have to take the arroyo back the way we came, hike uphill over the shoulder of the ridge we camped on last night, and down to the bigger creek."

"I could walk right into them."

"Exactly." In the yellow light from the flash, her eyes looked hollowed out, and her face drawn. "So what I think you should do is go southeast a ways, hang a right, and climb over this ridge. From there, you can follow these canyons back to the Mogollon and avoid Bartlett and his guys. Do an end-around on 'em. Just have to be careful of the sniper, who'll be somewhere high and to your right when you're climbing the ridge."

"You make it sound so easy. All I'd need is a tube, and I could float down the river."

"Well," I said then ran out of sentence.

"Well."

"Take one of the packs. Some food and a water bottle. Better fill me up the other one before you head out. You keep at it, don't stop, you can make that distance in a day, maybe two if you have to backtrack around any obstacles."

"Two days?" Jade glanced at Marlon. Her look said it all.

"I know," I told her then shrugged. "Who knows? Maybe we'll get lucky and the cavalry will come save us. Could be, I'll be sitting up in a fancy hotel room, drinking a beer, and you'll still be humping through the mountains. Stick to the route we outlined, and I'll send the troops to come get you."

She nodded. Scratched her nose. Scrubbed her hair. Glanced around like she'd forgotten something.

"What?" I prodded.

"Bartlett's helicopter," she said. Her eyes held mine, reminding me how tough this woman really was. "What if I could find that? I could force—"

"Don't even think about it." I held up a finger. "One, you don't know where it is." Another finger. "Two, it could come down to kill or be killed, and neither outcome is good for you. You're already on the hook for one self-defense killing; two would be a stretch. Especially if you could have avoided it. You go looking for trouble..." I shrugged. "Could go bad, is all I'm sayin'."

She didn't look completely convinced, but she said, "Okay, Sam. We'll try it your way." She took a deep breath, inflating her chest, and I kept my eyes above her collar with an act of supreme effort. "I'm so tired, but I should get moving."

"Let's get you packed." I busied myself organizing supplies. "Then you can power nap for an hour. Moon should be up by then anyway; give you more light to see where you're going."

We didn't have much to begin with, so packing took less than three minutes. I told her to keep the pistol she carried. If she ran into any of Bartlett's crew, I didn't want her unarmed.

"But if you see a bear," I warned her, "don't shoot it with that puny nine-mil. Mr. Bear will be picking Jade out of his teeth for a week."

"Roger that," she said with a grin.

"Cut the light and catch some z's. I'll keep watch."

She clicked the switch, and blackness slammed down around us. I lay back to give my sore body a rest, worried I would relax too much and fall asleep.

I jumped a little when Jade snuggled next to me. She rested her head on my shoulder, threw an arm over my chest, and pressed the length of her body against mine. Her hair tickled my chin.

Holy cow. At least I wouldn't have to worry about falling asleep.

"Sam," she murmured, "you're so stiff."

"Jesus, Jade."

Her low chuckle rumbled against my chest. "I meant your body, big boy. Relax. I won't bite. Anything you need to keep, that is." She chuckled again.

I wrapped an arm around her and rested a hand against the silky muscles of her back. She was warm and soft, and she fit just right against my side. And I was about to send her off on a thirty-mile hike through rough terrain populated by bears and Bartlett's bad guys.

I stared into the darkness without moving, listening to her breathe, for a long time.

Chapter 24

"Undoubtedly, criminals' use of role-playing games for exchanging money with each other will only increase." — Imran Khan, *Fraud Magazine*, June 2016

Rita

Rita Goldman bulled her way through a herd of sluggish, tired passengers disembarking from American 1053, the connecting flight from Dallas, at El Paso International's Gate A2. Her heels clicked on the smooth tile, echoing in the nearly empty terminal. She passed a Latino guy running a buffer and dodged a family—mom, dad, grandma, and sixty-eleven kids—ambling in a cluster between her and the baggage claim exit.

A wizened, squinty-eyed Marlboro Man in a Western-cut suit and cream Stetson waited by the luggage carousel, one foot propped on the rubber edge. As weathered and lean as a barbwire fencepost, Captain Les Marshall stood six inches taller than her only by virtue of his black cowboy boots.

Next to Marshall, a pro wrestler in his late thirties, wearing a sport coat and slacks, scanned the area with eyes like a gun turret. He spotted her first and nudged Marshall, who nodded.

"Glad you could join the party, Goldfarb." Marshall shook her hand. "This is Trooper Duncan. C'mon. Car's waitin'."

Rita fell in step next to Duncan, trailing the fast-moving Marshall. The captain was the only Texan who seemed to move like he had a purpose. "Are you a Ranger, too, Duncan?"

"No, ma'am." Duncan's voice was surprisingly soft for someone with his build. "DPS, plainclothes. I'm here to help the captain interact with the twenty-first century, ma'am."

"Huh?"

"I work his cell phone for him."

Marshall's rental car was parked by the curb in the passenger-loading zone, flashers blinking. Wade Duncan held the passenger door for Rita, took her suitcase, tossed it in the trunk, then climbed into the back seat.

"You don't want shotgun?" Rita asked.

"No, ma'am, you go ahead, please."

She shrugged. *Texans. Slow but polite.*

Dry, desert air instantly evaporated the moisture in her sinuses and made her wish she'd remembered to bring bottled water. The dark shoulder of Franklin Mountain, outlined in twinkling lights, rose behind the glow of El Paso. Rita shut the car door, cutting off the roar of jet engines spooling up for takeoff.

"What about—*Holy fucknuts!*" Rita's head snapped back when Marshall floored the gas, barking the rental's tires and spooling up its own little engine in sympathy with its big brothers on the airfield.

He made a right onto a six-lane divided road with barely a tap on the brake then took a left at the next traffic light, mashing Rita against the door. "Goddamn Japanese piece of shit. Turns good but no guts."

Duncan leaned forward. "Now you know why I prefer the back seat, ma'am."

"Lesson learned."

"Y'all knock it off," Marshall growled. "Wade, get Dolph on the phone, put him on speaker."

The lean captain powered up the I-10 entrance ramp and nipped in front of a semi rig at somewhere near the speed of sound.

Rita adjusted her seat belt. "Now that we're going fast enough for time to run backward, would you mind telling me what the fuck has happened in the last five hours I've been stuck on planes?"

"Nothing on the plane crash." Marshall cracked the window, dug out a pack of cigarettes, and lit one up, holding the steering wheel with his knee while he cupped the flame. When he spoke again, smoke drizzled from both nostrils. "What's happened, Agent Goldberg, is that Dolph's picked up one of Bartlett's boys down in Houston and found a warehouse fulla smuggled cigarettes."

"Cigarettes?"

"I have Dolph, sir." Duncan reached over the seat and held the phone between them.

"Bring us up to speed, Dolph," Marshall ordered. "Use small words because I got the FBI here."

"Goldman? That you?"

Rita leaned closer to hear over the rush of wind from the open window. "Yeah, it's me."

"All right, then. Let me see..." Dolph cleared his throat.

Rita thought, *Oh my God, he's gonna tell a story.*

"Donald Ray Adams is a civilian employee of the Bureau of Alcohol, Tobacco, Firearms, and Explosives. He is responsible for the destruction of confiscated goods seized by that agency, under the supervision of sworn agents of, well, that agency."

"Don't make this an all-nighter, Dolph."

"Hold your horses, you old coot. Here's the good part, anyway." Dolph sounded a lot like Slim Pickens in *Blazing Saddles*. "Bartlett and some of the other agents from the Houston office been die-vertin' the evidence instead of destroying it. They're supposed to witness the destruction, sign off on it, but they been fudging the paperwork and stealing the contraband. Cigarettes and liquor."

"Guns?" Rita asked. The back draft of lingering smoke in the car made her eyes water.

"Naw, strangely enough, Donnie says Bartlett's against guns being sold back to criminals. He ain't above traffickin' in tobacco and booze, but he won't do weapons."

"A crook with a conscience?" Marshall said. "What next? Aliens from Mars?" Marshall flicked his cigarette butt out. When he reached for the pack on the seat, Rita stopped him.

"You light up again, Captain, I'm liable to shoot you and take my chances in the wreck."

"Hah!" Dolph laughed. "She got you there, you damned fossil."

Wade Duncan looked away, holding the phone like an offering to the spirit world, tucking his smile into a shoulder.

"Keep talkin'," Marshall growled. He snapped a glare at Rita but kept his hand off the pack. The car rocketed through light traffic, passing through the residential section of El Paso. Shopping malls. Car dealerships. Except for the preponderance of signs in Spanish, it looked to Rita like any city in the US.

"So where was I?" Dolph said. "Oh yeah, the criminal conspiracy part. Ah, okay. The crime part is simple: steal the stuff, sell the stuff. Takes no great smarts to figure that part out. Where it gets interesting is how they washed the money. Y'all ever heard of Em-porgs?"

"What?" Rita and Captain Marshall said in chorus.

"Wait, let me look at my notes. Uh, here it is. M-M-O-R-P-G. More-pigs."

Rita squinted in confusion; the captain shook his head.

Duncan said, "Massively multiplayer online role-playing games."

"Yep," Dolph agreed, "that's it. See, here's how it goes: People use real money to buy what they call in-game money. Gold doubloons or fairy gold or whatnot. They use the in-game money to buy, uh..."

"Enhancements," Duncan supplied.

"Enhancements. The genius part is there's no physical product sold, no inventory records, not a shred of accountability. The gaming company can report whatever income they want. I mean, who's gonna track to see how many people are actually playing the game and see what all they're buyin'?"

"A perfect placement strategy," Rita mused.

"Exactly," Dolph agreed. "The first stage of money laundering. Get the funds from an illegal source to a legal one."

"Isn't creating games expensive?" Duncan asked.

"Not these games," Dolph said. "They paid high school kids to build a few More-Pigs. Donnie says they're junk, but who cares. Nobody's really playing; they're just buying the game tokens themselves. Bartlett's people bought prepaid cards with their dirty money then spent them in their own games. Presto-chango, real money rolls into the company bank accounts."

They rode in silence for a full minute. City lights had faded away to black desert, leaving them with only the glow of the dashboard and the screen of the cell phone held by Duncan.

A sound of shuffling papers came from the phone, then Dolph cleared his throat. "I asked Donnie who all was in on this, and here's the list he gave me: Bartlett, of course, as the ringleader. Then a cat named Dan Luksa of the BATF. All these guys are BATF, except for Tommy Grace, the Dallas detective. Then there's Reuben Naranjo, Ray Fuentes, James MacKenzie, Dominic Lazzari, Lee Bragg, and Toby Glenn. That last guy is a civilian contractor, works for the bureau as a chopper pilot."

"That's a lotta damn people," Marshall said. He reached for his pack of cigarettes, cut his eyes at Rita, and slid his hand back to the steering wheel.

"Lookit," Rita said, "this is all very interesting, and it looks like the fugitive lawyer—whatshername, Stone—was maybe right about the conspiracy and this and that, but it don't mean they brought down Sam's plane. I mean, c'mon, right? Maybe they wanted to shut her up, maybe they didn't, but we got nothing to tie them in to crashing a plane in New Mexico."

"The Feeb's right, Dolph." Marshall steered around a slow-moving semi, and Exit 155 flashed by. On the left, the neon lights of a truck stop flooded a small patch of desert. "You got enough for a warrant; get the US ADA, and start rounding these assholes up. Sweat 'em and see what they have to say about all this."

"Can't."

"Say what?"

"Well, boss," Dolph drawled, "here's the real interestin' part. According to the BATF, Bragg and Glenn are undercover and can't be reached, on assignment by their Supervisory Special Agent, John Reed Bartlett. All the others, including Bartlett, suddenly took PTO and quote-unquote went on a hunting trip."

"All of 'em?" Marshall met Rita's look with one of his own.

"Ever' stinkin' one. I had the boys do some checkin', and six guys led by a man matching Bartlett's description chartered a plane out of Houston night before last."

"A plane," Rita spit. "Do we know where they went?"

"Yep. Same place y'all are goin'. Silver City, New Mexico."

Sam

I WOKE TO A HAND WORKING my belt loose.

"Stop," I hissed at Jade Stone. Then my words came out in a rush as her hand dug under my waistband and found the prize she sought. "What d'you think you're doing?"

"Shh," she whispered. "You'll wake Marlon."

I glanced over at the trooper, who snored with a bubbling wet sound. The reflected light of a full moon shone into the mine through the gap above the door, allowing me to see Marlon's covered body. I pitched my voice low. "Don't, Jade. This is a really bad idea."

"You can stop me anytime you want." Her breath warmed my ear, and her body pressed into my side. My hand at her back slid down and discovered she was naked below the waist.

Jade's hand continued its mission, working me into fullness. A groan escaped me, and the tension flowed out of my back. I cupped her bare bottom and lifted my hips as she worked my jeans down. Moments later, she added the soft warmth of her mouth to her stroking fingers.

I didn't stop her. I thought about it... right up until the moment she swung a leg over me and pressed the soft lips of her sex against me. At that point, it was fair to say I gave up thinking.

I held Jade's bare hips as she rocked atop me. The silky flesh under my fingers flexed with her movement, and I marveled at how firm and strong she was. My hands traveled up, and I covered two pebble-hard nipples with my palms. She bit off a moan and rocked faster, her breath coming in short pants.

I clamped down on the urge to drive into her, letting her set the pace, which had grown desperate, almost frenzied. Jade covered her mouth with both hands to hold back the noises coming from deep in her throat. Her eyes fixed on mine, glittering in the dark. They were wide open, her expression reflecting surprise, delight, need, and a bunch of other emotions I could only guess at.

And then her stomach clenched, and she shuddered. Jade buried her face in my shoulder and bit down, stifling the cries that erupted from her as she twisted her hips and shook from head to toe. I held her tight and let her spasms subside.

"That never... happened before..." she whispered.

"What never happened?"

Jade touched my lips with a finger. "Shh. Never mind."

And then she was sliding up and down again, moving with me, urging me. I didn't need much urging. I braced my legs and exhilarated in the sensation of being inside her, filling her up, and taking her. Being with her. Having her...

All too soon, it was over. Both of us together this time, gasping into each other's shoulders. The scent of her damp hair and two-day-old sweat struck me as the finest of perfumes right then. If I never stopped smelling Jade Stone pressed against me, well, that would've been just fine.

We fell asleep that way, her on top of me, our bodies loosely joined, with me breathing her in and her whispering small words that made no sense but conveyed her pleasure just the same.

"COME ON, STONE, MOVE your ass." I waited outside the mine-shaft, one hand holding up a tree.

"Hey, I'm not the one who fell asleep on duty."

"Ain't that just like a woman," I muttered.

"I heard that." Jade emerged from the shaft, backpack over her shoulders, the Glock in her waistband. She spotted me under the tree, stepped in close, and slipped her arms around my waist. "That's okay. I always wanted to sleep with a real cowboy."

"Many do."

She stepped back and slugged me in the arm. "Jerk."

"But few succeed."

"Nice save." Her eyes glittered with reflected starlight. "But it wasn't enough."

"Next time."

"Yeah. Next time."

I stood like a stork, balanced on one foot, and soul-gazed with Jade. Two teenagers on a first date couldn't have been more sappy. I knew a microscopic movement was all it would take for us to start kissing and not stop until we were a tangled heap on the rocky soil of the New Mexican mountain. The same way a few ounces of muscle pressure on a trigger will fire a gun.

The voice in my head spoke. *You've done enough dumb things for one night.*

I eased back, and the moment was gone.

"Well," Jade said.

"Well."

"I better go."

"Ah, yeah. Good idea." The outside temperature had dropped since we entered the cave, and a fresh breeze made it almost chilly. "You gonna be warm enough in that T-shirt?"

"Once I get moving, I'll be fine."

"Okay, come with me. I scouted around a little while you were fixing your makeup."

I hop-stepped from under my tree and led her along a narrow trail that hugged the base of the slope, angling left and upward away from the mineshaft. My right leg seemed to work as long as I didn't test it with too much weight.

A half-moon and an ocean of stars lent enough light to follow the trail without tripping, but I still used the Mini Maglite in places where the overhanging foliage blocked the sky.

About fifty hobbling steps from the mine, the hill on our right was split, creating a natural shortcut pointed toward the summit.

"Here," I said. We stopped and locked eyes again.

A century or two later, Jade whispered, "You know what my daddy would say at this point?"

"Huh-uh."

She reached up, and cool fingers laced the back of my neck. "He'd say, 'Fish or cut bait.'" Jade pulled, and I didn't resist.

Despite our dry, cracked lips, two days of unbrushed teeth, and the sour smell of our bodies, Jade's kiss blasted enough fire through me, my socks started smoking.

When we broke apart, she touched my face with her fingertips. "I wish..." She looked down and stayed silent.

"What?"

"Nothing. I need to get going."

I squeezed her shoulders. "Be careful. Watch out for Mr. Bear."

Her smile flickered for an instant; she turned and walked away, a dark shape in the night.

My knee was screaming at me, so I found an ottoman-sized rock, eased my butt down, and stretched my leg out to give it a break. The scuffing and scraping of Jade's footsteps on the sandy trail continued for a time. Then she was gone.

Dominic

LAZZARI SETTLED INTO the third observation post in the last two hours, having systematically moved from position to position to scan different segments of the valley. The FLIR RS32 thermal scope was a joy to use, but the battery life allowed a limited window of opportunity. Eight times, he'd frozen on a hot spot, only to see it resolve into a deer or a raccoon. The image quality through the FLIR left no doubt, once he zoomed in and his eye focused on the shape. He panned the rifle in methodical arcs, sweeping from farthest distance to nearest, then back again. When he completed the terrain sweep, he would move to a different spot and try again.

For the ninth time, a dot of white crossed his field of view. Lazzari froze and centered the image. The FLIR had no rangefinder, and estimating distances through a thermal scope was more magic than science, but his experienced guess put the target somewhere between two hundred fifty and three hundred meters away, near the scope's maximum range. Even zoomed in, the shape was nothing more than a white blur, smaller than a diamond-stud earring on a saltine.

Lazzari centered the image and controlled his breathing, reducing the jitter and achieving a Zen state of calm. The blob moved-shifted-resolved into a tiny human form, standing erect from seated position. He or she—Lazzari suspected a male, though he couldn't say why—moved awkwardly, as if injured.

Lazzari smiled. "Got you, you bastard."

Chapter 25

"And whether we shall meet again, I know not.
Therefore our everlasting farewell take:
For ever, and for ever, farewell,
If we do meet again, why, we shall smile;
If not, why then, this parting was well made."
— William Shakespeare, *Julius Caesar*

Bartlett

"Six, this is Eagle. Come in."

Bartlett snapped out of a light doze when Lazzari's voice crackled over the radio. At first he thought—hoped—it was Donnie Adams, calling him back. He'd left four messages, and so far, nothing. Then his brain caught up to the message.

"Six, Eagle. Do you read?"

Cocooned in a warm sleeping bag, he focused on the luminous dial of his Breitling Chronomat and read the time: 12:35 a.m. He'd slept for over two hours.

The campfire had died to the thinnest of orange, smoking embers, rendering the men no more than bundled shapes in the dark. On the other side of the campfire, Luksa and MacKenzie stirred.

"Six, this is Eagle. Copy?"

Camping near the water had been a mistake; fog veiled the riverbed in a chilly shroud. Bartlett fumbled with the handset, which was slick with condensation. "Go for Six."

"I have a tango. I think it's one of them."

Bartlett sat upright. "Roger, Eagle. One tango only? Can you give me a position?"

"Uh, approximately two klicks south of your pos. Eastern slope of the mountain I'm on. About... half a klick upslope from the river bottom."

"Can you ID?" Bartlett glared at the Motorola logo, willing the radio to tell him what he wanted to hear.

Luksa was up, propped on one elbow. Mack gave no indication, but Bartlett sensed he was awake, as well.

"Negative, Six. Has a limp, could be injured. I, uh, have a limited window here. Battery low and target moving. I need to take a shot now."

"Eagle," Bartlett snapped, "do not engage. Repeat, do not engage." The last thing he needed was another civilian decorating the landscape with the remains of .50-caliber finger painting.

"Six, I..." Lazzari paused.

"We'll check it out. You sit tight. Six out."

Luksa and Mack were already shoving their feet into boots. Good men, they didn't need orders.

"Lazzari sounds cranky," Luksa said.

"He's pissed he missed the shot yesterday," Bartlett told him. "Hustle it up, before he loses his mind. I want to get eyes on who this is before he cuts loose with that elephant gun."

Dominic

MOVING, THE GHOSTLY image in Lazzari's thermal sight looked more like an amoeba under a microscope than a human form. A number of challenges presented themselves when night-shooting through a thermal scope. Besides distances being hard to estimate, things like tree branches were invisible, increasing the odds of a deflection.

Lazzari's lips twitched. *With a Barrett, not so much.* The thumb-sized bullet took more to deflect it than the average round.

The figure moved with a halting, uneven gait. Definitely hobbled, probably injured. The FLIR was amazing. When the target paused, the image coalesced into a tiny human shape. With most thermals, anything beyond spitting distance was a blob of white.

Lazzari clicked the safety off and caressed the trigger with the pressure of a fly landing on a pillow. All it would take was one... tiny... squeeze.

"Shit and fuck," Lazzari muttered. The battery indicator started flashing a warning. All his zooming in and out earlier had burned up a lot of juice. He had a minute, maybe two, before the scope died and he lost sight of the target.

The figure paused and rubbed his knee. Lazzari steadied the crosshairs on the biggest section of white in the scope. *Bartlett's gonna be pissed, but screw him. I want this shithead.*

The dirty secret he kept to himself: he loved the hell out of shooting people at long range. In the Sandbox, Lazzari had served with some hard-asses, snipers as cold as Arctic pack ice who could drop a dozen hajis like punching a time clock then have a beer and a smoke later as if coming home from a shift at the factory.

His buddies joined up for love of country. The Stars and Stripes, apple pie, and all that "America, the Beautiful" shit. Not Dominic. Mama Lazzari's youngest had enlisted to get away from the North End docks and the ripe dumpster stink of the alley under his tenement window.

When he discovered how much he liked blowing the turbans off the camel-suckers in Iraq, Lazzari knew he never wanted to do anything else. And he did it well, until the REMFs rotated him back to the US.

Opportunities to ply his chosen trade were few and far between. Any chance to shoot with the long gun, he wanted. And he wanted this one, here and now, for extra special reasons. As much as he'd ever wanted anything. He ached for it the way a reformed smoker craved a hit of nicotine when he walked into a smoky bar.

"Fuck it," Lazzari muttered. His finger pressed ever so gently against the trigger, and he let out half a breath. Then squeezed.

Sam

I MASSAGED MY ACHING knee, which did nothing for the pain, but it made me feel proactive and in charge. Pain was weakness leaving the body, and I had a lot of weakness on its way out. Without Jade, the night seemed colder, less enchanting, as if all the life had drained away. All my aches and pains—

Bam!

The Father, Son, and Holy Spirit reached out with an open palm and bitch-slapped me upside the head. I sprawled in the dirt, my ears playing a high-pitched whine at full volume.

How? What?

I remembered a flash of heat—my left ear was warm—followed by a concussion, then... pretty stars overhead. A tree branch exploded in a shower of splinters, followed a heartbeat later by the boom of a rifle.

Ah. Sniper.

I squirmed deeper into the underbrush, burrowing like a mole, blind and panting. Gravel scraped my chest, and dust filled my sinuses. Where could I hide? The guy was on an IR or thermal scope; he could be pinning me with his crosshairs right now, and I wouldn't know it until a missile-sized bullet blew me apart.

Another round smacked the far side of a tree on my left. It shivered, mortally wounded, and pine needles drizzled over me. *Damn, that's a big gun.*

The first round had passed so close to my left ear, the pressure wave alone had knocked me silly and flash-burned my ear. Based on the slight sound delay, the shooter was close, within two to four hundred yards. Elevation unknown. Was he still at the top of the ridge, or had he moved down? The last three rounds had felt more probing than target-ed, like he wanted to flush me from cover.

No, thanks. I think I'll stay right here, becoming one with Mother Earth.

Except I couldn't, could I? His buddies would be hot-footing it in my direction, vectored in by the guy upslope. Out in the open, pinned down by a sniper, I was like a Ranger-shaped piñata just waiting for Bartlett and his crew to surround me and beat me to a pulp. Marlon lay in the mineshaft, defenseless. He had weapons—the M4 was there, not in my hands, where I needed it—but I doubted he was conscious enough to defend himself. I had to move, get back to the mineshaft, and fort up with Marlon.

How many rounds did the sniper fire? Four? And how many in a Barrett clip? I... couldn't remember. *Five or ten? And did they make extended magazines?* My brain refused to focus on the problem. Counting rounds was pointless, anyway. I had to make a run for it, gimpy knee and all.

Another bullet whip-cracked through the branches, this one behind me, and high. I moved.

Jade

JADE FROZE AT THE FIRST shot, lifting her head to test the air. She wasn't the target; that was obvious instantly. The trail Jade traveled lay deep in a rocky split, resembling the arroyo she'd followed with Sam and Marlon earlier. Anybody shooting at her would have to be right on top of her, at cursing range, and that shot had come from a distant rifle.

Who was shooting? And at whom?

Another dull boom started Jade moving again. She'd climbed about halfway to the top since leaving Sam. By her best guess, she had another hour to reach the summit, longer if the trail vanished and she was forced to ad lib a route in the darkness.

Growing up in rural Mississippi, Jade had heard hunters firing all manner of weapons from distances near and far. That sound had come from somewhere to her right. After the third report, she decided it was a high-caliber rifle. It lacked the flat crack of a .223 or similar cartridge.

It wasn't hard to guess who was shooting. *Lazzari.*

Of all Tommy's pals, Dominic creeped her out the most. Sandy hair and light-brown eyes, with a jock's physique, the sniper should've been a chick magnet. Whenever she was in a room, Dominic's eyes followed her like the eyes in a painting in a bad horror movie.

Jade shivered. She'd lied to Sam when she said movement would keep her warm. Sweat patched her light T-shirt, and whenever a mild breeze funneled down the narrow split, it chilled her to the bone. She touched the Glock in her waistband.

One way or another, she wanted this little ordeal to be over. No way did she plan to hike another two days to get out of the mountains. Not when there was a faster way.

Boom!

The shot echoed, and Jade moved faster.

Bartlett

"GODDAMN IT, EAGLE," Bartlett snarled into the radio. "What did I tell you about engaging? What part of 'do not engage' failed to penetrate that thick skull of yours?"

No answer.

"Fuckin' Lazzari." *What a clusterfuck this mission is turning out to be. Bragg, Fuentes, Naranjo: dead. Two civilians: dead. Donnie: out of touch, unreachable. Lazzari: off the fucking reservation, busting caps in the middle of the night at a target he can barely fucking see!* "Goddamn it!" Bartlett squeezed the radio tight enough to crack the plastic. He cocked his arm, one breath from smashing the handset into a rock.

Mack and Dan stared at him, as immobile as granite statues. Bartlett couldn't see their expressions, but he could imagine them. *Has Reeder Bartlett lost it?* they had to be thinking. *Can we count on him?*

Bartlett took a breath and tried a chuckle. It came out shaky but serviceable. "Sorry, boys, don't mind me. A little pissed is all. You all ready to move? Good. Let's haul ass, see what we can find."

Nods in his direction were tiny motions in the night. His two team members pivoted and fell into line, paralleling the stream with their weapons at the ready.

Bartlett waited for a long count of ten, getting his breathing under control. That was the only thing he felt he could get under control; everything else was crumbling like sandcastles on the beach.

Is it time to run? Bartlett examined that thought seriously for the first time ever. He'd always been in charge, never fearing arrest, always one step ahead of everyone else. *Don't all crooks feel that way?*

"Heh." Bartlett's lips pulled into a thin smile. Sure enough, he'd busted enough guys who thought they had the tiger by the scruff of the neck, only to learn that tigers didn't give a shit what they thought.

I should turn around. Head the other direction and hike out of here. Two, three days, I can catch a bus to Galveston. Dump the hidden cash from the Sugarland accounts into an offshore, gas up the boat, and head out to sea.

Bartlett remained in place, shifting his weight from one foot to the other, for a full five minutes, scanning the foggy darkness for an answer. *Dawn. I'll wait until dawn. This isn't resolved by then, I'm outta here. Fuck the guys. They can take care of themselves.*

Jaw set, Bartlett shouldered his pack and moved out, striding forward with an outward façade of resolute leadership. As commander, he had to set the right example. Otherwise, the troops might sense betrayal, and performance would be degraded.

Dominic

LAZZARI WAITED, EYE glued to the scope. The gray field of view was his entire world. He'd zoomed out enough to ensure he didn't miss any movement when it happened. The first shot had whiffed—that much he knew. Even a touch from a .50-cal would wreck a human body, and this guy had squirreled away so fast, he couldn't have been hurt.

Probing shots had done nothing to root him out. Yet. The guy couldn't stay hidden forever. Then again, Lazzari couldn't stay on the scope much longer; his battery indicator had already been flashing way longer than he'd expected it to last.

He fired again, bracketing the area where his target had gone to ground—

There!

A blob of white blurred through the lower left corner of his scope. Lazzari shifted the rifle instinctively. Centered, he led the target and squeezed. The rifle hammered his shoulder with a solid thump.

God, I love this shit.

Chapter 26

"Only John can make somebody that crazy." — Holly Gennaro McClane, *Die Hard*

Sam

The ground in front of me erupted, and something hard smacked my forehead. It made a damp thumping sound inside my skull, like hitting a pile of wet newspapers with a baseball bat. A spike of pain split my head, my legs quit working, and I tasted dirt for the second time in as many minutes.

Panicked and blinded, I fought the urge to curl up in a ball and scream. I scrambled in the darkness, clawing earth. The sniper had me in his sights. *Move.* There was a short drop-off to my right that—

I hung weightless for a split second before gravity caught. I plummeted through a screen of bushes and belly-flopped hard enough to hammer the wind from my lungs. The world spun. The smell of dust and weeds tickled my nose. I tasted blood from where I bit my tongue.

Somewhere in my head, an alarm rang with a steady beat of *sniper-find-cover-sniper-hide-sniper-crawl-away*. I could no more move than a cat could drive a car. I'd had the wind knocked out of me enough to know what to expect, though experience didn't help recovery. I could only hope the rock at my side sheltered me from the sniper's view.

Remember to breathe. Simple. Open mouth, suck air. After several seconds of not being blown to bits, I managed the first lungful of air, then the next. The ringing in my ears receded, and my vision came back into focus.

I'd dropped from a six-foot-high rock bench into a tangle of bracken. My hands were scraped raw, and wetness—correction, blood—trickled from a stinging lump over my left eye.

I crawled closer to the man-sized bluff and squeezed against the cool stone. The night was too dark for me to tell how far in either direction the projection extended. In the run from the sniper, I'd become disoriented and had a hard time placing myself in a spatial relationship to the terrain. In other words, I was lost. For the moment.

A breeze ruffled the weeds, and their acrid scent made my eyes water. I wanted to sneeze. But relief pulsed through me when I touched the walnut-checked grips of my Kimber in its high-rise holster. At least I wasn't completely helpless, cowering in the dark, waiting to see which would find me first—a sniper's bullet or Bartlett's band of douches.

I blinked my eyes wide open and scanned the darkness for threats. The sniper fire had ceased, so I was probably hidden for the moment. The shooter was no doubt moving to another position and would reacquire my heat signature, sooner rather than later. Once he did, Bartlett could zero in on me based on the sniper's report.

Time to move, Sam. Need to get back to Marlon. But… which way is the mineshaft?

Dominic

IN THE SECOND BEFORE the scope blinked off, Lazzari saw the white ghost of his target spin sideways and fall, disappearing into the terrain of trees. The scope blinked once then died. Lazzari pulled his eyes back to reality. Downslope, he saw nothing but a faint outline of pines, aspen, rocks, and wilderness in the moonlight. He only knew the trees were pines and aspens because he'd seen them earlier. At night they became "tree, black, type one."

Might as well try to find a light switch in a basement as see a human figure at a quarter kilometer in the wilderness. From the way the guy had tumbled, it looked like the last shot had hit, but Lazzari had no way to know for sure. *Well. Shit. Bartlett's gonna be pissed.*

"Eagle to Six."

"Six!" Bartlett came back like he had his finger poised over the talk button. "What the fuck, numbnuts?"

"Target down. Status unknown. Same relative position as earlier reported." Grimacing, Lazzari waited for the biting comeback. For all his Coach Lombardi bullshit, Bartlett could be a real prick when annoyed, running a guy down in front of the squad with sarcastic comments.

No wonder Tommy moved to Dallas, with a brother like Reeder.

Nothing came for a long time.

"Copy, Eagle. Go back to the bird and await further. Six out."

"Huh," Lazzari grunted to himself. "Await further what, asshole? Instructions? Genius thoughts from our fearless leader, the dick-sucking sack of shit?"

Lazzari engaged the rifle's safety and levered himself off the ground with a huff of effort. He patted his pockets and took a mental inventory. Leaving anything behind for other law enforcement types wouldn't be wise. His XM500 had a brass catcher attached, so at least he didn't have to wander the forest, looking for shell casings.

Fucking Bartlett. Lazzari didn't know why he put up with the guy. Besides the money, of course. He could never forget the money.

Lazzari shouldered his rifle and followed the hooded beam of his flashlight to the game trail he'd followed to his overlook position. Stars washed the sky, and a glowing half-moon rose over the eastern range of the Mogollon Mountains.

Bartlett thought no one knew he was gay. What a joke. Everybody knew he and Luksa were fucking. Nobody gave a shit. It was creepy, but as long as they kept it private, Lazzari didn't care. *Not like I gotta shower with them.*

No, Bartlett's whole persona might have been copied from a wall of motivational posters and have as much depth. *Well, screw Bartlett and his dick-breath buddy. If the fake fuck wants to chew on Mamma Lazzari's boy, he's gonna find the XM's muzzle stuck down his throat. See how he likes sucking on that.*

There was nothing else he could do tonight. Time to get back to Toby Glenn and his helicopter, eat some chow, and grab a few hours of shut-eye before dawn. Lazzari found the stack of rocks marking the main trail back to the helicopter. He turned left onto the path and quickened his pace.

Bartlett

THE SECOND TIME LUKSA fell face-first into the creek, Bartlett called a halt. After an hour of splashing through freezing water, stumbling over the uneven streambed, exploring dead-end trails with eyes peeled to cue-ball size, they hadn't found jack-all.

"Huddle up, men." They gathered by a fallen pine. Luksa, sodden and dripping, plopped his butt on the tree and hung his head. Bartlett's spine crackled when he stretched to relieve the tension. "This effort, my friends, is class-A stupid."

"Agreed," Luksa said.

"No shit." Mack faced outward, scanning the forest, though Bartlett doubted he could see a foot past his nose.

Bartlett checked his watch. "It's two or three hours till dawn. You boys find a spot and catch some shut-eye. I'll stand watch until we have enough light to see what the fuck we're doing."

The hair on the back of Bartlett's neck tingled when he found Mack staring at him, two disembodied eyes in the surrounding darkness. The big man stood as silent as a totem pole.

"Roger that." Luksa groaned and limped to a sandy spot, where he dumped his pack and stripped out of his wet clothes, which he hung on nearby tree limbs.

"What?" Bartlett demanded when Mack said nothing.

The black man matched stared at him for a long moment. Mack snarled up a wad of mucous, leaned to the side, and spit. "Nothing. I'll see you in the morning."

After Mack vanished into the forest, Bartlett seated himself on the fallen tree and slipped off his pack. From a side pocket, he pulled a flask of brandy and took a hit. The fiery burn soaked through his blood-stream like water into a dry towel. He capped the flask and put it away.

Not far away, Luksa snuffled and grunted, settling into his sleeping bag. A few minutes later, he quieted, and Bartlett had the night to him-self. The smell of pine and sage, carried by a light breeze, washed over him. A fish plopped in the stream. Bartlett vacuumed air into his lungs through his nose then expelled it through his pursed lips. He did it over and over, until a slight dizziness tickled the edges of his consciousness.

How did it come to this? Itchy and tired, hiking a forest beyond the back of nowhere, hunting the skinny bitch who'd shanked his brother. Two guys left he could count on, and he wasn't so sure about Mack.

Best case: they find Stone and her detail early, right after first light, and manage to drop Stone and the Rangers... something they hadn't been able to accomplish all day, despite their best efforts. Then they would have to pack out six bodies, bury Stone and her bodyguards, and somehow get his guys back to the swamps to stage a crime scene that would stand scrutiny. All without being seen by anyone.

This mission had crumbled like dry cake. Had the woman already spilled her guts? Was there already an investigation underway? Their operation was covered by the thinnest of tissues, hiding in plain sight. It wouldn't take much to cut through the skin and find enough evidence to land them all in jail.

"What was I thinking?" Bartlett murmured.

Luksa grunted in his sleep and rolled over. Bartlett glanced at the mounded shape. *Too bad. Dan's the one thing I'll miss.* Bartlett uncapped the flask and sipped again. *But not for long.*

Sam

NO MORE PESKY CANNON shells tore up the quiet night while I hugged the ground, breathing dust and weed pollen, trying not to sneeze. Bugs buzzed, and leaves rustled. No rogue alpha male federal law enforcement agents stalked the night. I nearly blew away an armadillo who snuffled out of the bushes without warning. He scuttled across my field of vision and vanished into the weeds.

It was so peaceful, I almost dozed off. I waited a solid twenty minutes before I moved from my little patch of Sam-shaped New Mexican dirt, inching through the brush as carefully as a naked man climbing a cactus. Every few feet, I paused and listened. The same bugs buzzed, and the same leaves rustled.

My back muscles clenched tight, in expectation of a bullet the size of a cruise missile. I burrowed into the incline on my left, following the base of the drop-off until it petered out and rejoined the main trail I'd followed earlier. Then I paused for another listen. Bugs buzzed. Leaves rustled. No bullets cutting the air. No feds sneaking around.

I scrabbled up and sprinted—hobbled, really—across a bare patch to the shelter of an oak. Pressing into the rough bark, I panted harder than the effort was worth. The run had made me dizzy, and more blood trickled into my eye. The cut hurt like hell, had for a while. I tuned it out, crouched under the oak, and waited for my head to clear, listening hard.

Nothing.

Either the sniper had run out of ammo, or he'd lost me in the clutter when I went over the edge. I had to accept as a given that the shooter had some form of radio or sat phone and had given his buddies my approximate position. Bartlett's gang of misfit agents couldn't find me in the dark, despite the sniper's report.

Adrenaline ebbed as I waited with my back against the tree. My eyes drooped, and a whole can of tired poured over my head. I wanted nothing more than to sit there and take a nap. Somewhere on the slope above me, Jade Stone was climbing for her life—for all our lives—and the odds of her making it to help in time were... not good. My partner was down, held together with nothing more than a ton of guts.

Back in the old days, when a Comanche warrior was up against it, his back to the wall and facing impossible odds, he would sing his *habbe we-ich-ket*, his death song.

If I'd known a good death song, I would've sung it right then. I yawned. *Maybe Blue Oyster Cult's "Don't Fear the Reaper"?*

The molasses of drowsiness seeped into my muscles, and I yawned again. *What about...* My head snapped up, and I jerked awake, looking around. Bugs, leaves, yadda-yadda. Nothing else moved. I leaned my head back and closed my eyes. *What other good death songs are there? "Stairway to Heaven"? Would that one count? "Wreck of the Edmund Fitzgerald"? How did...*

Chapter 27

"I've cheated the Grim Reaper more times than I know."
—Eddie Rickenbacker

Jade

Maybe an hour away from true dawn, Jade found the clearing with Bartlett's helicopter. The sky had just begun to lighten in the east. For the last quarter mile, she'd followed the scent of wood smoke from a smoldering campfire. Jade crouched at the edge of the clearing and surveyed the quiet camp.

To her left, a moderate sprint across open ground, the faint outline of a Bell helicopter stood out against the forest backdrop. Black outlined in wet silver. Condensation pearled its windows, concealing the inside. On the right, closer to the edge of the mountain overlook, a shape huddled in a sleeping bag near the smoking remains of a fire.

Jade watched, using her peripheral vision, and scanned the ground with care. The shape on the ground was either Glenn or Lazzari; both should be present, given that Lazzari was the sniper and Glenn the pilot.

She slid the Glock from her waistband and eased the pack from her shoulders, allowing it to settle silently behind her. She shivered. Despite having told Sam she would be warm enough, this time of day was the coldest, both physically and psychologically. The mild breeze, fitful and random though it was, chilled the sweat dampening her thin cotton T-shirt.

She'd fired a Glock before and knew how it operated. The Glock used a trigger-mounted safety; the act of squeezing the trigger disengaged it, allowing the gun to fire without a lot of preparation. The pistol had a round chambered. Jade had checked it before leaving the mine.

She glanced over her shoulder at the way she'd come, picturing Sam Cable down there somewhere, waiting for her. It tugged at her, the feeling of loss. She hadn't expected that, nor had she expected the orgasm that had surprised her when they made love. The only time she'd experienced that particular sensation was with herself, alone, and so she'd marveled at the sensation of coming with a man buried to the hilt inside her. It had been... remarkable. It was too bad, really.

After scanning the clearing one last time, Jade slipped from the tree line and strode across the open ground in a direct line to the man sleeping near the fire ring. No one challenged her. The shape in the bag didn't move.

It was Lazzari. Jade stood over him. She looked around again. Glenn had always struck her as a bit of a wuss. He wasn't likely to be sleeping rough, out in the open. Probably bunked out in the helicopter. That left only one threat.

Jade shot Lazzari twice in the body and once in the head.

The flat crack of the pistol slapped her ears, and the muzzle flash leaped from the barrel in streamers of sparkling fire. Downy fluff puffed from Lazzari's sleeping bag and drifted away. Blood from his head sprayed the ground in a black fan.

Jade spun on her heel and marched to the helicopter. Before she reached it, the side door cracked open, and a muzzy-headed Toby Glenn stumbled out. He wore a rumpled flight suit and white socks, no shoes. Ginger hair spiked around his head.

"Wah? Who?" He blinked and rubbed his eyes. "Holy shit. Jade?"

She stopped a few steps away and leveled the Glock at the pilot's face. "Hello, Toby. Miss me?"

Luksa

DAN LUKSA DREAMED OF his mother's old washing machine. It used to chatter in the spin cycle and vibrate the entire house. "But, Mom," he said, "how're we going to get the clothes dry in time?"

His mother, frail at sixty and darn near skeletal at eighty, said, "Don't you worry—"

"Get up." A kick in the foot snapped Luksa out of his dream, and his eyes popped open to see Mack looming over him in the pre-dawn light.

"What?" he groaned.

"Bartlett's gone." Mack stalked to his pack and started shoving things inside.

"Gone?"

"Split. Left. Booked it. Y'know? Gone."

Luksa sat up and looked around, half expecting to see Reeder come sauntering back into camp. He didn't, of course. "Maybe he's, you know, reconnoitering."

Mack snorted.

"Well? Why would he just leave?"

"You that dumb?"

"Is his pack gone?"

"He took everything. Including his smell." Mack hefted his pack and settled it on his shoulders. "I dunno 'bout you, but I'm getting the fuck outta here."

"But—"

"Look, dumbass. He gone. Bartlett ain't comin' back. He done hiked his ass up that hill, grabbed Glenn, and choppered the fuck away. You not hear the bird take off a few minutes ago?"

Luksa scratched his ribs and looked around. He found his radio and keyed it on. "Six, come in... Six, this is Two. Come in." He returned Mack's glare with one of his own. Maybe Lazzari would know something. "Eagle, this is Two. Come in." He waited a couple of seconds and tried it again. Then again.

Mack sneered. "Shee-it, that boy done gone too."

Luksa worked the radio a few more times while Mack urinated against a tree. Nothing but faint static came back through his earpiece.

"Now what?"

Mack snorted and spit. "Now what? Now I'm walking my black ass outta this here forest and getting me back to civilization. I'm taking what I got in the bank and heading for Mexico and points south. You got a brain in your head, that's what you'll do too." He didn't wait, either. The last sentence was thrown over his shoulder as he hiked toward the river.

Luksa crawled from his bag, and his skin goose-pimpled when the cold air hit him. He found his shirt and pants and drew the still-damp garments on while shivering. He buttoned his shirt in a hurry then fumbled his belt together.

No way in hell did he want to try to find his way through the wilderness on his own. Luksa hated being in the woods. He hated being alone even more, and with Reeder gone, he was as alone as he'd been in a long time. Mack didn't count for companionship.

Luksa clenched his jaw and fought the pre-tear tingle behind his nose. If Mack saw him crying, he would keep walking for sure. He could be a real prick sometimes.

"Wait up, Mack," he called. "I'm going with you."

Rita

RITA GOLDMAN AND THE Rangers had arrived at the Silver City airstrip in the wee hours and located the head of the local Search and Rescue, a forest ranger named George Wells. He told them nothing they didn't already know then offered some sandwiches and blanket-covered cots, both of which they accepted.

Rita napped long enough to take the edge off then met Wells in the briefing room he'd commandeered from the airfield manager. "Anything new?"

He shook his head, mouth set in a straight line. A paunchy forty-year-old, Wells had hangdog eyes and a scruffy beard. Dark stains marked the underarms of his green forest service uniform, and something that looked like dried egg stained the breast pocket.

"Only thing," he said, "we seem to have lost contact with two of our people on the far northern side of our search grid. Radio's prolly out, but I'm fixin' to go find 'em, make sure they're okay."

"How're you going to find two more people"—Rita gestured toward the Gila National Forest looming in the darkness outside the window—"out there?"

"All our people carry GPS trackers. Mainly so's they can call in their position, they find something. Sometimes so's we can find them, they get themselves boogered up out there."

Boogered up? Rita smiled. That sounded like something Sam would say. "You from Texas?"

Wells winked one droopy eye. "Don't tell no one 'round here. Every single New Mexican will piss in a Texan's beer, given half a chance. Anyway, I'm headin' out shortly to take a look. Y'all want to go? I'm taking the chopper; maybe we'll spot something on the way."

"Yeah, sure."

She'd left Wells "fixin' to get ready" and wandered outside. The rising sun lit the tarmac at the Silver City airstrip, giving Rita her first good look at the tiny field. Captain Marshall appeared beside her with an extra cup of coffee strong enough that the fumes alone could cause a jump in blood pressure.

A helicopter skimmed in from the north and settled on the far end of the airfield, too far away for Rita to make out any details. For an instant, she thought it might be bringing in news of the search, but when nobody got out and the rotors spooled down, she gave up the fantasy.

"My nerves," Marshall said, "are jumping like electrified frogs."

"Mine too. Though I wouldn't know from frogs. Never electrocuted one."

"It's a sight," Marshall admitted.

Her eyes grated in their sockets. The hot coffee hit her stomach and instantly turned to acid. She drank more anyway, took a breath, and turned to the captain to ask a question.

"He'll be okay," Marshall interrupted her half-formed thought. "Sam's tougher than algebra."

Rita nodded and brushed her hair back from her face. "What I was gonna say—"

The office door banged open, and Wells bustled out, Trooper Wade Duncan in tow. The forest ranger's eyes were lit up, and he practically beamed good cheer.

"Guess what! We got a phone call, came in a few seconds ago. The caller phoned in a tip about where to find your people. It's not far from where my own folks went missing. If we get moving, we can be there in a hour, maybe less."

"Who called it in?" Rita asked.

"I dunno. She hung up when I asked her name."

"You think it's legit?"

Wells seemed taken aback. "The caller was pretty specific. Gave us GPS coordinates, said Trooper Boggs was hurt bad and Ranger Cable had a bum knee. Said they was holed up in a mine at the base of the mountain. I got 'er pinpointed on this here map." Wells waved a folded map in illustration.

"Anything about the prisoner? Jade Stone?" Marshall wanted to know.

Wells pursed his lips and shook his head. "Why, no, nothin' but the other two."

Rita and Captain Marshall exchanged a look.

"Let's go see," Rita said. "We have to check it out, one way or another."

Marshall squinted and nodded. To Wells, he said, "Any way to trace that call?"

"No," the forest ranger said. "We're not set up for that here."

"All right." Marshall nodded again, firmly this time. "Let's do it. C'mon, Wells, we're burnin' daylight here."

Sam

"HUH?" I SNORTED AWAKE, instantly aware I'd screwed up and fallen asleep. A squirrel bounded away when I sat up, shooting into the underbrush and disappearing with a flash of bushy tail.

The sky had turned a pretty magenta. The morning sun wouldn't be far behind. That meant I'd been out for three or four hours. Luckily, no one had shot me in my sleep. I would've deserved it, though.

Marlon.

Damn me for a fool. No telling what Marlon was thinking, everyone having run off and left him alone in a dark cave. With any luck, he would still be out cold from his dose of herbal tea, but I had to get back before he freaked out.

I tried to stand and sat right back down again. My knee reminded me it hurt like hell. I stifled a groan and flexed it—very gently—until a marginal amount of stiffness went away.

I found my left eyebrow itched with crusted, dried blood. When I scratched it, the wound open again, and fresh blood trailed down my cheek.

"Jeez, Sam," I said to myself. "You're in some bad freakin' shape."

With a little help from my friend the oak tree, I stood upright and tested my bad wheel, wincing when I attempted a hobbling step. I tried another one then a few more, using whatever I could to help keep my balance. Tree here, rock there. Soon I was moving pretty well and following the right trail back to our little corner of heaven in the mountains. *A dark hole in the ground. Yay.*

I ducked under a low limb then straightened up, and an enormous black man in full tac gear appeared on the trail in front of me. He stopped so suddenly, the guy behind him, a much shorter white guy in his mid-forties, bounced off the big man's back.

Both men were armed with tactical rifles, packs, and weapons harnesses. They might just as well have been wearing big signs in bold letters: Crooked Federal Agent.

The lead man swung his rifle up. I clawed at my Kimber. We fired at almost the same instant.

I didn't see where my shot went. A bullet slapped me in the left collarbone and spun me around. I went with the momentum and let the spin turn into a tumble. I rolled off the trail to my right, hunting cover, gripping my pistol in a white-knuckled fist. Bushes scraped my clothes. I burrowed behind the shelter of some rocks and took a breath to steady my nerves.

I risked a quick peek from cover and saw... nobody. The trail was empty.

A voice carried from somewhere deeper in the forest. "Mack! Back here!"

A deeper baritone answered. Closer, but it was still hard to pinpoint. "What?"

"There's a cave or something here. Looks like tracks. Stone may be back in here somewhere. Keep the guy pinned down while I go check."

Damn it. I clenched my teeth to keep from screaming. The numbness in my shoulder drained away, and pure hellish acid pain filled the vacancy. My collarbone ached like hell, and my left arm was practically useless. And the bad guys had found our mine, where Marlon lay in a drug-induced stupor.

Chapter 28

"It'll be just like Beggar's Canyon back home!" — Luke Skywalker, *Star Wars*

Sam

The vegetation grew wild and thick where I hunkered in the rocks next to a piñon tree, my face stuck into the tall grass around its base. The sun had yet to penetrate this deep in the valley; if I stayed quiet, I would be hidden from anyone without IR goggles.

I couldn't stay hidden, though.

Squirming around, I tugged my shirt loose to look at the bullet hole in my shoulder. Blood saturated my collar, and I hissed when the cloth pulled loose from the wound. More blood welled up from the jagged hole midway along the collarbone. The bullet had struck bone and glanced up and to the left, tearing a gash in my trapezius muscle.

What luck. Two inches to the right, and it would've taken out my jugular. And then where would I be?

The bone grated when I moved, feeling like sand in the gears, and a little mobility seeped into my left arm. All kinds of feral noises escaped through my teeth as I experimented flexing it.

It hurt, but it worked. Some. Gentle—very gentle—probing made me suspect the bone wasn't shattered. Maybe the clavicle was cracked, not busted to hell like I'd thought at first.

Now, where's the guy who shot me? I suspected he was the one called Mack. The guy in the rear had shouted his name, and because he was smaller, he seemed more likely to own the higher voice that had announced he'd found the cave. *Did I hit the lead guy?* He hadn't sounded hurt when the two exchanged words.

And shouldn't there be more agents? I ran through a mental recount of the men I'd seen disembark from the chopper, and not counting the sniper and pilot, there should be three left, not two.

To paraphrase Will Rogers, there were three ways to find something out. The first and second methods—reading and observation—wouldn't work in my current circumstances. The third way a man gained wisdom, according to Will, was to keeping peeing until you peed on an electric fence—a learning method I seemed to employ way too often.

The sandy-haired dude was closing in on Marlon, and blood was leaking out of me faster than a vampire humping a porcupine. I had to move and get this over quickly. The third method it would have to be, then.

Keeping low, forcing my right knee to bend and take the strain, I crabbed away from the piñon and danced the drunken monkey shuffle through the low brush and far-too-rare tree trunks. Pausing to catch my breath, I tried to Elmer Fudd myself behind a skinny pine. Sweat stung the cut in my forehead and ran into my eyes. I wiped it away with a sleeve. My shoulder throbbed, and my knee squalled. Overall, I was a symphony of body parts singing in harmony. My death song had turned into a Johnny Cash rendition of "Hurt."

A mourning dove cooed as shafts of sunlight splintered through the trees. I recognized the terrain. The entrance to the mine was thirty yards away—maybe a four-second sprint for a healthy man. For me, it would be a minute-long hop-skip-hobble.

On the left was a tall slope that offered no place to hide. On the right, thick brush clogged the gaps between scrubby trees and bare rock. A Mongol army could've hidden six feet away, and I would never know it.

In the middle was a bare patch of ground. Beyond that, a left turn at the gravel slag heap, and then I would be home sweet home.

Halfway between me and the slag heap, a trail joined the main path and veered down toward the creek. I'd missed it in the dark the night before. That must have been the path the dynamic dimwits from the arroyo had taken. They'd walked within smelling distance of the mine-shaft and never noticed it until they bumped into me. When the short-er guy ran for cover, he must have found the shaft entrance.

If I hadn't taken a really long beauty sleep, I never would've run into them. I would already be back in the cave, snug and happy, never having enjoyed the pleasure of Mack and Mr. Sandy's company.

A pee-on-the-electric-fence type of guy would walk right down the middle of Broadway and wait for incoming fire to reveal the enemy. In the business world, they called that "being proactive." A better ap-proach would be to sneak through the brush alongside the trail and...

The back of my neck prickled with that feeling of being watched. I could almost sense his presence behind me, as if his mass affected the local gravity. If he could project a menace that well, the Force was strong in this one.

It was hard enough to spin and fire with four working limbs. Suf-fering from appendage deficit syndrome, I would be lucky not to fall down and shoot myself. I tensed, mentally rehearsing the moves: pivot-spin on my good leg, center weapon with one hand, line up sights, pull trigger, and blow up Death Star. *Just like Beggar's Canyon.*

Ready, set—

A deep, maple-syrup voice drawled, "Freeze, muthafuckah."

Luksa

DAN LUKSA'S STOMACH churned when he contemplated the open mouth of the cave. A rectangular tomb in the side of a mountain, the entrance was big enough for two men to walk in side by side and spooky enough to scare them both right back out.

Was Jade Stone in there? And did he really care one way or the other? Bartlett had run for the hills. Lee, Ray, and Reuben were dead. Everything had pretty much gone to shit. Did he really have a good reason for sticking his nose down that hole and killing Stone? Assuming he could.

He'd never liked the woman, not from the first time they met in her office in Dallas. A junior partner the big boys had do their scut work, Stone had the kind of looks that would get her whatever she wanted. She was smart, fashion-model pretty, and—Luksa had thought at the time—as deadly as a coral snake. He'd warned Reed and Tommy both about her when she started cozying up to Tommy. He wasn't surprised when he found she'd gutted Tommy and left him to bleed out on her kitchen floor.

And now I have to go in a dark hole and kill the snake before she bites?

That made no sense to anything except his pride. "Leave no job unfinished," his dad always said and reinforced the message with a granite fist. *About the only one of Dad's lessons that stuck.*

Luksa sighed, dropped the magazine on his rifle, cleared the chamber, and propped the rifle against the timber support near the mine entrance. He had no way to handle both the long weapon and his flashlight comfortably, so he figured he might as well lose the weight. He entered the cave with his 9mm crossed over his Maglite-carrying hand, sweeping them both in wide, irregular arcs.

When he wasn't shot in the first tentative steps inside, his lungs deflated, and he drew a shaky breath. Inside the mineshaft, the walls narrowed a tad, and the air had a musty smell: dust, old timber, dry rot, and... urine?

Luksa crouched and studied the floor. The dust and debris had been disturbed. Fresh footprints and scuffs indicated recent usage. "So they *have* been here," he said under his breath. "But are they still?"

He crept forward, eyes peeled so wide, they almost bulged out of his skull. He followed the flashlight's yellow beam farther from sunlight, tensed for the blaze of a muzzle flash from the black tunnel ahead.

Luksa put one foot in front of the other. Powder-fine dust, milled by time, puffed at each step. He froze when his light skittered over, then snapped back to, a sleeping bag heaped a dozen feet away.

Sam

I PUT AS MUCH SNEER into my voice as I could muster. "'Freeze, motherfucker'? Seriously? Wow, that is *such* a cliché."

"You like that? Well, try this: throw your gun off in them bushes, and put your hands on your head."

I engaged the Kimber's thumb safety and tossed it about as far as a toddler could spit.

"Cute," the voice behind me said. "Don't matter. You try for it, you make a move—in fact, you twitch, scratch, or even per-*spire* too heavy—I drop you."

"I can't do the hand-on-head thing." I turned in a hippity-hop circle and saw who I expected to see.

Darth Vader in tac gear scowled and centered a semi-auto rifle on my chest. I gestured at my shoulder.

"Collarbone's cracked, maybe broken."

"Where's the woman?"

"Died in the plane crash."

"Bool-shit." The black agent smirked. At six-two, he was almost my height, and he packed an impressive stack of muscle. Bull-necked and flat-faced, he had wide, flaring nostrils and hooded eyes. He seemed as nervous as a corpse on Prozac. A boom mic circled from the headset on his left ear. "Wasn't no dead body in the plane."

I shrugged then wished I hadn't. "Internal injuries. She held on for a while, but... you know. I buried her last night." I nodded behind him. "Back yonder a ways, where I was coming from, before I met you two fine gentlemen. You're the one called Mack, correct?"

"How'd you bury her? No shovel."

"Dug into the sand a ways with my hands, far as I could go." I almost shrugged again. "Piled rocks on top."

Mack appraised me with a skeptical look. The muzzle of his M4 remained vise-steady. My shoulder had commenced throbbing—jabs of lightning pain, hot and heavy enough to make my hands tremble and my eyes water. I measured six long steps between me and him—steps a normal man might take. It looked more like twelve limps and a shuffle for me. And what would I do when I got there? Use my dead-weight left arm as a club and beat him to death?

"C'mon." Mack gestured with his chin. "Let's get on to that cave back there, see if my partner done found the woman. She not there, I just shoot you in the head, call it a day."

"Why don't y'all just run off back to home and leave me be?"

"Get moving, or I'll shoot you right here. I ain't a patient man."

"Typically a result of poor toilet training."

The echo of two distant shots thudded, faint and muffled, from the tunnel. Mack touched the radio headset by his ear. "Two, this is Three. Come in."

Garbled squawking responded, loud enough I caught a bit filtering through the big man's earpiece. *Crackle-pop.* "Camp—" *Crackle-crackle.* "Blood trail—" *Crackle.*

"Say again, Two."

Crackle-whine.

"Two, come in."

Nothing.

"Shit." Mack focused on me and gestured with the rifle. "Move it, Huckleberry. Let's go find your friends."

Luksa

LUKSA'S EARS RANG FROM the two shots he'd pumped into the sleeping bag. He hadn't believed it was occupied—too flat—but shooting into it from a safe distance was good insurance. He played his flashlight over the bag and stalked closer. Definitely empty.

Although... Luksa leaned closer. A smear of blood, black and wet, trailed away from the bag. Someone injured had crawled away. Recently, too, by the look of it.

He could barely hear Mack's query, both from the poor reception in the mine and the high-pitched buzzing in his ears.

"I found their camp," he radioed. "Looks like there's a blood trail leading deeper into the mine. I'm following it now."

Luksa turned the volume way down so he could listen better. The charcoal murk ahead swallowed his flashlight beam, ate it whole, and sent nothing back. The tunnel reminded Luksa of a creepy carnival fun ride, like a tunnel of love where frisky teenagers would be slashed and slaughtered by a deformed guy in a mask.

"Too much late-night TV, Dan," he told himself.

Luksa crouched and followed the scrape marks in the dust, rewarded now and again with the reflection of a new smear of blood. He touched one, and his fingers came away damp and tacky. Fresh. The wounded person had to be close.

When he looked behind him, the glow from the entrance had faded, leaving him alone in an island of light created by his Maglite. Heart thudding, Luksa crept forward.

Chapter 29

"It is often hard to distinguish between the hard knocks in life and those of opportunity." — Frederick Phillips

Rita

In the forest service helo, squashed between Marshall and Duncan in the middle of a row of jump seats against the rear bulkhead, Rita closed her eyes and swallowed to keep her guts from turning inside out. The hammering of the rotor sent a vibration up her spine that built the foundation for a solid headache on top of her roiling stomach.

The helicopter bounced and wallowed in the mountain updrafts, shaking her insides and turning the coffee in her stomach rancid. Medical contraptions and rescue gear jammed every square inch of extra space, adding to her mild claustrophobia.

Her eyes snapped open at a shout from the front. From the cockpit, Ranger Wells contorted into the bulkhead gap and pointed emphatically to his right. Marshall and Duncan craned forward at the same time she did, all three of them straining to see through the starboard window.

At first, Rita saw nothing but green trees, tan rocks, and red soil. The pilot banked right, and her heart froze. The burned-out hulk of a tiny plane, wings and tail still attached, lay crumpled in a meadow. A long strip of torn earth arrowed from the plane downslope, showing its final landing path.

"That's ours," Marshall yelled. Wire-taut, the Ranger captain nearly vibrated in his seat. A grim look pulled at the corners of his eyes, deepening the crow's-feet. He shouted at Wells, "Set 'er down! We gotta make sure!"

Wells was already motioning at the pilot, and the rotors changed pitch. Rita's stomach floated as the helicopter dropped, pitching through the air as if the pilot were being docked for every spare second of fuel used. At shoe-top distance, the rescue helicopter flared, and Rita's stomach bounced the other direction.

"Where did you learn to fly?" she shouted at the pilot, who wore radio headphones and no doubt couldn't hear her. "Disney World?"

That earned a nod from Duncan, who looked a little pale and clammy himself.

The chopper settled, and Rita was out of her restraints and tugging the door handle before either of her companions could move.

Luksa

LUKSA PASSED THROUGH a timber arch braced on either side by wood so dark, it looked black. He chose not to examine the dry-rot eating away the edges. The rock tunnel reflected a dull sand color from his flashlight beam. Roughhewn walls and a curved roof indicated the rock had been hand cut with muscle-powered tools.

Occasionally, things skittered away the instant before his light hit them, meaning he never really saw what kind of critters he disturbed. Scrapes in the dust, marked with fresh blood, led him onward. His breathing echoed, harsh and uneven. The ceiling height forced him to stoop; apparently, the mine had been drilled by the seven dwarves when, hi-ho, off to work they went.

But where's Snow White?

Luksa was so focused on following the trail, he didn't see the side passage open up until he was three quarters past it. A sense of space tickled his right cheek and jangled the alarm bells. He gulped in a startled breath and spun right.

His light beam swung, jittered, then steadied on a figure slouched against the wall. Black face. Red-rimmed, glittering eyeballs. Pistol muzzle pointed at him.

Fire bloomed from the pistol, and a bullet burned Luksa's ear.

"Ahh!" he screamed and dodged away. Another bullet shattered the wall beside him. He dove and rolled, feeling the pressure wave of another shot boom in the tiny space. His flashlight spun loose when he hit the ground, the light beam flying in a dizzy circle.

A round clipped the back of his calf, and Luksa scrambled to his feet and ran, deeper into the mine, hunched over to avoid low timbers. Blind, panicked, Luksa stumbled forward, staggering, careening, bouncing off the walls. He wanted distance between himself and that—

The ground fell away beneath him. Flailing his arms, he screamed when he dropped... and kept dropping. Stars flared behind his eyes when he banged his head on something wooden in the darkness. The sensation of falling continued for a moment before Dan Luksa lost consciousness.

Sam

I SCUFFED TO A HALT, the sound of shots booming from deep in the pit squeezing my chest with greasy fingers. We'd just passed the entrance —called a portal by mining types, I finally remembered—and been swallowed by the darkness. Mack clicked on a flashlight and held it against the foregrip of his tactical rifle.

My shadow capered ahead of me in the halogen beam.

"Keep moving," Mack growled. He repeated his radio calls for the elusive Two while I shuffled forward. Getting no answer, he cursed a blue streak.

"What's the matter? Can't find your buddy?" I chuckled and tried out a Dracula voice. "Maybe zee wampires got heem."

"You as funny as hemorrhoid."

"Really? What got up your ass?"

I came to the place we'd camped. Marlon's sleeping bag lay to my left, bunched up and torn by a couple of bullet holes. The bag I'd rolled out to nap on was to the right, rucked into a pile. No Marlon. Anywhere.

A shaky breath whistled through my nostrils, taking with it some of the tension in my shoulders. Somehow he'd made it down the mineshaft, and Two must have followed him. *Now, were the shots fired by Marlon or the other guy?*

More importantly, did Marlon take my rifle when he went? I'd left it on my sleeping bag when I escorted Jade to the jump-off point. I could picture it, as plain as a teenager's pimple, lying there locked and loaded, two thumb-clicks away from full auto. Ahead of me, the tunnel narrowed, and the maneuvering room went from not much to none. I had a feeling if I kept limping down that mineshaft, I wasn't coming back up.

"What the hell?" I muttered, pretending shock and confusion.

"What?"

I sensed Mack creeping closer, my radar picking up body heat and bad breath. Without looking back, I slammed an elbow into his gut then head-butted straight back. A good shot to the face could blind a man with watery eyes, doesn't matter how tough he is.

Contact with Mack's forehead sent a shockwave through my skull. Using the momentum, I powered off my good leg into a full-on belly flop atop my sleeping bag. The hard metal outline of the rifle slammed me in the chest—it had gotten twisted sideways under a layer of goose-down-packed nylon.

Mack cranked off a shot, more out of hope than planning, I suspected. It went wide, and the bullet zinged off the ceiling of the mine.

My fingers slipped blindly along the shape of the rifle until they found the handgrip. I spun the other direction, popping out of the bag like I was unrolling a burrito.

"You dumb son of a bitch," the BATF agent roared. A bullet punched the air an inch from my face.

Mack fired again. My bad leg took the hit. I wobbled and fought gravity. He fired again, and a bullet punched me under the nipple on my right side. A frozen ice pick stabbed me in the chest. The guy was good. Blinded or not, he was scoring hits.

I buckled to one knee. My left arm hung, useless, and I forced the M4 barrel up, flinging aside the last of the clinging bag.

I screamed in rage and pain, struggling to stay upright. To stay alive.

Mack's weapon flared again and again. I didn't see where the bullets went.

My thumb found the safety and pushed it all the way down—two solid clicks. I squeezed the trigger. The muzzle tracked from right to left in an arc of hellish orange lightning bolts. I snugged the rifle's butt into the crook of my arm and rode the muzzle-climb as it thundered out a solid stream of fire.

My throat was raw, and I realized I was still screaming. I stopped.

Mack tumbled, loose and boneless. The M4 ran dry, and the bolt locked back. My ears rang.

Mack's light had skittered away. It painted a wall like a stage foot-light. Enough light reflected to see the BATF agent lay in a heap. Not moving. A black pool spread from under him, pulsing from the hole in the back of his head. A dark curtain came down, and I couldn't see anymore.

LUKSA HAD NO WAY TO tell time. When he woke in blackness, his head splitting from the pain, he discovered his cell phone was smashed to bits. He had no flashlight. No matches. Nothing. He'd lost his pistol somewhere along the way as well.

The lack of light was complete. His eyes strained so wide, seeking even the tiniest glimmer, they began to pulse with a pain of their very own.

He sat in six inches of freezing-cold water. Exhausted from searching his surroundings, he shivered and hugged himself, chafing his upper arms for warmth. Best that he could tell, he'd fallen down a shaft. How far, he had no way of knowing. He picked bits of crumbly wood from his hair; somewhere along the way, he'd clocked his head on a wooden ladder. His ankle screamed with pain, probably broken.

For the first hour after he'd come to his senses, Luksa had screamed for help. He'd nearly torn the lining from his throat, he'd screamed so loud and so long. Nothing happened, and no one responded. Luksa sat in the cold water and shivered.

FOUR DAYS AFTER LEAVING Mack and Dan behind, John Reed Bartlett hiked out of the Gila National Forest and found US Highway 180. The sun was high, and the day had grown steadily warmer. Sweat soaked his arms as he paced the road's shoulder, ignoring the whoosh of passing cars. The last thing he wanted was to hitch a ride.

Half a mile from the Gila River crossing, Bartlett had passed a house with a motorcycle on the porch. A hand-lettered For Sale sign indicated an asking price of five hundred dollars, which Bartlett dickered down to four hundred with a helmet thrown in. He paid with the cash in his pocket.

The ancient Honda had soft brakes and near-bald tires, and it smoked a little on acceleration, but it held the road and ate up miles. He made Las Cruces as the sun was going down behind him.

Checking in to a budget motel, Bartlett used the only fake ID he had on him, one made out in the name of Stephen Gibson, and paid for the room with a clean credit card in that name.

"You have a business center?" he asked the chipper Native American girl behind the counter. "With internet?"

"Yes, sir, we sure do." She pointed it out, and Bartlett nodded his thanks.

He slipped into the leather chair in front of the hotel's computer and jiggled the mouse to bring the screen to life. Bartlett was very aware of his own sweat stink. After six days without a bath, he reeked.

Well, no matter. He was within minutes of a long shower. All he had to do was move some money from his hidden accounts to his Stephen Gibson account, and he would be set. All the business proceeds from Sugarland Enterprises, after a thorough laundering process, went into offshore accounts so deeply hidden, a team of forensic accounts could make a career trying to find them. With Tommy gone, only he knew the passwords to those accounts. That money would finance his getaway and set him up for a long, long time.

Bartlett typed in the bank's URL and went through a lengthy dual-authentication process. Once he'd proven to the bank's satisfaction that he was who he said he was, it allowed him into his account-summary page.

He always got a special thrill when the page loaded and his balance, usually well north of six million dollars, showed up. He used to joke with Tommy about them being the Six Million Dollar Men. His brother, younger and less inclined to television in general, had no idea what he was talking about.

Bartlett grinned and waited for the summary page to load.

"What the hell?" He clicked the refresh button and watched the page reload. Something was probably screwy with the hotel's web browser. Bartlett stared, his jaw loose and his eyes growing hot in their sockets. No matter which way he looked at it and no matter what he did with the website, the balance stayed the same. Zero.

Eight minutes later, after reviewing the last week's transactions, he sat back and rubbed his tired eyes. In a weak voice, he mumbled, "That... *bitch.*"

THREE DAYS AFTER LAS Cruces, Bartlett rode his tired Honda through the gates of the Pelican Bay Marina in Galveston, Texas. His insides felt hollowed out at losing all the money he'd worked so hard to hide from everybody. The feds, the police, his co-workers... even his accomplices didn't know the scope of the take he'd stashed offshore. Nobody knew.

But Jade Stone had somehow wormed it out of his stupid brother.

One thing he still had, though, was his boat. There was over two hundred grand in gold coins stashed aboard. That plus a well-stocked bar and some fishing poles were all he really needed to be happy. *What was that Frederick Phillips quote? "It is often hard to distinguish between the hard knocks in life and those of opportunity."*

Consider this a hard knock and move on.

Bartlett parked the Honda and left the keys in it. He wouldn't ever be using the motorcycle again. He strode across the parking lot and onto the plank dock, footsteps booming with determination. The Gulf waters lapped and sloshed against the pilings, bringing a fishy, salty smell with them. The bright, glittering reflection from the water made him squint.

All I need to do is swing by the marina office, settle up the berthing fees, gas up, and I'll be on my—

"John Bartlett?"

Bartlett froze mid-step and focused on the man in front of him. A polar bear in a rumpled, Western-cut suit was his first impression.

Big, dumb, and somewhat simple-minded was his second. The guy had small-town cop written all over him.

"I'm sorry, friend," Bartlett said with a full-bore grin. "I don't know anyone by that name."

The polar bear smiled under his gray Stetson. "Ah'm sure you'd like me to believe that," he rumbled. "Good thing I got me someone knows how to follow the money, else I might never have found this here boat." The man touched the brim of his hat. "Dolph Ahlberg, Texas Rangers, sir. I'm here to arrest you for, let's see, conspiracy, fraud, murder—well, shit, about two-thirds the damn penal code. Why bother trying to remember all that fine print?"

Ahlberg leaned to the side and spit a long stream of tobacco juice into the water. Bartlett shifted, settling his weight and letting his hand dangle loose. His pistol rode in a high-rise holster at the small of his back. Not the best place to get to it in a fast-draw competition, but against this guy? *You gotta be kidding me. A glacier could out-draw this guy.*

"Well, now, Ranger..." Bartlett cranked up his smile to megawatt voltage. Nothing disarmed people like a bright smile and a winning personality. "I don't know who you think I am, but—"

Bartlett drew. His hand swept back, thumb hooked to lift his shirt, and gripped the butt of his sidearm. With the same motion, he broke the retaining snap and pulled. It was a clean draw, one of the fastest pulls he'd ever attempted.

Two sledgehammers hit him in the chest, side by side over his heart. Bartlett looked down, stunned. His gun thunked to the dock. Two holes, so close together, he could've covered them with a silver dollar, pulsed blood from his chest. Until the pulse stopped.

Epilogue

"What doesn't kill you gives you nightmares and all kinds of bad coping skills." — Anonymous

Three months after they pulled me off a mountain in New Mexico, I pushed through the screen door and onto the Ahlbergs' back patio for what I hoped to be the last time in a long while. The morning sun cracked the horizon and shot golden beams across the twenty acres of rolling Hill Country property. Three deer—two does and a fawn—ambled between their pecan and sweetgum trees, pausing now and again to nose the native buffalo grass for a tasty fallen nut.

"You all set?" Dolph asked.

I nodded and dropped my hat and duffel next to my accustomed chair at the round patio table, expecting to feel the stab of ghost pain from my shoulder when I moved. The trapezius had healed long ago, and weeks of physical therapy had worked out all but the memory of pain, which didn't seem to want to go away, along with some residual stiffness.

I watched the deer for a time, soaking in the first cool morning breeze of the fall. It had been a long, hot summer, filled with sweat and pain, and I was glad for it to be over. For therapy, I'd built a fence around Audrey Ahlberg's garden. Five-foot posts and four sturdy rails, designed as a deer deterrent. The three morning visitors meandered to the fence, and the biggest of the three gave me a dirty look, as if to say, "What's up with this shit?"

"I don't think Ginger likes your fence," Dolph said.

"No, she don't," I admitted. Early on, Dolph had confided in me that he planned to shoot the deer for venison stew, but once his wife named them, he threw that plan out the window. Ginger, Mary Ann, and Gilligan had the run of the yard but no longer the garden.

The screen door squeaked, and Audrey came out with two china mugs and a Mr. Coffee carafe. I took my seat and thanked her while she poured.

"When you comin' back, Sam?" Dolph's wife asked. Audrey and Dolph were a physical match; together they reminded me of the Berenstain Bears.

"I reckon you'd be glad to be shut of me, Auddie. Three months is a long time to put up with an invalid."

"Oh, pshaw," she sniffed. "You ain't no invalid. You're family, boy. Don't forget it." Audrey shambled away in her print housedress and Wal-Mart slippers. Before she turned, I would've sworn her eyes glittered with tears.

The door thumped closed behind her, and Dolph said to me, "She's gonna miss havin' the comp'ny, I think." He grunted a laugh. "Miss havin' somebody to fuss over too."

"Truth is, I needed a lot of fussing over. Especially at first."

When they found me in the mine, I'd bled about two pints more than was good for me. The bullet Mack had fired into my chest hadn't been the biggest problem; that one had hit at an angle, broken a rib, and torn out under my shoulder blade. No, the bad one was the bullet that ripped through my calf and nicked the posterior tibial artery, which would make a lot of trauma doctors use technical language like "Oh shit."

I heard tell they carried me out while Rita Goldman held the tourniquet and cussed all of them to move faster. I didn't remember any of it, but apparently, I'd raved long enough about Marlon that they went back and found him too. He'd dragged himself from deep in the mine, close to the entrance. He was passed out when they found him, and the paramedics had to shock him a couple of times on the chopper ride back to the hospital. *Which reminds me...*

"I talked to Marlon yesterday," I said.

"Yeah? How's he doing?"

"Says he's fine, but I don't know. Marshall told me he'd be lucky to walk without a cane. They nearly took his leg off above the knee but, in the end, pinned it up with baling wire and thumbtacks. I expect he'll retire on full medical or issue driver's license tests for the rest of his career."

"That sucks."

"Not as bad as Bartlett's guy." I was ashamed to admit I'd forgotten all about the last man from Bartlett's crew until six or eight days later. When the searchers went back in the mine, they'd found Daniel William Luksa of the BATF at the bottom of a deep shaft, dead from hypothermia. Since he'd been trying to kill Marlon and me, I didn't spend a lot of time feeling guilty. A bad way to die, though.

"You know what Marshall has in mind for you?" Dolph asked, snapping me back to the present.

"Not a clue," I admitted. "All he said was special assignment, whatever that means."

"Hah! The last special assignment got you lost in the Gila National Forest."

"No kidding. Let's hope it's nothing like that."

"Maybe he's gonna send you south, after that fugitive you lost. Stone."

"Humph. You think?"

"Could be." Dolph shrugged and sipped his coffee. "What a piece of work she was, huh? Ices that cop in Dallas, puts two in the back of the head of that chopper pilot. Killed that guy in his sleeping bag up on the mountain. Stole all that Bartlett feller's money." Dolph whistled. "Whew-howdy. That's a cold bitch right there."

"Yep." I watched Ginger and Mary Ann tour the outside of the garden fence, adjusting to their new reality. "Ice cold."

"Be glad she didn't pop you and Boggs too."

"And yet she called in where we were."

"How 'bout that?" Dolph marveled. "There's just no figuring people. I hear she crossed into Mexico about two days after they found y'all up there. Hadn't nobody seen her since." He reached across the table and slapped me on the shoulder. I almost flinched before I remembered it didn't hurt anymore. "Maybe she was sweet on you!"

"I'm sure that's it," I deadpanned. "Go figure."

"Speakin' of sweet on you, whatever happened to that Yankee gal? Goldman? While you was in the hospital, she guarded you like a mama bear over her cub."

"Went back home."

I could feel Dolph watching me. Their old farm dog, Fred, wandered up from the barn and passed the deer family without a second glance. His deer-chasing days were long over.

After the silence built and my coffee went cold, I said, "She's just a friend, Dolph. Nothing more."

"Hmm."

Fred negotiated the patio steps and made his way to the table. He laid his white muzzle on my thigh and activated his tail in a slow wag. I scratched his head and told him he was a good dog. His tail beat faster, and he sat down to accept his morning attention.

"Dog's gonna miss you too," Dolph said.

"He's a good ol' boy." I cleared my throat and told Fred, "Look after Audrey and Quick Draw McGraw here. One of these days, he won't be as fast as the outlaws."

"Bullshit on that," Dolph grumped. He cracked giant knuckles on both hands. "You about ready to head to town?"

I gave Fred a final rub and stood, grabbing my bag. I didn't feel a twinge when I hoisted it onto my shoulder. I nodded and settled my new hat squarely in place. "Let's go."

Also by Scott Bell

An Abel Yeager Novel
Yeager's Law
Yeager's Mission
Yeager's Getaway

A Sam Cable Mystery
May Day
April's Fool

Standalone
Working Stiffs

Watch for more at snapshooter4hire.com.

About the Author

Scott Bell has over 25 years of experience protecting the assets of retail companies. He holds a degree in Criminal Justice from North Texas State University.

With the kids grown and time on his hands, Scott turned back to his first love—writing. His short stories have been published in *The Western Online*, *Cast of Wonders*, and in the anthology, *Desolation*.

When he's not writing, Scott is on the eternal quest to answer the question: What would John Wayne do?

Read more at snapshooter4hire.com.

About the Publisher

Dear Reader,

We hope you enjoyed this book. Please consider leaving a review on your favorite book site.

Visit https://RedAdeptPublishing.com to see our entire catalogue.

Don't forget to subscribe to our monthly newsletter to be notified of future releases and special sales.

Made in the USA
Monee, IL
18 January 2021